How much worse could this get?

First a stalker, and now Anthony Bracco in her *home.*

There was still anger simmering between them, and no matter how many ground rules they hid behind, it would eventually boil over.

Worse, anger wasn't the only thing simmering. Already she'd felt that familiar separation of brain and body. Her brain would tell her to keep away, but her body couldn't possibly get close enough.

And now, sitting beside him, she could feel herself responding. Emma had never understood why he affected her this way, but apparently it was something that would never change or lose its power.

When his eyes had fallen to her mouth a few minutes ago, she'd known she wouldn't have rejected his kiss. Struggling to pull herself together, she rushed into the hallway with Anthony in pursuit.

With no place to hide…

Dear Reader,

This is definitely a month to celebrate, because Kathleen Korbel is back! This award-winning, bestselling author continues the saga of the Kendall family with *Some Men's Dreams,* a journey of the heart that will have you smiling through tears as you join Gen Kendall in meeting Dr. Jack O'Neill and his very special daughter, Elizabeth. Run—don't walk—to the store to get your copy of this genuine keeper.

Don't miss out on the rest of our books this month, either. Kylie Brant continues THE TREMAINE TRADITION with *Truth or Lies,* a dicey tale of love on both sides of the law. Then pick up RaeAnne Thayne's *Freefall* for a haunting, mysterious, page-turner of a romance. Round out the month with new books by favorites Beverly Bird, who's *Risking It All,* and Frances Housden, who'll introduce you to a *Heartbreak Hero,* and brand-new author Madalyn Reese, who gives you *No Place To Hide* from her talented debut.

And, as always, come back again next month, when Silhouette Intimate Moments offers you six more of the best and most exciting romances around.

Enjoy!

Leslie J. Wainger
Executive Editor

Please address questions and book requests to:
Silhouette Reader Service
U.S.: 3010 Walden Ave., P.O. Box 1325, Buffalo, NY 14269
Canadian: P.O. Box 609, Fort Erie, Ont. L2A 5X3

No Place To Hide

MADALYN REESE

Silhouette®

INTIMATE MOMENTS™

Published by Silhouette Books

America's Publisher of Contemporary Romance

SILHOUETTE BOOKS

ISBN 0-373-27312-6

NO PLACE TO HIDE

This edition published by arrangement with Harlequin Books S.A.

Visit Silhouette at www.eHarlequin.com

Printed in U.S.A.

MADALYN REESE

has always had a cast of extras roaming through her head. Imagine her relief when she started writing and realized they were characters!

She lives in beautiful central Minnesota with her husband, three children, two cats and a dog, but can be found playing at eHarlequin.com in her twenty seconds of spare time. She loves hearing from readers, and can be reached c/o Harlequin/Silhouette Books, 233 Broadway, Suite 1001, New York, NY 10279, or online at madalynreese@madalynreese.com.

For my Beautiful Things:
My family, my friends and Susan Litman,
whom I could never thank enough for giving me
their support, patience and guidance.

Chapter 1

"I don't know why you insist on canary diamonds. Your skin tone needs cool colors like sapphire or deep amethyst," Emma Toliver said.

"Amethyst?" Ginny Lewis balked, her lined, pixie face crinkling with distaste. "Isn't that a semiprecious stone?"

"Ginny, it's the new millennium. It's not about showing off your money anymore. It's about showing off your*self*."

"Don't give me that bunk, young lady. I want the most expensive piece you've got."

"Having a spat with Mr. Lewis again, are we?"

"He wants to buy a motor home."

"Ooh, that's serious. I have just the thing."

Mrs. Lewis leaned eagerly forward, her voice fallen to a hush. "One of your own designs?"

"Of course, but don't tell anyone. I'm supposed to be out of stock right now. This piece is fresh from Charles's hands and the only one I'll have for a while," Emma said, producing a black velvet box marked with her private design label's logo, Beautiful Things.

"My lips are sealed," Ginny said. "But I wish you'd quit running out of material. Weren't you bidding on some huge stone and metal auction thing? Please tell me you got it."

"Yes, by some miracle, we did. But it's been held up in the insurance process forever. They always seem to have trouble with rough, uncut stones, and of course that's what we need before we can get started again."

"Quit whining and show!"

Emma lifted the lid, watching Mrs. Lewis's face light up.

"Oh, Emma… Black orchids! How did you do it?"

"Enameled gold setting, the petals are carved obsidian and lab-darkened purple jadeite. See how beautiful semiprecious stones can be?" she asked reverently, casting critical eyes on the bracelet. It was one of her favorites, a seven-inch line of miniature sensual blooms strung end to end.

The telephone drew Emma's attention from the unveiling. "I'm on phone duty. We'll haggle in a second."

"Toliver's Treasures," she said, watching Mrs. Lewis's expression turn more acquisitive by the second.

"It's me, boss lady."

Wrinkling her brow, Emma turned to see her caller standing twenty feet away, speaking on his cellphone.

"What's the problem?" she asked. Brady, her jewelry department manager, looked positively dour. As always.

"Get rid of Mrs. Lewis. We need to talk."

"If it's about the auction lot—"

"Save that argument for later. You got another e-mail from the Creep."

Emma's stomach lurched. "Lovely. Any luck tracing it?"

"None. I called the Internet people again, but if you don't call the police today, I will."

"I don't… Never mind. I'll call as soon as I'm through."

Emma hung up and took a few deep breaths. Definitely a cheesecake in her near future. Between her crazed schedule, Beautiful Things's material shortage, constant attitude from Brady and the world's scariest e-mails, she deserved at least three pieces.

Brady was right, though. They should have reported the e-mails immediately. He and the Internet guys had done everything they could. Now she'd have to involve the authorities.

But not until she'd dealt with her friend. Putting on her game face, Emma turned and calmly fastened the orchids around Ginny's wrist. "There you go."

"Please tell me this costs as much as a motor home."

"Sorry," Emma replied, hoping she didn't sound distracted. "I'm asking twenty-five hundred. Not a penny more."

"Five thousand."

"Three. Final offer."

"Sold. But you're never going to make money if you don't take advantage of your clients, dear."

"Who says I'm not?"

Ginny's face split into a grin. "That's my girl. I don't suppose you could make a necklace and earrings to match?"

"Of course. You'll have to be patient, though. Charles and crew can't start carving until we have more jade."

"Fine by me, long as I can wear them for the motor home's maiden voyage." Ginny shrugged.

"You're very good to me."

"Nonsense. I'm a superstitious creature. At this very counter your great-grandfather sold my grandfather his wedding set. That marriage lasted sixty-three years. Given my husband's retirement plans I need all the help I can get. And speaking of—"

"Don't start."

"I will start, thank you very much. A pretty girl like you should be married with children."

"I *am* married. To this store. And Beautiful Things is my baby. I barely have time to breathe, let alone start a real family, and if you don't stop harping I won't have time to fast-track your necklace and earrings, either."

"Tyrant. Keep acting this way and you'll be single forever."

"God willing," Emma replied with a wink.

Ginny clicked her tongue and bent to sign the charge slip, muttering, "If your parents were alive I'd tell them how rotten you turned out."

Pulling a tolerant but affectionate face, Emma handed over the bag and leaned forward to accept Ginny's peck on the cheek.

"No more bickering with Mr. Lewis."

"Bah. He loves it and you know it. Behave yourself," the older woman ordered, then scurried away in a waft of expensive perfume.

Emma put the charge slip in the till and faced the stairs. They loomed, beckoning her to another of the Creep's e-mailed photographs, which would make her flesh crawl.

The Creep had been following her with a camera, and over the last six days he'd sent forty-two pictures.

Being followed was bad. The photographs were worse. But the big black Xs superimposed on her face in every shot were downright creepy. Hence the nickname.

It wasn't really necessary to look at this morning's new arrival before calling the police, was it?

No, she'd spare herself that much. Dealing with the police could turn into an all-day project, but at this point Emma didn't care how long it took. Her apartment was on the fourth floor of the Toliver's Treasure's building, and she'd already lost an entire weekend, waiting for the Internet company to track this person down.

The e-mails had stopped over the weekend, probably only because she hadn't gone out. No opportunity, no photos, right? So Friday's trip to the bank had been her last venture until this morning's coffee run, when the promise of caffeine and a crowded sidewalk had lured her from the building.

Obviously, the Creep had been waiting.

Every hair on the back of her neck prickled at the thought, and Emma's eyes narrowed. She dared whoever it was to keep this up. She'd be more than happy to introduce the Creep to the infamous Toliver temper. And her stun gun.

Squaring her shoulders, she marched for the stairs. No way would she let some whacko ruin the most important week of her life.

But she never made it to the stairs. A few feet away those suspicious hairs snapped to full attention.

She was being watched. She could feel it.

Turning instinctively, Emma found herself eyes-to-chin with Anthony Bracco.

She had to be imagining this. Fate couldn't be this cruel.

Emma blinked and prayed the apparition would disappear. It didn't. And he was angry. Muscles along a sharp jawline pulsed like a heartbeat as he ground his teeth.

Her day now completely destroyed, Emma looked up. Anthony hadn't changed. Not male-model handsome, but close enough. His eyes were an odd, indefinable color somewhere between brown and gray, like rich, dark smoke quartz. Framing them were thick lashes even blacker than his hair, and his eyebrows had a natural, devilish arch.

How fitting, considering the man was Satan.

''What fresh hell is this?'' she snapped.

''A new record,'' Anthony replied in his raspy, chocolatey voice. ''It only took you ten seconds to quote Dorothy Parker. Get upstairs. We have a problem.''

''No, *we* don't have a problem. *You* have a problem. If you don't get away from me I'm calling security.''

''Go ahead. You'll undoubtedly need them in a few minutes.''

''Are you threatening me?''

''Hold the tantrum, please. Believe me, if this wasn't urgent I wouldn't be here. Go. God forbid one of your precious clients should discover how awful you really are,'' Anthony said, forcibly turning Emma and propelling her up the stairs.

Emma felt as if she'd been struck by lightning. She was

numb everywhere but her waist, where Anthony's hands transferred their heat through thin yellow silk.

What was he doing here? This was insane.

Arriving at the top, Emma batted his hands away and turned into her office, barely giving him time to step inside before she slammed the door.

"What do you want?"

He ignored her to hurry behind the desk. Too stunned to react right away, she stared. What a waste of gorgeous male. Wide shoulders in an expensively shiny white T-shirt, and tight, narrow hips in button flys. Sinful. He was even more gorgeous than he'd been two years ago, when he'd lived in hand-made Italian suits.

But she hadn't fallen hopelessly in lust with the man for his looks. It was the way he crackled with energy that had initially caught her attention. In second place was his self-confidence. She'd learned too late it was actually cold, hard arrogance, but he'd been enchanting up till then.

Emma's temper gauge shot straight to the red when Anthony shoved her chair out of the way and started fiddling with her computer.

"What the— All right. That's it," Emma spat, lunging for the telephone.

In one deft move Anthony caught her wrist, then quickly captured the other as she went for the security button.

A brief, futile tugging match ensued, ending when Anthony landed on the desk chair with her in his lap. Glaring at him, she warned, "Get your hands off me."

"Mmm," Anthony murmured, far too close to her mouth, "just like old times."

His eyes were hooded as he watched her. Waiting. Daring her to do her worst.

Much as she'd love to accommodate him, her hormones had other ideas. Damn the man. He had some colossal nerve, showing up here like he owned the place. He'd disappeared two years ago after trying to seize control of her store, and she'd prayed daily that he'd stay gone.

No such luck, but she had to be careful. If she mashed him into a pulp he'd probably sue. Leaning away, she said, ''There'd better be a point to this.''

''There is. Look,'' he ordered simply, swiveling the chair so Emma faced the computer monitor.

On the screen was the Creep's latest e-mail, a picture of Emma in the yellow dress outside the local coffee shop. And as usual, there was a big black X superimposed over her face.

Forgetting herself for a moment, she slumped in his arms. ''I was only outside for three minutes.''

''That's all it takes.''

Emma turned to lock narrowed eyes with Anthony. Seeing a certain smugness there she tried to wriggle free, demanding, ''How did you know about the e-mails?''

''Your Internet provider called the FBI for help. How long has this been going on?''

''Let me go. And how did you know my Internet—''

''Would you stop digging your bony butt into my thigh? That hurts.''

Her temper blew and Emma pushed at him, grinding the heels of her hands into his chest.

''Ow! You—'' Anthony said, cut off by Emma's yelp as he let go.

Silk slid on denim, and she would have landed on the floor if he hadn't grabbed her arms. But as soon as she had a foot on solid ground she stumbled away, choking on angry words.

Anthony followed, asking, ''Why didn't you report these? If you don't start explaining I'll tie you to the couch.''

''Try it, Anthony. You think I fought dirty last time? Try me again and see what happens.''

''A deliberately provocative statement. I might take you up on that offer someday.''

''Lucky me.''

Anthony huffed out a laugh. ''Okay. We've established that I still hate you and you still hate me. Very productive.

Can we move on now? I have a lot to say and not much time to say it.''

''Start with how you knew my Internet service called the FBI.''

''I've been getting e-mails like this for three weeks,'' he said. ''Pictures, mostly.''

''Yeah? And?''

''And I don't have time to explain everything right now, so close your mouth and listen. We're in trouble, Emma. The FBI's right behind me and you need to promise you'll cooperate.''

''Oh, I'll cooperate, all right. Just as soon as you get out of my store.''

''I can't. They'll be here in a second. I'm under FBI protection until this guy's behind bars,'' he told her.

He looked sincere, but Emma knew that meant less than nothing. He'd looked sincere last time, too.

''Do you think I'm stupid? I have no reason to believe a word you've said.''

''You're impossible.''

''I'm impossible? After what you tried to pull last time you were here, I think I'm entitled to a little skepticism. So why don't you tell me what you're really doing here? And cut to the chase so I don't have to waste my time foiling your evil plans again.''

''Fine. We'll do it your way.''

Emma's eyes widened as Anthony began pulling his shirt from his jeans. ''What are you—are you insane? If you think I'm going to—''

''You asked for this,'' Anthony said, dragging the T-shirt over his head, leaving his hair a shiny mess. ''Just remember I tried to be reasonable.''

He locked eyes with her again, twisting around to expose the back of his left shoulder. Raw challenge shone from those eyes, and Emma felt her anger seep away in a moment of breathless regret. Why could she never rein it in until it was too late?

Disobeying every order issued in her head, Emma's eyes fell to Anthony's back.

This couldn't be happening.

But the gruesome evidence on Anthony's left shoulder was all too real.

A scar. A very big, very fresh, X-shaped scar.

Chapter 2

"Oh my God."

When those words wheezed from Emma, Anthony knew he'd gone too far. He'd come prepared for the temper, but he'd forgotten an actual human being lurked beneath its fire.

A brilliant diamond quivered on her right ring finger, shooting rainbows as she lifted her hand to touch his back.

"Don't. It itches like sin."

Emma's normally glowing complexion blanched, almost matching her icy green eyes as she jerked her hand away. "What happened?"

"Self-explanatory. Are you ready to listen now?"

"Yes. No. I..."

At the sudden unfocused look in her eyes, Anthony dropped the shirt to grab Emma. "Oh Lord. Don't faint."

He registered the feel of ropy muscles beneath cool skin and felt a surge of powerful disappointment. This wasn't how he remembered her at all. The Emma Toliver he recalled had been lusciously ripe and tough as nails. She was still beautiful, but she looked wrung out. Tired.

Tired was bad. When she reached her limits, Emma always came out swinging and God help her target. The fight wouldn't end until she was the only one left standing.

He should know. He was still recovering from the last time he'd backed her into a corner.

As she blinked away the haze, Anthony regrouped. "Emma, I'm sorry. I didn't mean to scare you, but I need your attention."

"Mission accomplished," she said, shaking off his hands to swoop down for his shirt, then slam it against his chest.

Anthony grunted at the impact and while he hurried back into the garment, she said, "I understand this is serious, and I can only imagine how you ended up with an X on your back. Finally messed with the wrong person, did you?"

"Is that your version of 'I told you so'?"

"That's beneath my level, Bracco. I'll cooperate with the FBI, but if you set foot in my store again, I swear to God I'll—"

"Hold it," Anthony interrupted. "If you'd stop ranting for three seconds I'll explain why I came here alone."

Emma's haughty, expectant expression made him want to howl. Letting the sarcasm flow, he said, "In case you weren't aware, you have a tendency to fly off the handle, and the people trying to catch this guy don't deserve the wrath of Emma. They're stretched so thin they can barely cover me, let alone produce a second team for you. So that means you're stuck with me, and there's something I want to say before this gets any worse."

Hands on hips now, Emma inquired, "What?"

Against his wishes, his body recognized that parts of her were still as lushly feminine as he remembered. The pose stretched silk across her breasts, highlighting a wispy lace bra barely containing the objects of many an unwanted erotic dream over the last two years.

Oh God. Total disaster. Why had he let himself panic like this? The FBI would protect her. He didn't have to, and she wouldn't let him anyhow.

But making sure she was safe wasn't the only reason he'd come. The agents didn't need her attitude, so he had some work to do before they got here. After a deep breath, he said, "I apologize."

"Are you feeling all right?"

"Why?" he asked, praying his reaction to her wasn't visible.

"I figured you must be gravely ill if you're apologizing. Or is that scar finally showing you the error of your ways?"

He couldn't help it. "And I suppose you consider your own actions completely justified."

"Let's compare, shall we? You tried to seduce me out of my store. I simply allowed you to tie your own noose. I'd say I was completely justified."

"You would say that. All I wanted was the businesses, Emma. Nothing personal."

He watched as a red taint bled up her neck into her face. "You made it personal."

"All right, let's stop this," Anthony said. "If it makes you feel better, I admit what I did was unforgivable. I was an ass, and believe it or not, I am truly sorry. Are we understood?"

"Yes. I get what you're saying. Now that you need something, you're trying to kiss up."

"Fine. If that's the way you want it to be, so be it. But I refuse to spend this entire investigation sniping with you, so either we agree to act like adults or we don't speak at all."

"Can I have that in writing?"

Anthony squeezed his eyes shut and visualized throttling that long, skinny neck. Ten minutes. That's all it took Emma to drive him nuts.

How was he supposed to survive this? First some psycho calling himself the Doppelgänger had sworn vengeance for the companies Anthony had chopped up. And now he was face-to-face with the biggest wrong he'd ever committed.

All he wanted to do was find the nearest corner and die

quietly of guilt. But no. Dop meant to punish him, and making him deal with Emma again definitely took the cruel and unusual prize.

And he'd just made it harder on himself by lying straight to her face.

Coward. She'd find out how he knew about those e-mails and tear him apart with her bare hands. And considering this newest nightmare she'd been sucked into, he wouldn't blame her one bit.

Watching Emma stare at him with one eyebrow raised, Anthony marveled at his own stupidity. God help him. Lies told in the heat of the moment were the least of his worries. There were other lies she could uncover. Like what had really happened two years ago.

He had to tell her. He owed her that much. But how did you tell someone they'd been nothing more than a convenient pawn, a casualty in the cold war between you and your father?

Still not the worst of it. If she found out what he'd done more recently, he was a dead man. Why couldn't he have left well enough alone?

Footsteps sounded in the hall, preempting self-recrimination hour. He knew who was outside the door: a group of seriously unhappy FBI agents who were about to encounter one of the bigger challenges of their careers.

They didn't even knock. Jim DeBerg came in first, followed by Layne Crawford and Walter Hornsby. The three of them looked at Anthony accusingly, while Emma's angry expression shifted to tolerance.

Stepping forward, she seized control. Huge surprise. "Good morning. I'm Emma Toliver. You must be the FBI."

She shook hands with Jim first, Anthony's best friend and a man very young to be where he was in the bureau. Thirty years old, and already in the Behavioral Sciences Unit.

Jim introduced himself. "Special Agent Jim DeBerg. I don't know how much Anthony told you, but we've certainly got a mess on our hands, Miss Toliver."

"So I hear," she acknowledged, turning to Layne Crawford.

Layne scared Anthony to death. She was a tiny little thing, sixtyish, with brilliant blue eyes that never stopped watching. Jim had summoned her a week ago and Anthony still knew nothing about her. He didn't even know what position she held in the Bureau, if she even held one. All he knew was that she loved to make people talk.

Not a big fan of talking himself, Anthony avoided her at all costs.

He waited for Layne to introduce herself by title, but she gave only her name and stepped back in deference to Walter Hornsby. A giant in his mid-thirties, his job was to coordinate the practical aspects of the investigation—security and communication with the police.

Hornsby gave his usual muttered greeting while Anthony watched Emma. She was an expert at reading people, but this time he could see her struggling. Good luck. He would enjoy watching her realize these three lived to annoy.

Jim began. "Do I need a warrant to look at your computer?"

"Not necessary," Emma responded. "Be my guest."

While Jim clicked through messages, Layne's eyes burned into his skull. Silence thundered through the room until she finally glanced at Emma.

"Miss Toliver, is there somewhere I can speak to Mr. Bracco in private?" she asked.

"No one will disturb you in the boardroom," Emma said, "Anthony knows where it is."

He led Layne from the room like a man leading his own executioner to the gallows. Two doors down on the right was the boardroom, brightly lit by wide, paned windows and dominated by a long walnut table. The room smelled of aged wood, and the old leather chair he slumped into creaked beneath his weight.

Layne sat primly, ankles crossed. She stared at him

awhile before saying, "You were placed in protective custody for your own safety. I thought that was understood."

"It was."

"Interesting, as you completely disregarded our cautions this morning. Jim said you were already halfway here by the time he called you with the Internet service info, so I'd dearly love to hear how you knew about Emma's e-mails before we did."

"I'm psychic?"

Layne smiled. "She's a beautiful woman. Lovely bone structure, and all that delightful blond hair. Given your rather...colorful past together, I would assume there's unfinished business."

Anthony bobbed his chin, neither denying nor admitting anything.

"You're right," Layne said. "It doesn't matter, does it? But I must insist you share your insight with me. Frankly, I'm concerned I might have missed something in your e-mails."

Knowing he was being played with, Anthony lied, "It wasn't anything concrete. There was a lot of publicity on what I did to Emma, and Doppelgänger could have seen it. Then Jim was talking about sympathetic symbols, someone this guy might relate to as one of my business victims, and it got me thinking. That's all."

Layne shocked him by uttering two syllables that crisply defined her disbelief. "Pardon my French," she added as an afterthought. "But I wasn't born yesterday. Tell me the truth or I'll start digging. You know I'll find...something."

Purposefully mirroring Layne's speech patterns, minus the French, he asked, "Hypothetically speaking, if I admitted I'd found out about the e-mails in a less...intellectual manner, would you find it necessary to inform Emma?"

"That remains to be seen."

"Why are you threatening me? I'm not the criminal in this equation. I haven't done anything wrong."

"Excuse my need to poke holes in your reasoning, but

there's a very dangerous man out there who disagrees,'' Layne said. ''In his mind you've done many things wrong. Now, I fully appreciate the fact that you've turned your life around, and believe me, I applaud and respect you for it. But if you hide things from us we can't move forward.''

With a sigh of defeat, Anthony said, ''I have an insider here at the store. Charles, Emma's goldsmith.''

Layne's brows shot to her hairline. ''Dare I ask why?''

''I tried to call Emma about four months ago. She was out so I got Charles instead, and we talked. I told him the truth about what really happened back then, and it sorta developed into something else. Anyway, Brady told him about the e-mails this morning, and Charles called me. You were gone. Jim was out. I panicked.''

Ignoring his admission, Layne asked, ''Sorta developed into what, exactly?''

Anthony rubbed his eyebrows. ''Emma didn't have enough capital to get this auction lot of metals and stones she needed for Beautiful Things, so Charles and I rigged her bid. I've got about half a million sunk into her design label and she doesn't know.''

Layne was silent for a decade or so, then observed, ''You can't help yourself, can you? Emma's a proud woman. If she finds out she won't be amused.''

''No, she won't. After what happened two years ago you can imagine what she'll think, but I took measures to make sure she'd never find out.''

''Is there a chance she'd understand why you did it?''

''Are you kidding?'' Anthony asked. ''I had my reasons, but at the time I didn't know any of this would happen. So what's done is done. There's nothing I can do about it now.''

''Agreed. However, we have a problem. If we're to continue baiting this Doppelgänger creature—''

Anthony interrupted, ''No way. Forget it. I may not care much for the woman, but I can't condone using her as bait.

Besides, sooner or later her temper will take over and she'll run for the hills. Maybe that's for the best."

"You *cannot* allow that to happen. This is a game for him, Anthony. A sick, twisted game. He's become fixated on Emma and we need to maintain his target area—the store—in order to trap him. If it closes or she leaves, he'll believe we've cut off access, and I don't want to imagine what might happen next. However, Jim, Walt and I have better things to do than play referee between you and Emma. That means you have an occupation now—to ensure the store stays open and she stays here, come hell or high water."

"I can't!" Anthony argued. "She hates me."

"Then I guess you'd better remedy that, hadn't you? Whatever you have to do to keep her here, you'll do."

"No way. It won't work. You haven't witnessed her in action, Layne. If you want my honest opinion, Emma might be put to better use. Get her talking to this guy on the Internet. She'll have him crying for his mommy inside of an hour."

"Interesting, but let's put it this way. Either you keep Emma here or I'll tell on you."

Anthony ground his teeth. "Speaking of sick, twisted games..."

Layne smiled.

Left alone with Jim and Walter, Emma worried at a thumbnail while the two men crowded over a file on her desk.

This was insane. Absolutely insane. One minute she was stressed over business and now this. And no one seemed too interested in telling her anything.

Taking matters into her own hands, she slipped behind the agents to see what was in that file.

Neither of them objected as she watched them flip through printed-out e-mail photographs of Anthony. There were twenty or so, and it turned Emma's stomach to see the big black Xs over his back in every shot.

Don't think about it. If she thought about it, she'd lose more than her cool.

But she couldn't believe her eyes. Not a single suit in any of them. And in all the pictures, Anthony's hair was much longer than it was today. He hadn't shaved, either.

Anthony scruffy? What the heck was going on?

She had to admit the fresh-out-of-bed look was no insult to the eye, but back then, Anthony had always been preening, his appearance like an arsenal for corporate warfare.

The smile was his nuclear warhead and the scruff would steal some destructive force.

The scruff was gone now, but her curiosity was on full alert. If he was gearing up for a return to Bracco Inc., his father's Chicago-based acquisitions company, he wouldn't be running around looking like that. And Toliver's Treasures was gossip central. It seemed inconceivable she wouldn't have heard he was back in St. Paul after his highly publicized disappearance.

But with Anthony looking like that, no one would have recognized him. He'd better not be up to something. If he was, he'd have much more urgent problems than a stalker.

And she couldn't get that scar out of her mind. The sight of it was burned indelibly on her brain, and a very unwanted pang of sympathy whispered to the surface.

Stop it, she scolded herself. Don't let him get to you again. Even in the throes of an unhappy reunion he still had that annoying aversion to explanations, and the live-wire quality was so subdued she could hardly believe he was the same person.

And what was that apology about? It was two years late but she suspected he'd actually meant it.

Something was wrong with him. Something more than a scar.

"You keep at this," Jim told Hornsby. "Write down anything that strikes you even if it seems coincidental. I'm off to depose Miss Toliver."

"Depose?" she repeated. "Will I need an attorney?"

"Nah. Is there another private space available? Someplace comfortable. We probably won't take that long but you never know."

Emma led him up a discreet staircase tucked in one corner of her store office. They emerged into what used to be a guest room but was now her design office. Passing through it, they entered a hallway and finally convened in her living room.

"Colorful place," Jim said. "Jewel tones. No surprise there, I guess."

Emma shrugged. "I love shiny things."

He sat in a Queen Anne armchair, spreading a file open in his lap. He scanned a few pages and Emma stole the opportunity to examine him more closely. Not what she might have expected an agent to look like. He was way too young, for one thing, and handsome. Not quite in Anthony's league, but handsome.

"All right," he said, catching her staring.

He raised his eyebrows and she crossed her arms over her chest. If he planned to grill her she should at least be allowed to stare.

He began again. "I'll just index the info we already have. If we need to make corrections, go ahead and stop me. Emma Rae Toliver. Age, twenty-six. Five foot ten and I'll spare you the weight estimate. Blond hair, green eyes. Owner, Toliver's Treasures. Beautiful Things, too. Started the design business three years ago. No siblings. Mother, Meredith Sullivan-Toliver, deceased—let's see. Twenty-two years ago. Aneurysm?"

Emma nodded.

Jim continued, "Father, Marshall Toliver, no middle initial. Remarried one, two, three times. Deceased four years ago. Passed in his sleep. Cardiac arrest at age fifty."

She nodded again and Jim scratched his cheek before saying, "Says here the final Mrs. Toliver, Vivian, retained the family residence upon his death. How's your relationship with her?"

"Fine. We don't see each other much but we're very close."

"What about the other two wives?"

"We talk once in a while, exchange Christmas cards. That's about it."

"It doesn't say if there were any children," Jim stated.

"There weren't any."

"Why not?"

Emma fought a rising tide of irritation and answered, "My father didn't want more children."

"Is Vivian remarried?"

"Excuse me." Emma stopped him. "What does that have to do with anything?"

"It's just a question. I might ask a lot of seemingly irrelevant things, but please answer anyway."

"Why? Trying to catch me in a lie or something?"

The agent gave her a tolerant look. "Can I do my job without the hostility, please? I understand you're less than thrilled to be involved in all this, but the sooner you cooperate, the sooner it's over."

Emma sat back in the chair, unrepentant but answering, "Yes. Vivian is remarried. Twin boys, obviously quite young. I baby-sit for them occasionally but I don't know her husband very well."

"Better," Jim said. "Toliver's Treasures. Opened 1876. Hasn't changed much. China, silver, art and books still on the main floor, jewelry on the second floor balcony. Famous for its loyal clientele and architectural features like original oak paneling and staircase. Very beautiful, by the way. I was impressed."

"Thank you." Emma said. "Now will you humor me by answering a technical question?"

"Maybe."

"If you didn't know I was getting e-mails, why do you know so much about me?"

Jim gave her a long look. "Shouldn't be a surprise that you were a suspect until this morning. Never our chief suspect. You don't fit the profile. Too much to lose."

Emma absorbed that as Jim went on. "Next, the security system. Major upgrade when you expanded the workroom for the design business. Many a service call since then. What's the problem?"

"If the roof component's set to full sensitivity, it goes off all the time. Thunder, planes, anything can trigger it."

"Risky. I'll have Hornsby take a look. See? Something positive. You'll get your security system fixed for free."

"Be still my heart," Emma muttered. The security system worked just fine the way it was.

Jim watched her down the length of his nose. "Sarcastic, aren't you?"

"Not usually. It's been quite a morning."

"Well, we'll try to keep this as painless as possible. And I should bring you up-to-date quickly...."

He hesitated at the sound of footsteps in the hall.

"That would be Brady," Emma explained, just before Brady hollered.

"Emma? You up here?"

She said, "He's my right hand, so I'd appreciate it if he's allowed to hear whatever you have to say."

"Saves time." Jim shrugged.

Emma got up to meet Brady in the doorway. Seeing Jim, he asked, "What's going on? Who's that? And who's the guy in your office?"

"I'll explain in a minute. Brady, this is Jim DeBerg, FBI."

"That was fast," Brady said, crossing to shake Jim's hand. Emma watched them size each other up. Jim calmly scanned Brady's dark features as Brady disguised his wary expression.

As the department manager headed for the couch, she

caught Jim's eyes on his ponytail. It stretched halfway down his back, just a few inches shorter than Emma's hair. Over the years they must have gone fifty rounds about the danger of long hair in a jeweler's workroom, but Brady refused to cut it off.

Too bad his wife liked it or Emma might actually have an ally in harping about safety.

The two men muttered social niceties while Emma sat down next to Brady, groaning as Jim produced another file.

Same drill as last time. "Brady Edgar Wilson. Age, thirty-eight. Married to Tanya. No children. You manage Toliver's Treasures' jewelry department. Supervisor for Beautiful Things. I see that your father, Edgar, worked as a goldsmith here as well. Fifty years? Is that correct?"

"Yes," Brady answered. "He was very happy here."

"Must have been. Anything to add before we get started?"

"Nope."

"All right then, here's the deal."

Jim proceeded to explain that their suspect referred to himself as "The Doppelgänger," a German word meaning a ghostly double that haunts its earthly counterpart. They'd taken to calling him simply "Dop."

The situation began when Anthony was attacked just over three weeks ago, on June fifteenth. Dop claimed responsibility the next day, telling them in a virtually untraceable e-mail that Anthony was evil and Dop had marked him so the world would beware.

"But it's been two years since Anthony was fired from Bracco and no one's heard a peep from him since," Emma said. "Why now?"

Jim said, "We're guessing Dop couldn't find Anthony before he came back to St. Paul. Very few people knew where he was and they weren't real likely to share."

"Any *guess* why this person's after Emma now?" Brady asked.

Emma frowned at him. Jim might be young but at least

he was finally giving them details. And she couldn't help but be impressed when Jim took Brady down a couple pegs with, "Let me be honest. We're not dealing with your garden-variety stalker. It would be irresponsible on my part or yours to assume there's a logical reason for what Dop does. So what I need you to do right now is listen. Let me get through the facts and maybe something will ring a bell with you. Until then, bear with me."

Brady relaxed while Jim backed up to clarify a few things. Anthony hadn't had any warning. No e-mails like Emma was getting. They hadn't started until afterward but the pictures had been taken beforehand, showing them that Dop had been following Anthony for at least two weeks prior to the attack.

Emma couldn't help it. "Where was he when it happened?"

"At home. But he'd spent most of the night at his parents' house. Well, his mom and stepfather's, actually. I understand you've met Sophia and Geoff?" Jim asked.

"Yes," Emma said. Geoff Turner was a thoracic surgeon at the hospital where Sophia was Director of Nursing, and they'd gotten married shortly after Anthony disappeared. "We're on a charity board together. American Red Cross."

"Oh yeah." Jim nodded. "You have a fund-raiser this Thursday night, right?"

Emma looked at Brady again. The Red Cross charity auction was a loaded topic around here. During the festivities, she was supposed to meet with Trenton Neville, one of the world's most influential jewelry merchandisers. He needed to be in St. Paul that day and he'd added the auction to his agenda so they could discuss Beautiful Things.

And he wasn't messing around. Neville planned on bidding upward of twenty-thousand dollars on whatever she'd donated.

But last week, Brady had accidentally sold the gardenia necklace earmarked for the auction, forcing Emma to sacrifice a piece she cherished. Not only was the rose necklace the first piece Charles, her master goldsmith, had ever crafted for Beautiful Things, but it held other, more personal and private meanings.

Thanks to Brady and their material shortage, she had to give it up.

And now it seemed all the arguing and juggling might have been unnecessary. With this psycho on the loose, they probably weren't going anywhere Thursday night and it was to be hoped Trenton Neville had a heart. Or a really good sense of humor.

Her temper meter nudged upward a bit. She'd seen Anthony's mother, Sophia, a week ago at a fund-raiser planning meeting. All things considered, Emma understood why she wouldn't have said anything. But if Sophia had, the Creep's e-mails would have been reported instantly to the proper authorities.

She turned her attention back to Jim, who told them Anthony had stuck around after his parents' party, talking with his stepfather into the wee hours. He went to sleep there for a while, but around four-thirty in the morning he drove home.

Anthony remembered seeing movement in the backyard as he pulled into the garage and was jumped almost the second he stepped outside to investigate.

Dop made the first slash immediately from Anthony's neck to the base of his shoulder blade. Blood trail evidence showed Anthony had fought for an extended period of time before blood loss and a blow from his attacker rendered him unconscious.

Anthony couldn't remember Dop finishing the X. The working theory was that the second cut had been made after he'd gone down.

"Dop's calling card, presumably," Jim said.

Listening in horror, Emma felt her stomach begin to churn again. Even if Jim was an agent and had probably told worse tales, she couldn't believe his nonchalant delivery.

But she'd seen Anthony with her own two eyes. She knew the outcome, so there was no reason her stomach should be performing acrobatics.

"Problem," Jim said. "It was a new moon, and Anthony's yard light was out. Probably not a coincidence. At any rate, the only physical description he can give us is that Dop is fast, taller than himself, and wore black clothes and a ski mask. Finding someone taller than six-two does narrow the field, but that's all we've got for a physical description."

Still in gruesome narrative mode, Jim explained that Anthony had been found two hours later by his housekeeper. The X itself hadn't been deep enough to damage bone or muscle, and the EMTs didn't find another knife wound. But time had been Anthony's enemy. The fight had cost him copious amounts of blood and his prognosis at the scene had been "grave."

Emma's stomach seized. Thank God she'd skipped breakfast. Her entire mind was flooded with a vision of Anthony lying helpless on the ground, bleeding and unconscious. He might have been ambitious and unethical, but no one deserved that.

This couldn't be happening.

And then Jim said, "The worst part was, those people who'd been at that staff party were on duty when Anthony was brought in. So everyone was shook up and Sophia was a wreck. Luckily, Geoff kept his head and was calm enough to resuscitate him."

Emma covered her mouth, feeling bile rise into her throat.

"Emma?" Jim asked sharply. "Are you all right?"

"Oh, no." Brady panicked, dragging her off the couch and explaining, "Weak stomach."

Emma stumbled along after him, limp as a rag doll. Her mind seemed to have exited stage left with the word *resuscitate.*

Brady herded her into the hall bathroom, propped her against a cool tile wall and asked, "Are you gonna throw up?"

Unsure of the answer, Emma bobbed her head vaguely and closed her eyes to avoid his inspection. The last thing she needed right now was Brady asking why she was so completely shattered.

But that's exactly what she was. Horrified. And eaten alive by guilt and shame.

Her stomach lurched again at the thought that the only thing separating her from Dop was a push over the edge of sanity. They both hated Anthony Bracco with a passion, but she wouldn't wish this on anyone.

Anthony was just a man. A bad man, but she should have listened to her therapist. It was time to let go. If she didn't, ancient history would taint the rest of her life and she'd never get rid of her temper.

"Deep breaths," Brady ordered. "As soon as they're gone I'll get you the biggest cheesecake I can find... Oh. Sorry. We'll wait until your stomach calms down. But for now, sit down, and for once in your life, let someone else take the wheel."

He stopped to wet a washcloth and press it to her forehead. They'd spent so much of the last three months arguing over the business that Emma almost started bawling at the simple act of kindness.

"I'm gonna go speak with what's-his-name out there for a few minutes," Brady said soothingly. "I'll give you time to pull yourself together, but don't leave this room until I come back."

Emma nodded, hoping he was aware that Anthony was in the building. She could read between the lines. Brady looked calm, his square face stoic and watchful, but if he came across Anthony, his perpetual bad mood might turn ugly.

Chapter 3

The boardroom had fallen quiet. Only the sound of Layne's pen scratching on a legal pad could be heard while Anthony stoically picked at a brass rivet on his chair arm. He didn't know what came next, but the day had to take an upward turn soon.

But not quite yet. The door opened for Jim and Hornsby, followed by Brady Wilson, who hadn't changed one bit. He still had that snooty demeanor. Anthony had no idea why Emma put up with the guy.

"Where's Emma?" Layne asked after chilly introductions.

"Upstairs," Brady answered. "I hope you're proud of yourself, Bracco."

"Mr. Wilson," Jim cautioned, "Your personal grievances with Anthony can wait. Right now we have business to discuss."

Brady sat down at the head of the table, the snootiness evaporating before their eyes as he said to Jim, "Look. Let me be straight with you. There's a lot going on around here that you don't understand, and I'm not at liberty to share. But I have to ask that you keep Emma out of this. She's got enough on her plate."

"What do you mean?" Jim asked.

Brady looked down at the table. "Just understand that if she's not real cooperative, it's not her fault."

"So how do you suggest we make things easier?" Jim asked.

Turning his eyes on Anthony, Brady said, "Get him out of here, for one thing."

"I'm sorry but we can't do that," Walter said. "I appreciate the warning but you need to understand what we're up against. We're trying to install a reliable security system at Anthony's house, and we've had to tear out and upgrade all the electrical wiring to support it. The same drill you went through when you upgraded the store's system."

Brady grimaced.

"Yeah. It hasn't been a small or easy task. So until that's finished we simply don't have the men available to protect two people at separate sites."

But Brady started shaking his head. "We've got security here at the store. Can't we use them?"

"No," Jim said, "They have their own job to do."

Layne said, "Anthony, why don't you step outside for a while? See what you can do to smooth things over?"

He got up while Brady protested, "It's not that simple. He can't just—"

"Give him a chance," Layne said. "Trust me, Brady, none of us wish to upset Emma. But this is the hand we've been dealt, so we've all got jobs to do, including you. You're in charge of protecting Emma's businesses during this investigation. The Bureau's job is to protect her from the suspect. But none of us can protect Emma and Anthony from each other. That's something they have to work out for themselves."

Brady sucked his teeth, took a deep breath, then shot Anthony a glance full of defeat and frustration. "She's in the guest bath upstairs."

Anthony left and stood in the hall, thinking about what Brady had just done. Pretty shocking, considering what Emma might do if she found out what Brady had told them.

What did he mean by "a lot going on around here that you don't understand"? Was it business or personal? Charles had told him Emma was ready to rip the roof of the insurance office to get at the stones they'd helped her acquire. But that would hardly be enough to send someone like Emma over the edge.

Hoping Brady was exaggerating, Anthony headed toward the office steps, and on his way upstairs he gave himself a pep talk. He wasn't the same person he'd been back then. Not everything was win or lose. There were degrees now, and he had rules.

Rule number one: Keep life simple. That was laughable under the circumstances. Dop aside, Emma was as complicated as it got. Keeping her here wouldn't be easy because he was already fighting the urge to run rather than tangle with her again.

The woman was flat-out vicious. He hadn't known how vicious until that night they were supposed to sign the contracts giving him fifty-one percent control over Toliver's Treasures.

Not for one second had he planned on actually taking the store from her. He may have been jealous of her for who she was and what she had, but he'd never intended to let things go that far. He'd singled her out for one reason and one reason only. The temper. He'd been counting on her to use it. But not the way she had. *She* was the one who'd made things personal.

When he got to the apartment that night, he found candles, champagne on ice and Emma in a filmy black silk dress that didn't hide one dang thing. And she'd stroked his ego, thanking him for solving the crisis he'd created.

He should have seen it coming—should have known

she'd mercilessly use their powerful attraction against him the same way he'd used it against her. Giving him hungry looks and touching him, whispering things that made his blood roar after ten days of a strict hands-off policy.

She'd ripped his original plan completely off the rails. Made him believe, if only for a few minutes, that he could pull it off. Get what he'd come for, and keep Emma and the store, too.

By the time dinner was over, she'd had him so drunk on his own power, and so beyond ready to rip that dress off with his teeth, he'd never considered he might already be in her temper's grasp.

Idiot. Just before she'd nuked him, the only thing on his mind was feeling her beneath him, making her surrender everything until his greed for Emma Toliver had been sated.

And nuke him she had. One nanometer away from a kiss and she'd punched him so hard his jaw was sore for weeks afterward.

Then she'd started yelling, things that were carved into his skull to this day. Sadistically awful things, like he destroyed companies to make him feel as powerful as his father.

One ego brutally murdered. Granted, it had needed killing. But for a couple weeks, he'd refused to relive what she'd said. Why should he? Emma hadn't really known anything about him. She couldn't understand the pressure he'd been under or the hell his father put him through. She'd been his ticket out of the war with Maxim Bracco, and another casualty had meant nothing to him. Especially a casualty who had a fiercely loyal clientele, a perfect life and a respectable business to run.

She'd made a fool out of him, and since that's what he'd singled her out to do in the first place, it shouldn't have hurt quite so much. Somehow those moments where he'd believed he could defeat his father and win Emma had never completely gone away, despite the nuking. And her judgment of him hadn't been exactly accurate, but she'd been right enough that two years later he still judged himself by it.

Anthony took a deep breath and let it out. Sometimes it floored him to remember the way he'd been. He couldn't even conceive of that mind-set anymore and he'd spent most of the last year trying to make up for his former life, donating time, money and brain power to the people he'd hurt.

Emma had been a problem, though. He'd had no idea what to do about her. Eventually the guilt goaded him into picking up the phone and the rest was history. Charles had been a godsend. When he'd called about that material auction, it seemed like the perfect solution: a way to make amends without having to see her again.

Face it, pal, he told himself. You're scared of her. And if that auction comes back to haunt you, you'll have no one to blame but yourself.

Which reminded him of rule number two: Never take yourself too seriously. Also laughable. Between Jim and Emma, there wasn't a slug's chance in a salt mine he'd be allowed to regrow the ego.

And in light of the reunion with Emma, Anthony wouldn't even touch his third rule: No women for a while. Now that he'd seen her again, his sacred, final law was dead as a doornail. He might be afraid of her, but she owned him.

Reaching the top of the staircase, Anthony hesitated, finding himself in an office that hadn't existed two years ago. It wasn't really a surprise that the business was invading her living space, nor that it was right next door to her bedroom.

Don't peek. Get your mind right before you go any farther.

Pressing fingertips to his forehead and grimacing, Anthony tried not to look. But he couldn't help himself. He peeked into her bedroom, and all he could see was that evil black dress.

It took more than one deep breath to clear the image from his mind. The war is over, he told himself. You don't have to be like your father anymore. You can't. You learned the hard way. Now be a real man and face the music.

Keeping his eyes out of her bedroom, Anthony moved on down the hall to knock on the bathroom door. "Emma, let me in."

"Go away."

"I'm not going away. In fact, I'm pretty certain you'll have houseguests for the foreseeable future."

There was no response.

"Are you gonna make me stand out here all day? What if one of your employees comes upstairs?"

That did it. "The door is open, Einstein."

Anthony drew one more deep breath and turned the knob. Stepping inside to find her slumped on a brocade bench, he said, "My mother did teach me some manners, you know."

The jade eyes turned on him and for a moment Anthony hardly recognized her. She seemed shrunken. Vulnerable. And white as paper. He'd never seen her this way and he abruptly realized why Brady was so concerned about Emma.

Not until that moment had he ever realized how much he relied on Emma Toliver being evil. It was easier to justify what he'd done to her when he thought of her as a witch.

Blowing out a breath, Anthony leaned against the door and stuck his hands in his pockets. He needed to get her talking, so he said the only thing that came to mind. "Did Jim upset you?"

"I'd rather not talk about it."

"Neither would I, but tell me anyway."

Emma bit her bottom lip, an action Anthony remembered well. She always did that when trying to control her temper. After a pause, she said, "He told me what happened to you."

"Jim has a tendency to be blunt. I'm sure the truth isn't half as bad as what he told you."

"It doesn't get much worse than nearly dying, Anthony."

"No, you're right. It doesn't. But you can see for yourself I'm fine. No harm done other than the obvious."

"How can you be so..."

Emma trailed off and fiddled with the big diamond on her right hand. Feeling relatively safe—safe enough to let his guard down a bit—he soothed, "I've had more time to deal with this than you have. Believe me, a week ago I wasn't quite so flippant."

Keeping her eyes on the gem, Emma nodded. "You're moving in?"

"I believe so. We've been hopping from one hotel to the next because they're still installing a security system at my house. Here, everything is contained under one roof, needs-wise."

"Yes, everything of mine. What happens if you need to work?"

"I don't work. My former life as a lecherous, corporate-raiding swine was very profitable."

He'd given her the perfect opportunity for sarcasm, but she didn't take it. Instead, she said, "How's your mother? She must have been terrified."

"She was, but Mom's resilient. So far she's doing all right. And she's got Geoff. My stepfather, in case you didn't know."

The platinum head nodded, but Emma still wouldn't look at him. "Do you like him?"

"Yes. I didn't always. We've gotten to know each other better, though, and that helps."

"I suppose saving your life helped, too."

Anthony grunted out a laugh. "Yeah, that helped, too."

He wondered about this gentle probing she was conducting. Asking after his mother was the last thing he would have expected. But he could handle this. In fact, it would almost seem restful if the subject wasn't so dire.

He shouldn't have relaxed. The next probe was not gentle.

"You said 'former life.' Are you asking me to believe you're no longer a lecherous, corporate-raiding swine?"

"I'm not asking you to believe anything."

Emma finally looked up, and to his relief there was color

in her cheeks. Not the blazing, angry stain he'd learned to fear, just an innocent, healthy glow as she said, "Try to understand. As much as I'd love to blame you for this, I know you're not really responsible for Dop's actions."

Anthony raised his eyebrows. Someone had been in therapy. She said, "But you and the FBI can't be here. I've got a storeful of employees who'll be in danger if I stay. And I know you want to scream every time I say this, but my clients are like family. I can't see any other solution than to leave. If we're gone, nothing will happen."

A silent curse echoed in Anthony's head. She'd already made up her mind, and it wouldn't be easy to sway her now.

"You can't leave," he said, buying time to come up with some leverage. "Mom said you have a Red Cross thing Thursday night. And there's a rumor going around that some jewelry honcho will be there to see a design that might earn you a patent. Well, it wasn't a rumor. Layne told me."

"How did she know that?"

"I wish I knew. She scares me senseless. I haven't gotten away with any of my usual tricks since she showed up," Anthony said, only half-joking.

"Liar. You managed to get here, didn't you?"

"Yes, but she probably let it happen. Look, I know this situation has to be overwhelming, but if you turn your intelligence on it, you might prove to be a valuable asset to—"

Oops. Anthony thudded to a halt at the sight of her hostile glare. He'd attempted to call on her pride, and she'd seen through him in seconds.

"Nice try," she muttered as he backpedaled, crouching in front of her to make eye contact she couldn't evade.

"If you run we'll never catch him."

"Run? That's your department. I'm protecting people because I care what happens to them, not saving my own a—"

"Emma." He cut her off, his eyes involuntarily dropping to her mouth. Blood pounded through his veins and a slow breath escaped as Emma's own eyes mirrored the action a moment later.

He had to get out of here. The attraction still had him in a stranglehold. If she did that again he wouldn't be able to stop himself from doing what he itched to do. Touch her. Feel her cool skin heat as his hands explored.

But if he did it, Emma would leave. Layne would find her, tell her about Charles and that auction, and then Emma would hunt him down.

"Listen," he said, starting again. "I know you're scared right now, but you need to understand something about Dop. If he feels you've cut off access, he'll take his frustration out on someone important to you. Or he could pick another victim who doesn't have the resources we do. How will you feel if that happens?"

She scratched at an eyebrow with a long pink nail, and the scar on his shoulder burned in response. Pushing harder, he added, "I know you don't trust me, and frankly, I don't blame you. But I haven't been idly sitting by and letting this happen. I've learned there are ways of surviving the FBI, and if you're not careful, your perverse nature might find it amusing."

"Jerk."

"Sorry, but I'm sick of being serious all the time. So how about this? We could work out some ground rules so we know how to act around each other."

"Can I ask you something first?"

"Can I stop you?"

Emma gave him a pained look and fired. "Is this whole attitude adjustment a near death epiphany or what? Because I find it very disturbing."

"There you go, sugarcoating everything again."

"Answer the question, smart aleck."

"Why do you want to know?"

"Why won't you ever talk about anything?"

"Isn't this where the nun smacks our knuckles for bickering in class?"

Emma sagged against the wall, looked up at the ceiling and shook her head. "I'd forgotten how irritating you can be."

Relaxing a bit, he scooted her over on the bench and sat beside her. "So you'll stay?"

"As if I have a choice," Emma answered, leaning away. She still couldn't believe this was happening.

How much worse could it get? On top of everything else, a stalker and Anthony Bracco had been added to the pile. Not to mention having him in her *home,* along with the FBI.

And was she supposed to be buying his act? He'd deflected the question about his attitude the same way he used to deflect any question that hit too close to his schemes. She wasn't blind. He might have changed, but not in any significant way.

All the same, he was playing the responsible role quite well, warning her about Dop and what he might do if she left.

But whether Anthony had changed or not, there was still anger simmering between them, and no matter how many ground rules they hid behind, it would eventually boil over.

And anger wasn't the only thing simmering. He hadn't been here more than an hour, and twice already she'd felt that familiar separation of brain and body. Her brain would tell her to keep away, but her body had its own ideas.

Even now, sitting beside him, she could feel herself responding. His energy may have been subdued but it was still there, if a little different. Emma had never understood why he affected her this way, but apparently it was something that would never change or lose its power.

When his eyes had fallen to her mouth a few minutes ago, she knew she wouldn't have rejected his kiss. Any form of comfort would have been welcome, but she must be losing her mind if she considered Anthony Bracco an acceptable alternative to cheesecake.

Struggling to pull herself together, Emma answered, "I need time to think."

"How much time?"

"You know what? Forget it. I can't believe I'm even speaking to you. I'm going back to work."

She rushed into the hallway with Anthony in pursuit, urging, "Emma, you can't pretend this isn't happening."

Just as he figured, reasoning with her was a waste of breath. By the time Emma reached the stairs leading to the sales floor a professional smile was plastered on her face.

Denial. Complete and utter denial.

Emma's attitude worried him, but Anthony knew he'd dodged the first bullet. It took him a moment to figure out how he'd accomplished that. And then he realized something vital as he watched her shake hands with an older gentleman and lead him gently toward a counter.

Quiet moments were the enemy. If Emma was angry, she'd run, just like he always did. Except she'd run straight downstairs to work, where he was supposed to keep her. And since angering Emma Toliver seemed to be Anthony's specialty, Layne might never get a chance to deliver on that threat.

"Where'd she go?" Jim asked from down the hall.

Anthony turned, gesturing toward the counter. "Downstairs."

"We'd better give her some time to recover before we take it any further. Hornsby'll be talking to store security in a minute. I'll have to help with the employees, but let's have a talk first."

Jim closed the door as Anthony sank into a creaky chair. "So," the agent said simply, his eyebrows raised.

"Would you accept a bribe in lieu of this particular conversation?" Anthony asked.

"Not on your life."

"Don't even think it. You know why I'm off women."

"Yeah, you screw up and run away," Jim said. "Been

doing it as long as I've known you. But Emma's got a lot going for her. She's smart, gorgeous and doesn't take any of your crap. Not too many women around with all those attributes."

"There's one key factor missing in your summation. She's a witch of the first order. You want her? She's all yours."

"Generous offer. I'd accept, but you'd probably rearrange my anatomy if I did. Anyway, Layne told me what you and Charles have been up to. Can't help thinking you went through an awful lot of trouble for someone you can't stand."

"I didn't do it for her," Anthony told him. "It was my version of making amends, which, translated, means I did it to make myself feel better."

"Okay." Jim sighed. "But you have to keep her here somehow. Are you grasping the irony? You, the speed and distance record holder, have to keep someone else from running away."

"Yes, one of those moments I'm convinced God's up there laughing."

Jim didn't bite. "You know, if you'd talk about things once in a while, you'd be better off. Emma's father wasn't exactly saint material, either. Maybe if you explained what happened—"

Giving his friend a wry look, Anthony interrupted, "Sorry, but I like to keep the number of people trying to kill me down to a bare minimum."

"Ah, yes, here comes the sarcasm. I'll stop. So back to business. We're about to get a whole lot more aggressive."

"How?"

"Several ideas are on the table. Dop's gotta make a mistake somewhere along the line. We'll help him do that."

Anthony held up his hands and waited expectantly.

"You and your results mentality," Jim complained.

"Well, it's a little hard to be patient, Jim. He's already

blown every profile you've come up with. It's like he's deliberately changing course just to throw you off base.''

''You're right, he is doing that. But meanwhile he's showing us he's done time in either law enforcement or prison. I'd guess the latter. Guys in there study how we work. He's also highly intelligent, efficient and patient. When we bring him down I'll definitely be publishing his case.''

''*If* we bring him down.''

''Oh ye of little faith,'' Jim commented. ''Look, I need to go help Hornsby. You keep an eye on Emma. Make sure she doesn't take off on us.''

''Yes, sir. Hey, wait a second,'' Anthony said. ''What did you make of Brady?''

''I don't know yet. I'm not sure I buy his altruistic act. He grew up at the store, same as Emma, but she's holding all the reins. And Brady's wife left him a couple of weeks back. Emma doesn't know that, though, so keep quiet about it.''

Anthony sighed. ''Did some digging before this morning?''

''It's a sickness. I can't help myself. And speaking of which…''

''I'm going!'' Anthony groused. He left Jim to his beloved cellphone, which seemed to be permanently attached to the man's ear.

Descending to the jewelry department, Anthony found Emma stubbornly immersed in work. She was still attending to the older gentleman, talking over a tray of rings.

Anthony took up position by the workroom door, receiving a flurry of suspicious looks from Emma even while she showed the utmost patience to her client. It was a learning experience, seeing her smile the way she used to when he'd first met her. Genuine. Kind. He found it hard to believe that striking face could turn so cold.

Wondering how, exactly, one got on Emma's good side, Anthony rubbed his shoulder against the doorjamb. The itching was a constant reminder of Dop, and though the doctors said it was a sign of healing, it was yet another irritant in an already full load.

As Emma moved on to the next client, Anthony decided to do double duty. There were ways to make this easier. He'd done enough damage in her life already and now he was adding a stalker to the tally. Right now, planning might do more good than an apology that would satisfy no one.

So he took out his own cellphone and got to work, spying as Emma milled around a constantly busy sales floor.

Her state of denial began to slip when Hornsby and Brady pulled a security guard from his post. She went white, then red, but didn't interfere. That was good, Anthony supposed, although she would almost certainly take it out on him later.

She handled the next round better, showing nothing but calm as Jim made off with department heads, one by one. Emma rotated to cover their absences, and it wasn't always easy for Anthony to find an unobtrusive vantage point. He finally gave up and sat on the oak staircase as she took over the china department. It was nearly noon by then and the hot, viciously humid weather had slowed down even the most avid shoppers.

Anthony was virtually alone with her now, watching as she tidied an already pristine set of displays. He wondered what she was thinking, but didn't mind the cold shoulder. It gave him a chance to stare.

The yellow dress was straight out of a Doris Day movie—sleeveless, tailored and prim, yet somehow managing to show a mile of tanned skin. His eyes moved to her legs, where high heels, nice ankles and the curve of firm calf muscles held his interest for quite some time.

And then suddenly she was walking right toward him, like a warrior on a mission. Anthony's spine straightened abruptly at the obstinate look on Emma's face. He was unprepared for another showdown.

"You need to answer a question," she said.

He raised his eyebrows expectantly.

"Did you really believe I was behind this?"

"At first, yes," he said. "And you thought it was me."

"The thought did cross my mind."

"Well then, that's out of the way. How's your stomach doing? Better? Feel like lunch?"

Emma eyed him warily for a moment. "No," she said. "But I suppose if I'll be having houseguests I'd better call the grocery store."

"Already taken care of. My housekeeper will be here later with provisions. And I'll make a deal with you."

"What?"

"I'll cook if you scratch on demand."

"If I what?" she asked.

"The scar. It itches and you have long fingernails."

There was another pause, but this time Anthony could see what she was thinking. Having houseguests was one thing. Touching him was another. They both knew they were in trouble under the enforced proximity. It only remained to be seen which one of them would slip first.

"Are you supposed to be scratching?" she asked.

"Probably not. But the deal stands."

"Fine."

"All right. Why don't you come upstairs for a while, anyway? I can scare up lunch and tell you what the FBI's been up to."

"I can't. When they keep pulling people off the floor we're short of help."

"You're also short of customers. Look, I know this is awkward, but I promise no mischief if you promise not to flirt."

"Excuse me?" Emma exclaimed indignantly.

"I'm only teasing. Lighten up."

"Easy for you to say," she muttered. "You don't have to watch your back every—"

Anthony laughed out loud at the horrified look on her face.

"What's so funny?" she chirped, then smiled sheepishly.

"Man, talk about putting your foot in your mouth. I'm sorry."

"Don't be. I think that's the first time I've laughed in weeks."

They started up the stairs, Emma's expression sour. "You must be pretty desperate if you're laughing at that."

Chapter 4

"A cantaloupe? That's it?" Anthony complained.

"There's some butter and mayonnaise, too," she said, watching him dig in the fridge. "I think there's some tuna fish in the cupboard and I know there's bread around here somewhere."

"Oh, good. And here I was hoping for actual food. Don't you ever eat?"

"Yes, I eat. I just don't have time to cook much of anything."

"Then my presence will serve a purpose. And it'll be a nice change from hotel food for me. If I ever see another room service tray again it'll be too soon."

"That bad? I would think hospital food would be worse," Emma said, wondering if he'd talk about the attack. Now that she wasn't quite so overwhelmed she was ready to hear the rest of the story.

But Anthony sidestepped the topic, saying, "I was only laid up for a week, then had to move into the Whitney for a night or two because Jim knew we'd have good security.

After that it was the St. Paul Hotel. The rest of that second week's pretty much a blur. Painkiller fog. But that ended after Dop's last swipe."

"What happened?" she asked, sliding a cutting board toward him when he pointed to it with a knife.

Emma refused to look at the melon while he cut it.

"Nothing much," he said. "Dop drew an X on the door across from ours. Hornsby turned the place inside out but there was no sign of him. Probably happened while we were all asleep. And then Layne decided to show up."

"You don't like her?"

Anthony shrugged a shoulder and Emma's eyes lingered on the shiny white fabric covering smooth, rounded muscle. "It's not that I don't like her. I just don't know anything about her, and Jim's being very tight-lipped. Hornsby hinted she's pretty high up the ladder, though."

"A surprise around every corner," Emma said. "But how did the FBI get involved, anyway? I mean, this place is gossipville and I never heard one word."

She snagged a piece of melon off the cutting board and nibbled, watching his arm flex as he worked. Her stare followed a line of tendon to his hand. She was an expert on male hands, after years of staring at them while fitting wedding rings on innumerable couples.

Anthony's had changed. Back then she could have sworn he got manicures, but now they looked beat-up, as if he'd been doing some sort of manual labor. Hard to believe, but scattered across the square backs, palms and long knobby fingers were calluses, scratches and a scar or two. Not too many. As with everything concerning Anthony, he seemed to have the exact amount to suit her taste.

Here we go again, she thought. Very depressing. Two years later and she was still hopelessly in lust.

But the bad things had not been forgotten. He may have changed somewhat, but it would take a heart and brain transplant for Anthony Bracco to be someone she could count as a friend. Or anything else, for that matter.

He explained. "Mom checked my e-mail while I was in the hospital and found it flooded with Dop's pictures. Pretty hard to miss the connection between the Xs and the assault. So since Internet crime is the FBI's jurisdiction, she had an excuse to call Jim, and he slapped a gag order on the cops right away."

"I take it you already knew Jim?" Emma asked. With Anthony one had to fish diligently or details had a tendency to be brushed over.

"Yes. We were roommates at college and kept in touch. Luckily, he had enough pull to get my case assigned to him."

"Does he have a specialty?"

"Criminal profiling, mostly. You know, where they try to discern personal attributes by a suspect's behavior, and then use it to predict what he might do. Not easy with Dop."

"Hmm," she murmured, trying not to think about that. "And who's Hornsby?"

"Jim's partner. A security expert."

"Ah. You said something about messages? Like word messages instead of pictures?"

"Yes, but not a subject matter to discuss while eating," Anthony said, turning away from the sink. "They came in fast and furious when I was in the hospital, then dropped off that second week. After the *X* on the hotel wall they all but stopped. Jim was starting to get concerned, but now we know what Dop's been up to. Following you around."

Emma sighed impatiently, "Are you *ever* going to tell me what he said in those e-mails?"

"There you are," Jim said from the doorway. "Brady was having a fit, thinking you'd been abducted."

Pressing one hand over her thumping heart, Emma exclaimed, "Do you have to sneak up on people like that?"

"Yes, it's a job requirement. Is Anthony bringing you up-to-date?"

"Sort of," Emma replied, sliding Anthony a piqued look.

"There's really not all that much to tell. Just the messages and the hotel thing," Anthony said.

"You're forgetting the phone calls," Jim stated. "But I need to get back downstairs. Just wanted to make sure you were up here, and hadn't run off somewhere again."

Emma raised her brows at the glowering looks that flashed between the two men, but Jim darted away before she could comment. Ignoring Anthony's irritation, she prompted, "Phone calls?"

"A few. Not pleasant. I know I'm leaving things out, but trust me, you don't need to hear the gory details."

"Isn't that my decision?"

"No, it's not. You might as well get used to guessing what's happening because no one tells the whole story. Not even Jim."

"Great. I ought to be crazy in about twenty-four hours."

"Slacker. I was there in twelve. But then I learned I was better off. And you, the biggest worrywart on the planet—"

"Ha," Emma said. "As if I don't have reason. Especially where you're concerned."

"You're just spoiling for a fight, aren't you?" Anthony challenged, sliding her a plate. He had the gall to smile at her as if it were *cute* that she was still angry after two years.

"I wasn't until you said that. Now that you mention it, maybe I am. I can't believe you're acting like nothing happened."

Anthony hooked his foot through the rungs of a stool and pulled it up to the island counter. "Fine. You want to yell? Go ahead."

Emma gaped at him for a moment, then said, "I hate it when you condescend."

"I wasn't condescending. If you want to yell, feel free. Get me mad enough and I might even yell back."

"Oh, can I?" she asked sarcastically, annoyed that she'd actually missed the way they used to bicker over nothing. Only this wasn't nothing.

"All right, Emma, listen. What's done is done. Neither

one of us can go back and undo what we did to each other—''

''As if I have anything to take back,'' she muttered, and took a bite of her sandwich.

''You have plenty to take back. Like shooting your mouth off and being a tease just for extra revenge. Not very nice after being Miss Don't-Touch-Me for a week.''

''And that compares to what you did?''

''I never said it did. I'm just saying you didn't play fair, either.''

''Do you think I'm proud of that?'' she asked, wondering just how obtuse the man was.

''Are you saying you're not?''

They stared at each other for a moment, and Emma noticed Anthony squirming a bit. His shoulder itched.

Let him suffer.

''No, I'm not proud of it,'' she sighed. ''What about you? If you could do it all over again would you bribe your way into owning my company?''

''Honestly?''

Emma let out a groan of sheer disgust. ''You *would!*''

''In a heartbeat.''

Rolling her eyes, she said, ''Some people never learn.''

''Right. So how would you do away with me this time?'' he asked, flexing his left arm.

Emma took another bite of melon, wondering how long he could stand it before he scratched. ''This time I'd probably sink you up to your thick skull in lawyers. What about you? How would you do it differently?''

''This time I'd bribe the entire building inspector's office so they couldn't tip you off.''

Emma laughed. ''That was your own fault, you know. Should have done your homework. The guy who told me someone must have faked the asbestos samples was my father's best friend.''

''Live and learn,'' Anthony said. ''Almost pulled it off, though. My people were all set to come in and look busy doing nothing. You never would have known I'd set the whole thing up if you hadn't replied to their noncompliance letter with a huge temper tantrum."

"Humph. I can't believe you thought you'd get away with it. I would've gone nuts being shut down for months. And even though you said you'd pay for everything, I never would have given you controlling interest," Emma said.

He laughed and Emma's throat tightened at the sight. She'd forgotten how utterly gorgeous he could be when he laughed. Smiling was bad enough.

Emma jumped when the phone rang. She stared at it a moment, debating whether to ignore it. This conversation was far too interesting to let drop, but no one ever called during lunch unless it was urgent.

"Hang on a minute," she said, fighting the impulse to scratch his shoulder as she passed.

Anthony's shoulder was on fire but he refused to contort himself into scratch position. It would remind her of the scar, and he didn't want to erase this last half hour's progress. They'd somehow managed to joke about the past in a way he never had, not even with Geoff, his stepfather, whose sense of humor had been Anthony's saving grace during the last two years.

But then it had always been easy to talk around touchy subjects with Emma, because she was always quick to smooth over unwanted topics herself.

Eavesdropping shamelessly as she picked up the phone, he heard her say, "Hey Brady."

With her back to him, Anthony felt free to scowl. But it melted from his face as Emma's voice turned sharp. "What? You've got to be kidding me! Put him through."

There was a pause and the scar began to itch again in earnest as Emma said, "Hi, Peter."

Peter was Peter Carlson, Emma's insurer, and a huge danger to Anthony and Charles. They'd made absolutely certain the New York auction house would keep their mouths shut about enhancing Emma's bid, but Peter's appraised value of the stones and metals would be way more than she'd paid.

Charles had been soothing Peter for a couple months now, telling him these things sometimes happened. But Peter wasn't on the phone with Charles this time. He was talking to Emma. And she wasn't known for being careless.

If either one of those two got nervous enough to dig deeper into that appraisal discrepancy, Anthony and Charles were toast.

"What do you mean we won't have them today?" Her voice was level but he could see her back tighten with tension.

Anthony, on the other hand, blew out a quiet sigh of relief. With Emma in no-excuse mode, Peter wouldn't dare hint at another delay.

"Yes, well that's what you said last week. I don't care how many stones there are. There's no way it takes three months to appraise one auction lot. With what I'm paying you... Well, are you sure your people aren't overvaluing the uncut stones? It's happened before, and our bid couldn't be that far off the value."

Oops. Holding his breath, Anthony watched as she put a hand on her hip and stretched sideways. He almost felt sorry for her.

But he could imagine how she would react if he told her the stomach problem and knotted muscles would disappear as soon as she stopped letting her career run her life.

She'd get mad if he called her on it, and that did not appeal, although he couldn't help recalling how spectacular she looked when angry. Full bottom lip red and glistening from the abuse, green eyes flashing, and that telltale blush of a steaming temper. She'd looked that way the night she'd tricked him into believing he was about to get a whole lot more than her businesses. Ravishing. A wild thing that could never be tamed.

Anthony dropped his sandwich. If she turned around looking that sexy he wouldn't be held responsible for what happened next. Taking no chances that his already battered rules wouldn't survive the next ten minutes, he cleared away his lunch mess as Emma listened to Carlson.

Since she hadn't turned around to bonk him over the head with the phone, he assumed Peter was doing some major kissing up. Good man. Emma needed it. And the sooner those stones were released, the better they'd all feel.

Maybe this afternoon he'd place a discreet call and persuade Carlson to speed things up.

The idea was quickly retracted when Emma said, "You know what, Peter? I have seven other insurance companies begging for my money, and right now you're costing me more than premiums. So let's do this. If that lot isn't in my vault by noon on Thursday, consider our contracts terminated."

So much for discreet, Anthony thought, as Emma said a quiet goodbye and hung up. He couldn't have done it better himself.

"Problems?" he asked.

"Nothing important. Not to you, anyway. Do you want help with the dishes or can I go downstairs now?"

"After you've kept your end of the bargain, you can," Anthony said, his shoulder screaming for attention.

"What bargain?" she asked. Then she brightened and said, "Oh. Is it bad?"

"Believe me, I wouldn't ask if it wasn't. I do still have some ego left, and my shoulder's kind of hard to reach without contorting myself."

"Then you should have said something instead of trying to be all macho," she scolded.

Emma stepped up behind him at the sink, and the second her fingernails came in contact with his back, Anthony's entire body screamed for that attention. This was a bad idea, he realized, as she laid her free hand on his ribs for leverage.

Mind-numbing relief and arousal dragged a guttural moan all the way from his toes, and he could feel her smiling tolerantly behind him.

''It's not funny,'' he groused.

''No, it's not,'' she replied with heartening sympathy. ''But if I'd known it was this easy to shut you up I'd have started scratching the second we got up here.''

He sneered over his shoulder at her and she smiled.

''Okay,'' she said, clapping him on the back. The impact of the playful smack was like flint on metal as she added, ''I'm going downstairs and you don't have to spy anymore. I've got enough work to keep me busy for weeks. Couldn't take off even if I wanted to.''

Anthony tightened his grip on the counter and nodded weakly. As soon as she was gone, he leaned his back against the nearest wall and slid to a crouch with his hands dug into his hair.

This was impossible. His rules had been hard enough to follow before, but now Emma had blown number three sky-high. Not only was he thinking about her, but he'd begun to want something he could never have.

He couldn't handle her. Not yet. She'd laugh in his face if he told her how he felt. Then he'd run. It was as inevitable as the sunrise.

Angry with himself for letting her affect him, Anthony stayed where he was for a while, telling himself this couldn't possibly go on much longer. Layne had a crew scouring the employee files of the companies he'd raided, and something was bound to turn up. Either that or Dop would finally make Jim's promised mistake.

Anthony's cellphone went off in his pocket and he dropped his head forward in frustration.

''What fresh hell is this?'' he muttered.

But it was only Geoff, on a break between surgeries, calling to make sure he'd survived the reunion.

Emma only managed twenty minutes downstairs before the reality of the FBI hit home. She'd counted to ten at least sixty times while Hornsby personally opened and examined the day's shipments. Every one of the packages had been expected, but the man just wouldn't listen to reason.

And then Layne had strolled by the office, peering in as though Emma were on display.

Sighing and shaking her head, she toyed with the idea of writing "only doing their job" on a thousand sticky-notes and tacking them all over the place. Maybe with the added reminder, she and the FBI wouldn't be at war by dinnertime.

Dinner. What would that be like? Emma was still trying to put lunch in perspective. Yes, she'd forgotten how annoying Anthony could be, but she'd also forgotten how he could claim her total attention for as long as he darn well pleased.

Deep breaths. Many, many deep breaths. She could do this. She could handle Anthony. She could handle the FBI. It was just difficult because she wasn't used to having so many people in her space.

Her cooperative spirit faltered a bit as Jim stuck his head in the door, waving her mail in his hand. "Gotta have a look through this before you can have it. Oh, and we've got ears on your computers, phones and your cell. We're required to hang up on calls that aren't relevant, but we gotta listen long enough to make a determination. So you might want to keep the personal stuff down to a minimum."

"Subpoena?" Emma prompted.

Jim patted the envelope sticking out of his shirt pocket. "Don't mean to be rude, Emma, but I'm a cautious guy. The courts make it harder to convict than to investigate. Relax. My bases are covered."

Emma stared after him, wide-eyed. She couldn't give a hoot if the bases were covered for court. She didn't want anyone listening to her phone calls, personal or not.

And they'd darned well better hang up if it wasn't relevant. She and her therapist could never manage office visits so they'd arranged phone sessions instead, and these days he was number one on her speed dial.

Dr. Dillon. She didn't know how she'd managed before

he came along. He deserved full credit for the fact that she hadn't screamed at anyone yet.

The man was a blessing. She'd almost given up finding a replacement for her last therapist, then finally threw herself on the mercy of an Internet referral site. She'd entered all her information and the next day she got a phone call from Dillon. Simple as pie. And she thought she'd died and gone to heaven when Dillon said he'd visit her at work if it was more convenient, since he'd just moved here from California and wasn't booked to oblivion yet.

And from the moment she laid eyes on the man, she'd known he was the right one.

Dillon was about forty or so, with animated hazel eyes that made actual contact. He was totally laid-back and equipped with a smooth, soothing voice—perfect for when she was ridiculously angry over something stupid.

She'd have to call him and warn him about the eavesdropping. And Anthony, of course. Talk about kamikaze therapy. But Dillon said forgiving Anthony was a baby step forward on her journey to get rid of her temper and she knew he was right, much as she hated to admit it.

She'd be nervous, though, wondering if someone was listening in. Would she be able to tell if they'd hung up?

Why does everything have to be so damned dramatic? Would one normal week be too much to ask?

With a cynical laugh, Emma picked up her cell phone and called, catching Dillon on his way to a conference in Wisconsin.

And she heard it. A soft buzz, then a click. Hoping those sounds meant they'd hung up, Emma started talking.

Forty-five minutes later she felt considerably better. Able to cope at least. The doctor was, naturally, concerned about her being in danger but pleasantly surprised at how she'd conducted herself.

Well, mostly. She'd been given a stern dressing-down on her attitude toward the FBI, and she hadn't missed Dillon's quiet chuckle when she finally admitted to sympathetic feelings toward Anthony.

A big fat "I told you so" was probably in order, but Dillon didn't say it. What he did say was she shouldn't confuse lust for emotions.

Reliving that comment, Emma grimaced. It was something they'd talked about before, always concerning Anthony, and no doubt they'd talk about it again as soon as she'd calmed down. Hopefully Anthony would be gone before the next therapy session.

Dillon promised to be available at any hour until Dop was caught, and rang off with a gentle reminder not to dump on Charles if things got ugly—a mistake she often made when the pressure got too high for her to handle. She and her goldsmith as were close as father and daughter, and while Dillon thought it was good she had someone to talk to, Charles shouldn't be subjected to her tirades when she lost it.

The desire to unload the entire, insane Dop and Anthony story on Charles right then was very strong, but Emma forced herself to dive into a pile of purchase orders instead. They kept most of her brain occupied, yet one small corner continued to think about all the things she and Dr. Dillon *hadn't* talked about. For once. Like her father.

Marshall Toliver had refused treatment for his depression from the moment he was diagnosed, and Emma had spent most of her life dodging his mood swings. She'd also spent most of her life compensating for his problems.

Every therapist loved this subject, but Emma was tired of talking about it. Dad was gone now, so in her opinion there was nothing to discuss. Dillon didn't agree but he never forced the issue.

He didn't have to. Emma lived it every day. A majority of the employees at Toliver's Treasures had been manning their posts since before she was born, and Emma wasn't blind. There'd been times when her father's out-of-control behavior had scared them, none of them knowing whether they'd have a job the next day.

Things had gotten better for them once Dad handed the store over to her. She loved the store. It was her entire life. But she'd only been sixteen at the time. Juggling school, boyfriends and a thriving business sometimes drove her straight over the edge.

So the employees were no stranger to the temper. They didn't deserve it, but they'd been putting up with it for years. For all intents and purposes, she'd been raised by these people, and they were the true heart and soul of this place. She owed them far more than job security, and if she didn't start managing her emotions better, one of them would leave, taking part of that heart and soul—*her* heart and soul—with them.

She'd already learned how devastating a loss like that could be. Brady's father, Edgar. The temper hadn't claimed him. Old age had, but he'd been more of a father to her than her own. He was the one who'd urged her to stop treating design sketches as a ''someday'' hobby. Beautiful Things had been a huge risk, but she couldn't imagine her life without that precious escape.

However, that escape was often a colossal pain in the butt. Material shortages, the capital she'd had to pour into it and the demands on her time were beginning to catch up with her.

''Why couldn't you have had more kids?'' Emma asked aloud, then felt silly. Dad couldn't hear her any better now than he had when he was alive.

A little help would be nice, though. Here she was, up to her hairline in paperwork, stalkers, Anthony and the FBI, and on Thursday night she'd be meeting with the most influential jewelry merchandiser in the country.

No worries. Oh, but let's not forget we're twenty-six and have no social life, she complained to herself. Could it *be* any harder to find the perfect man, settle down and start a family so there's someone to take over this place when you're gone?

Emma rolled her eyes, then jumped when Jim trotted down the stairs wearing an impatient, vaguely excited look. "Come upstairs. We need to try something."

"What?"

"We're gonna send Dop a reply to this morning's picture."

"Excuse me?"

"Just come on," he urged.

Reluctantly climbing the stairs, she donned a cynical expression as he added, "You never know. We might get a response, and bam, it's over."

They stopped at the top of the stairs, greeted by Anthony, who radiated disapproval.

"Don't even say it, Brac," Jim warned. "We've got to reopen our line of communication somehow."

"Why? Do you miss him? No juicy whacko to dissect all week?"

"Yeah. Thank God you were here to fill in," Jim replied.

Emma bit her cheek, trying not to laugh, then blinked innocently when Anthony asked, "What are you laughing at?"

"Not a thing," she told him as Jim pulled another chair behind one of several computer desks.

"All right, here's the deal," Jim began, leaning back in his chair until Emma was convinced he'd fall over. "I'm torn as to how we play this. My gut says we go for the throat. My head says we play it safe."

Anthony and Emma spouted opposite opinions at once.

"Why play it safe?" Emma protested. "I'm assuming you want him angry enough to make a mistake, right? Playing nice will only prolong the agony."

Anthony argued, "If we take it slow we'll learn more, maybe get a successful trace and avoid a dangerous retaliation. Jim can learn volumes from as little as a turn of phrase, so I say we give Dop a chance to dig his own grave. You, of all people, should appreciate that strategy.''

Emma gave him a sour look as Jim said, ''I agree with you on some levels, Brac, but I like what you told Layne.''

''What did I tell Layne?''

Anthony perched on the edge of the desk and tucked his hands between his ribs and arms. Emma, acutely aware of him, tried not to stare at taut biceps and the veins running the length of the muscles beneath his sun-kissed olive skin.

''You told her we should let Emma have a crack at him. That he'd be crying for his mommy inside of an hour.''

''What?'' Emma squeaked in outrage.

Jim dissolved into laughter and Anthony squeezed his eyes closed. ''When will I ever learn to keep my mouth shut?''

''Crying for his mommy?'' Emma repeated.

Jim, still chuckling, said, ''Well, if you can crush Anthony's ego, I'd love to see what you could do to Dop. You run with the idea and I'll touch it up before we send.''

''Maybe Anthony needs to leave the room so I don't offend his delicate sensibilities,'' Emma huffed, not surprised that Jim appeared to know every last detail of what had gone on two years ago, even though Anthony had only said they'd been roommates and ''kept in touch.'' Apparently a crowbar was needed to pry all the details out of the man, and his constant evasions weren't doing much for her trust.

''Oh, give him a break,'' Jim admonished, humbling Emma as he added pointedly, ''you deserve to be picked on just as much as he does, in my opinion. Now, let's get this thing rolling.''

They all worked together for the next half hour, and Emma found herself almost as interested in Anthony and Jim's relationship as she was in the e-mail. They were such typical guys. She fell quiet while they traded insults and laughed with a morbid edge about things that had happened during the investigation.

It was enlightening, if nothing else. She learned that

Dop's phone calls had been thankfully short. Caller ID had given them numbers instantly, but they were always placed from pay phones too far away to reach before Dop would hang up. And of course the calls were always made during rush hour traffic, so police cruisers couldn't get there, either.

By profile theory, the timing might mean Dop was getting off work around that time. Jim didn't know if he trusted that theory. It seemed more likely Dop was just being a pain.

However, the content of the phone calls was enough to wipe any hint of a grin off Jim's face. Dop threatened Anthony's life during each and every call. But when Emma pressed, neither Jim nor Anthony would elaborate on what, exactly, he said.

The e-mail messages were also brushed over. But it was obvious to Emma, watching Anthony, that the contents weren't pretty. Every time Jim mentioned the messages, Anthony's whole body would stiffen, and the leg he'd been carelessly swinging would start to bounce convulsively.

What must this be like for him? In his shoes, she'd be a raving lunatic, but aside from the knee bobbing, he was pretty calm. It had to be painful, though, having his past rise up to kick him in the butt like this. Paybacks were hell, but this was horrible.

"Well, we'll see what my computer tech can do with this," Jim said, reading the message one last time.

Dop—

I've seen Anthony's back. What kind of coward slashes a man from behind in the darkness? Did you need the advantage because you're weak? The least you could do was finish the job. Or weren't you smart enough to do that?

So why did you choose me to pester? I don't scare as easily as you do. And I don't back down. I may not care for Anthony, but if it came down to a choice between him and you, he'd win.

The FBI is watching. If you come for me I'll feel it. And be prepared for a fight. I'm not afraid of you.
Emma

"Hmm," Jim mused while Emma was still cringing at the first paragraph. "We got in some key words like *coward, smart, scare....* This should rattle his cage. What do you think, Brac?"

"I think you're both nuts."

"Duly noted. I've gotta go help Walter and Brady with the security system. What time is dinner?"

"About an hour."

"What are you doing to the security system?" Emma inquired.

"Some tests later tonight after the store closes," Jim answered.

She nodded, and Jim said, "Oh. Before I forget, I need Dr. Dillon's license numbers and address."

"Why?"

"If you're talking to him about what goes on here, I need to know who he is."

"Fine," she said.

Anthony asked, "Did we ever get my bags from the hotel?"

"Yep. Your stuff's already in your room."

"Which room?" Emma asked.

Just as she'd feared, Jim said, "The one across from yours. The other two guest rooms by the front door and that big den down there will be reserved for our use, if that's all right."

"As if I have a choice."

"Hey, she catches on quick," Jim told Anthony. "Okay. Get ready to live in Grand Central Station. At least two people will always be here. Walter and I have some other cases to deal with so we'll be in and out. Layne does as she pleases, by the way." He paused, looking over his shoulder at Emma. ''So it's gonna be a wild ride. Let's hope that e-mail gets some results.''

Jim was already halfway out the door when she asked, ''Do you want us to keep checking the mail or what?''

He turned abruptly. ''No. My tech's monitoring activity and she'll call if we get a reply.''

''But I have work to do tonight,'' Emma argued. ''How am I supposed to answer my legitimate e-mails if—''

''Can't it wait for tomorrow? Toil your little heart out but don't connect to the Internet. Got it?''

Chapter 5

Emma made a face at Jim's back while he walked out, then flinched when Anthony reached over to tuck a few stray hairs behind her ear.

She stopped herself from swatting his hand away even though he'd set that entire side of her face on fire.

He said, "Come keep me company while I cook."

"Aren't you afraid I'll make you cry for mommy?"

"There's no chance you'll forget that anytime soon, is there? In context it didn't sound nearly as bad."

"Uh-huh," she said. "I'll be there in a minute. I need to change."

Tipping his head to the side, Anthony asked, "You think I'm stupid enough to leave you alone with the computer?"

"No comment. But why can't I be left with—"

"Don't play innocent. Need I walk you to your room?"

"God," Emma muttered. He didn't trust her. How strange.

She got up and Anthony followed as she went to the door between her office and bedroom.

"Scene of the crime," Anthony said. "I see you've made some changes in here."

Shifting her weight uncomfortably, she asked, "What was that you were saying about keeping your mouth shut?"

Emma chewed her lip while examining his profile. She might learn to handle the FBI in her space, but Anthony's invasion was different. It looked as if he was reliving every moment of that night, seeing past the bold reds and greens that had replaced the yellow scheme. Yellow was her favorite color, but she'd redecorated to avoid painful reminders.

Warring with the anger that erupted every time she thought about that night, Emma guessed what Dillon would say if she flipped.

Okay. Whatever Dillon said about it, he'd be right. There was no longer any reason to stay angry.

Never having tried to be objective about Anthony before, she battled every dictating order of her brain to say "I'll change later. Let's go make dinner."

Her words didn't seem to penetrate, and Emma could easily picture what was going through his mind: everything that night had cost him. His career, a smear campaign in the papers and an exit from his powerful, successful existence.

As if she didn't already feel guilty enough about her performance that night, here was her penance—watching him relive it. The things she'd said and done had been totally uncalled for. But what was she supposed to do? Sit back and let him steal her entire life?

It had all started so innocently. Anthony had shown up one day, shopping for Geoff and Sophia's wedding gift. For Emma it had been lust at first sight. Three nights, three dates later, and she'd been sure she'd finally found someone who would accept the Toliver package deal.

Not that she hadn't had her suspicions. Sometimes he'd seemed a little too interested in the store and label, but she'd written it off as her own paranoia.

Fool. How could she have been so careless?

On the fourth day, a letter had arrived from the building inspector's office, stating that the Toliver's Treasures building would require extensive refurbishing, and they had the asbestos samples to prove it. If she didn't have the harmful substance removed at once they'd seize the property and dispose of it themselves. And she wouldn't be getting it back.

She'd freaked, ranting to Anthony about how she'd just sunk all available capital, and a good deal of her own money, into the design label, to remodel the workroom and upgrade their security.

Anthony had been ever so helpful, making phone calls until he'd found a removal company that could come in right away to survey the building. As soon as she learned the extent of work to be done, heard how long it would take and how much it would cost, she knew it was game over. No matter how loyal her clientele, neither Toliver's Treasures nor Beautiful Things could possibly survive six months without any income.

Anthony had given his breakout performance that day. He'd acted as if it pained him greatly to say it, but he would pay for the removal if she gave him controlling interest.

Emma's gut reaction had been no way, even if she was the only stockholder in Toliver, Inc. It felt totally wrong, no matter how desperate for cash she was.

Unfortunately for Anthony, she wasn't born stupid. She'd told him she'd think about it, then had sent a rather scathing demand for proof to the building inspector's office.

Fate stepped in when a friend of her father's saw her letterhead on someone else's desk and took a peek. And immediately called her to say something was screwy. Toliver's Treasures had passed asbestos inspection twenty years ago. He'd also tactfully hinted that the inspector who'd sent the noncompliance letter was under suspicion of taking bribes.

Busted. All the suspicion and doubt had erupted, and she

was so angry that Anthony had been lucky she didn't know how to work a gun.

She'd taken it too far, although she had to admit she still cherished the panicked look on Anthony's face when she'd demanded marriage.

She'd been positive he would slither back under his rock, but instead he'd agreed. Unbelievable. So she'd taken it even further, bringing him to his knees with the seduction bit.

But as soon as he'd tried to kiss her, she had, for the first and only time in her life, struck someone in anger.

And what had Anthony done? He'd laughed. When she'd accused him of everything under the sun he'd proudly filled in the gaps, telling her the removal team had been in his pocket, too.

It was the pride that finished her. When he stalked out she'd fallen apart. Had sobbed for hours, completely annihilated.

What made her the most angry, she supposed, was knowing she had no one to blame but herself. She'd known exactly who he was. The son of Maxim Bracco, the most notorious corporate raider of all time, so Anthony couldn't help acting on greed any more than a snake could help being a snake. He was a product of his upbringing. As was Emma, who had four generations of highly ethical businessmen to guide her actions.

Bottom line, it was her fault. She should have known better.

The aftermath wasn't pretty. Emma had called in every favor she'd ever done at city hall to hush up what had happened. The bribed inspector was fired, but no charges were filed.

And for three weeks Emma prayed it wouldn't hit the papers.

It did. To this day no one knew who'd gone to the press, but whoever it was had done a thorough job. The media had been ruthless. In the end, Emma wasn't really affected.

But Anthony... Everything he'd done wrong his entire life, and probably some things he hadn't, had been out there for the world to judge, and his disappearance had only added fuel to the fire.

In one highly private moment, Emma had found herself having brutally hateful thoughts about Anthony's father, Maxim, as well. He and his corporation should have been included in the mudslinging. Not only for shoddy business practices, but for cutting Anthony loose. Damage control. How could Maxim Bracco do that to his own son?

When all was said and done, if Anthony had felt a fraction of the guilt she had, he'd suffered enough. And had Emma been in Anthony's shoes she would have disappeared, too.

The unexpected empathy she felt freed her in some ways. She turned her eyes from the spot where they'd stood that night, only to find herself the target of his bitter stare. Emma shrugged and said, "Can't change it, right?"

"Right," he agreed, the look in his own eyes softening. "Did you know you bite your bottom lip when you're trying to control your temper?"

"I do not," Emma declared, even though she knew it was true.

One side of his mouth lifted into a wry smile and he pushed off the doorjamb, herding her toward the kitchen. "You do, too. When you were on the phone at lunchtime I thought you'd bite a hole in it."

"What does that have to do with anything?"

"Just making an observation. Sit," he ordered.

Emma sat on a stool, watching as he pulled things from the fridge. Rubbing her bottom lip, she worried. She couldn't remember biting it while she was on the phone with Peter. Maybe she did it so often the pain didn't register anymore.

But that thought dwindled at the sight of fresh walleye fillets and Anthony's behind as he bent for a head of lettuce.

Now that was just wrong. Emma averted her eyes, yet

somehow she was still watching as he switched on a small television. That helped. Now she could pray they wouldn't show up on the news.

Emma sat quietly staring at the tube until Anthony reached over and pulled her hand away from her mouth. "Stop that."

"Stop what?"

"Rubbing your lip."

"Sorry."

The word seemed to echo as Anthony lifted her hand. Emma tracked the motion as it neared his mouth, surprise and instant arousal holding her mesmerized. When the fingertip that was still wet from her lip was just a hairsbreadth from his, Anthony raised his lashes, watching her with charcoal-colored eyes.

My God. How could she have forgotten that look? Electricity swept through her, and her breasts tingled instinctively at the raw hunger on his face.

Emma hesitated only a moment before finishing the motion, touching him and feeling liquid fire race up her arm from a smooth, firm lip. With their gazes locked, Anthony exhaled a warm breath that bled between her fingers. She could feel herself melting, while a knot of anticipation tightened in her belly.

And then she remembered to breathe as Anthony trailed her finger down his stubbly chin. If she dared speak she would have said something. No doubt very incriminating. But he beat her to it, saying, "Get away from me."

It didn't happen instantly. Her arm didn't seem to be obeying orders, and he wasn't letting go. Ten more seconds and she knew she'd be biting *his* bottom lip, but neither of them moved.

Jim's voice in the hall shattered the moment, and Emma watched Anthony's expression change from heat to ice. She found it easy to leave then, telling herself Jim had just saved them from doing something moronic, even though her body was still in flames.

But the arousal died the moment Emma's bedroom door closed behind her. The chemistry was dangerous. She'd given Anthony the benefit of the doubt once before, to her great expense, and now that she had her future hanging in the balance, she couldn't afford to let that chemistry affect her decisions.

Get away from me, indeed. Thank God it had ended before anything else happened. Anthony obviously didn't want this complication either, especially with her, the woman who'd thrown his life into the garbage.

So with that in mind, Emma called Dillon, who seemed to have become a one-man cheering section. Still none too eager to face Anthony again quite yet, she changed clothes and stayed in her room until Jim called her to dinner.

Emma found Brady in the dining room, sour-faced as always, but chatting quietly with Crawford and Hornsby. She sat at the far end of the table, trying to remember the last time six people had been in this room at the same time. Probably never.

After Anthony came in conversation centered around the case. Emma listened, poking at her food. It was delicious, but she was very aware of Anthony's silence at the other end of the table. Peering at him every so often, she thought he looked tired, and wondered if his shoulder still hurt, or if he'd been getting enough rest. None of her business, but this was so unlike the Anthony Emma remembered that she was honestly worried.

He caught her watching him and she smiled vaguely just before Brady began grilling her about how she was doing and what, if anything, needed to be done differently during business hours. Emma let Jim and Hornsby answer, and when the exchange grew somewhat heated, she reached over and grabbed Brady's hand.

"This won't last forever," she said, although she'd been worrying about that possibility all day. "I know things are a little extreme right now but in a few days we'll be back to normal."

Brady looked down at her hand for a moment, then lifted them again to ask, "Normal? What's normal? And what will you do about the Red Cross auc—"

No way would she allow him to bring that up in present company. God only knew what Anthony would do with the information. Pulling her hand away from Brady's, Emma knocked over his water glass. She jumped up, fussing, and Hornsby, who could take a hint very well, said it was time he and Brady went back to work on the alarm.

Jim and Layne volunteered to do the dishes, and when Anthony excused himself, Jim said, "That's a good sign. I don't think he's slept more than three hours a night lately. Maybe he'll be rested tomorrow."

She nodded and escaped to her design office where she sat down with a feasibility report. Maybe if she finally got all her ducks in a row, Brady would quit grousing about the deal she had in the works with Trenton Neville.

Emma sincerely hoped the FBI would let her go to that Red Cross auction, because that night was do or die for the deal. Not only would Neville go home with the rose necklace, but Emma had a surprise for him.

She planned to wear her latest creation, and Neville would faint when he saw it. The necklace she'd designed was exactly the kind of thing he loved. Bold, colorful and completely unlike anything else out there. It wasn't just an artistic representation of a stargazer lily. It *was* a stargazer lily done up mostly in jade, tsavorite and spinel.

In order for her to make it look real, she'd gone through a meticulous process of weighting stones to create the perfect tension in a painstakingly designed setting. If the piece worked as planned, it could earn her a patent.

And if Neville took her on, she'd have to expand. Which wouldn't be much of a challenge. The building next door had been sitting empty for a year now, since the mortgage company who'd owned it went out of business. It hadn't cost her a dime. The money for it had been held in trust since before she was born, and luckily the interest it accrued had kept up with property values.

The raw-materials auction hadn't cost nearly as much as she'd expected, so there was plenty of money to cover remodelling next door. She could have done that ages ago, but she'd never had time.

And time was the reason Brady was dead-set against her going into business with Neville. She was already run ragged the way it was. So were Charles and Brady.

At bare minimum, they needed a general manager to preside over Toliver's Treasures, two more bookkeepers and at least four more goldsmiths.

Even if things fell through with Neville, she still needed to pump up the employee base. But it was extremely difficult to find people who fit in around here, and going without that extra help right now was easier than training a bunch of people who might not end up staying.

For more than two hours Emma scrambled scheduling scenarios, her nerves hopping from the steady chirp of the alarm panel, certain it would howl to life at any moment. But Walter must know what he was doing. More than one plane had taken off and the system stayed silent and armed, despite the vibrations.

Giving up on the scheduling issues for the night, Emma turned to the computer and pulled up the skeleton outline of a ring setting. She got lost in the design process for a while, but before long the lines on the screen began to blur. Resisting the urge to check the store's e-mail, she went to bed.

But not to sleep. Her mind wouldn't allow it, wondering how she'd get through this without losing her temper twenty times.

Anthony was a problem; the FBI was a problem. She had a horde of people traipsing through her store and home, and she wasn't sure how long she could withstand the invasion.

Dillon. What time was it? Emma rolled over to look at the clock. Midnight, far too late to call…

So she lay there with the prospect of Thursday night looming large. Not only was her schedule a concern, but they still weren't sure the lily's setting would support the piece as planned. Charles hadn't finished the piece yet and he never let her see anything until it was complete. But Emma had faith. Charles had never let her down before and this time would be no different.

And then a thought crept in, instantly rejected but hard to forget. If the setting didn't work they'd have a beautiful lily but no patent, and at this point failure might be a relief.

Blocking that out, Emma drifted off in a swirl of worries, and slept horribly, tying her sheets into knots worthy of Scout merit badges, until the sound of voices jolted her awake the next morning. She groaned and forced herself out of bed, straight into the shower, then into a coral linen suit she hoped made her look cheerful even though she was a disaster inside.

She clipped her hair back from her face and procrastinated over makeup until the smell of coffee lured her to the kitchen. Maybe roommates weren't so bad. Running down the street for coffee and bumping into clients was great, but only when she didn't have time to make her own caffeine infusion.

Anthony was leaning against a counter, laughing at something an unfamiliar man had just said.

The stranger—another agent—was put on hold while Emma examined Anthony. He looked like a different person—healthy and rested, almost like the old Anthony. But still no Armani. Today he was wearing a white button-down shirt and khakis. His untied high-top tennis shoes were the crowning touch.

Shaking her head, Emma stepped into the kitchen, to be greeted with the news that Layne had weeded a suspect from the employee files last night. She'd questioned him late into the evening, and the other FBI agents were still awaiting her opinion.

"You mean this person might be Dop?" she asked the new agent.

"If he's Dop I'm Mary Poppins," the man answered.

"Well then," Anthony said. "Ready for our walk?"

Emma, feeling her slight ray of hope die a quick, painful death, echoed, "Walk?"

"Jim said we're supposed to stick to your schedule, so we're doing the daily Starbucks sojourn. Supervised, of course."

"Fantastic. Speaking of Jim, where is he? I need to talk to him about Thursday night."

"Outside," the agent said. "We need to wait a minute yet. Want some coffee?"

"No, thanks," Emma replied. At least the FBI agents were nice. But no way could she drink coffee now. Fear and caffeine didn't mix well.

The two men talked about the weather while Emma frowned at Anthony's feet.

"What?" he asked defensively.

"Tie your shoes."

"Yes, ma'am."

A few minutes later they were ordered to the foyer of Emma's private street entrance. The agent went out, telling them to stay put until everyone reached their positions.

Emma stood in silence, staring into the street as though the second she stepped outside she'd be cut to pieces. Deep breaths didn't help and there was no way she would punish her bottom lip again in Anthony's presence.

She started when he said, "Yes, I can hear you perfectly."

"What are you..." Emma asked, looking up when Anthony cocked his head and pointed at his ear. Tucked inside was a tiny black earpiece. He then pried his shirt open between the third and fourth buttons to reveal what she assumed was a microphone taped to his stomach.

Feeling somewhat better about the walk, even though she was miffed he'd gotten the toys, Emma keep silent until

Anthony said, "Not a problem. We'll handle it when we get there."

"Handle what?"

"Nothing," he answered, then said, "sorry, I was talking to Emma. Let me know when you're ready."

Growing more and more tense as seconds ticked by, she nearly screamed when Anthony began rubbing her back. "Hang in there. We've got six agents on us, but only for half an hour."

"Do we really have to do this?"

"Jim said we won't get to see Dop's reply to last night's message if we don't. Wait... Okay. Let's go."

Emma went through the door with a helpful shove from Anthony, wondering what kind of reply they'd gotten. Hopefully nothing too awful. Her day wasn't starting out so well, and if she planned on managing her emotions like an adult for once, she might as well start right now.

The street looked the same as always, but today it felt sinister. Not knowing where the agents were or what they looked like was awful. She had no way of knowing whether anyone was close enough to help if something happened.

They'd covered half a block when Anthony stopped to peer at an oil painting displayed in a shop window.

"Emma, keep your eyes on me," he said, his voice capturing her attention with a commanding, hard edge. "Don't turn around, and for God's sake, don't freak out. About twenty yards farther down the sidewalk there's an X spray-painted on the ground, with my initials. Can you walk by without losing it?"

"I..." was all Emma managed in reply. The thought that Dop had gotten this close to the building made her skin crawl.

Anthony kept his eyes on the painting. "All right, Miss Go-By-The-Gut. We're doing this. Together. Just stay calm and trust me."

"I don't know if I can—"

"Do you want to see that reply or not?"

"Yes, but... Oh, all right. Hurry up." Emma didn't want to be out here forever, so she grabbed his hand. It closed around hers with comforting strength and he started walking. Fast.

It was a straight shot down the street, but the sidewalk seemed to stretch for miles. Looming. Glowing with an evil light produced by Emma's well-fed imagination.

She spotted the X a few moments later, air flooding into her lungs as Anthony propelled them ever closer. Oh God. Don't hyperventilate. It's just paint. Dop wouldn't dare come after them on a busy city street.

The logic didn't work. Emma's chest tightened painfully as she tried to control the convulsive gulps. People passed, but no one seemed to notice she was scared half out of her mind.

The X was just a few feet ahead when Emma's nails dug into Anthony's palm. "Ow! Emma..." he complained, looking down and feeling the fear he'd avoided up till now.

She was gasping for air, utterly terrified. Her eyes were wide, her neck cords strained.

They were in trouble. Emma was hyperventilating, and if he didn't do something fast, she'd pass out.

They were right outside a bakery, but Anthony knew he didn't have time to run in for a bag. As he scanned the street for an agent, it dawned on him that he had an alternative. A dangerous alternative, but an efficient one. Feeling slightly guilty, he dragged her the few remaining steps to the X.

"Emma, forgive me, but this is very necessary."

Emptying his lungs, Anthony cupped her face with both hands. The look in her eyes just before he kissed her was a mixture of shock and anger, and getting Emma to open her mouth wasn't easy. She fought his tongue, her hands fluttering up alongside his, but then grabbing his arms when she caught on.

Naturally, the inflammatory show appealed to her. Emma

opened her mouth, letting him haul in a deep breath to empty her lungs.

The spontaneous kiss didn't end when it could have. Or should have. And feeling Emma catch her breath between nerve-searing, rhythmic caresses was the most erotic sensation he'd ever experienced.

Emma wasn't helping his self-control. She'd draped her arms around his waist, clinging to him so tightly he could feel her heart pounding in her chest.

She kissed just like she did everything else: full tilt. Yes, she knew they had an audience, but after last night's light show in the kitchen, it was no surprise that a kiss would be this explosive. A simple touch had been enough to keep him awake for hours, wondering which one of them had been in the deeper state of denial for the last two years.

In the end he'd quit lying to himself. Much as he wished otherwise, Emma had walked into his life like a diva strutting to the front of the stage, blowing the competition away like so much smoke in a hurricane. Only he'd been too emotionally stunted two years ago to appreciate it.

However, several time bombs lurked between them—namely, their past and his more recent, idiotic amends tactics—and he knew it was already too late. He'd burned this bridge beyond repair.

So he kissed Emma as if it was his last chance, and she trailed her arms up his back, digging her hands into his hair.

Meanwhile, Jim was laughing his head off on the speaker. Another agent asked, "What the hell are you doing?"

The laughter continued, breaking into a chorus. Anthony would probably be stone deaf for a few hours, but he was so deliciously preoccupied with that sweet, demanding mouth he didn't care.

Emma must have heard the laughter. She pushed at Anthony's chest and he let go. No sense pressing his luck. As she blinked in confusion, he had to suppress a smile of triumph at the sight of her passionately swollen lips.

Deny that, he wanted to say. Instead, he took her arm and

dragged her toward the coffee shop. Emma, ever unpredictable, was quietly giggling and lurching along beside him.

"What are you laughing at?" he asked. "Right now you should be thanking God Dop isn't a sniper."

"I am, believe me. And I know it's not funny. It's just...can you imagine what his next message will say?"

"Yes. And rest assured, you won't be laughing then."

A valuable lesson, he told himself, wrenching open the front door to the coffee bar. He'd been kissing the great love of his life and a moment later she was laughing, completely unmoved, while he was still trying to calm certain parts of his anatomy.

Pure, unadulterated Emma. If she ever did the expected thing he'd probably drop dead of shock. A convenient outcome. He could be buried right alongside his sacred rule about women.

They were in and out of there in what seemed like a flash, and the agents urged them to hurry home. Anthony refused to say one word as they walked, his entire mind focused on the sad state of his rules. Number two, never take yourself too seriously, was a little bent and twisted, but in no danger of breaking.

Rule number one—keep life simple—was on life support, and Emma and Dop seemed to be wrestling for dibs on who got to pull the plug.

It didn't really matter who won. Whatever the outcome, within the foreseeable future both Dop and Emma would be out of his life. Dop would be someplace he couldn't hurt anyone again. As for Emma, she'd be back to business, where she was happy. That's where she needed to be.

He needed to be somewhere else. Her life was too complicated. He'd lived that way once, and to call it a disaster was an understatement.

So why had he done it? Why had he stepped hip-deep into her business again? He'd known damned well he was tempting fate.

"Hey." Emma nudged him with her elbow. "What's wrong?"

"Nothing."

"Yeah, nothing," she said, flexing the hand he was crushing. "You'll spill the coffee if you don't relax, Mr. Stay-Calm-and-Trust-Me."

He'd mangled the coffee holder's handle, he noted, forcing himself to ease his grip. Damn Dop. If it weren't for him, there wouldn't be the slightest chance Emma would ever find out about him and Charles.

No, he wouldn't let himself get away with that one. It was his own fault.

But if he ever got that lunatic alone, Dop had better hope and pray the FBI got there fast.

Emma spent the rest of the morning and part of the afternoon at her desk, buried in work. The phone was ringing off the hook and people were in and out of her office by the dozen. Simple tasks seemed to take twice as long as usual, but she couldn't blame the interruptions for her slow progress.

Her thighs were still on fire from that kiss.

She'd be able to get her mind off it for a time but her memory was relentless.

And then she'd recall the crushing pressure of his grip on the way back to the store. Emma supposed it was only natural that someone like Anthony would be simmering with frustration and anger after three weeks, but it only solidified the suspicion that the old Anthony Bracco was lurking very close to the surface. Not good.

By two o'clock, Emma needed a break and went in search of Charles. She could use some good news, and since Jim wasn't around to harass about Thursday night, she hoped Charles would finally show her the lily.

Dr. Dillon had issued a no-dumping order, and Emma wouldn't disobey. She just needed a megadose of Charles's objectivity.

Emma stopped dead upon entering the workshop. From the door she could see Charles's office window, and Anthony and Layne Crawford were inside. Charles was behind his desk and they were all laughing so hard their faces were red.

Why was it every time she found Anthony he was laughing?

Feeling inexplicably violated, Emma went to the door. The men got to their feet and Charles came forward to peck her cheek.

"There you are," he said in his lyrical accent.

Charles was a native of India, but learning his craft had taken him everywhere from Germany to China, and every stop had left its mark on his speech. "Your ears must have been burning."

"Talking about me?" she asked, inspecting Anthony and Layne. They looked very much at home, the older woman's blue eyes returning her perusal. A spark of dislike flared in Emma at Layne's blank expression.

"I was just explaining why you are banned from the workshop."

"Very funny, Charles."

"A little funny," he soothed. "I told them of the enameling fire, and it makes us all feel better to know there is one thing Emma Toliver cannot do."

She gazed at the intruders. "Yes, well, we all have limits."

Anthony took the hint, telling Layne, "Let's go have a talk before Jim gets back."

Charles and Layne exchanged niceties for a moment before Emma asked, "When are you expecting Jim?"

"Who knows?" Layne replied. "Is there something you need?"

"Yes. I have an event Thursday night and there'll be war if I'm not allowed to go."

Layne clearly wasn't intimidated at all. "That's presuming we don't have Dop in custody, but there's no reason you can't go. The Whitney's probably the most secure location in the Twin Cities."

"I told them all about it," Charles interjected. "Do not worry. Everything will go as planned."

"It better," Emma snapped.

Anthony's eyebrows shot up. "Well. If you'll excuse us."

When they were out of earshot, Charles observed, "Your Anthony takes direction quite well."

"He's not my Anthony and please tell me the lily's done."

"Not yet. One last stone to set. The largest, of course."

"Will the setting work?" she asked, slipping into a chair still warm from Anthony's body heat.

"Without all the stones in place, that is very hard to say. Now stop this incessant worrying and tell me how you've been."

Thanking God she'd scoured half of Europe and India to find this man, Emma poured out the story. Most of it, anyway.

When she was through, he said, "He seems harmless enough to me. I do not see why you cannot forgive him."

"But I have forgiven him. Well, sort of. I'm not angry with him anymore, if that counts. Business is business." She shrugged. "Had it gone any further I might feel differently."

"You know what I always say, Emma. Everything happens for a reason. Even this Doppelranger creature."

"It's Doppel*gänger,* and I don't suppose you have any specific reason in mind?" Emma asked.

A smug smile appeared on his face and Emma demanded, "What?"

"You go away now. I will work on the lily. But forget your unease about Anthony. He is not always what he appears to be, just as you often are not."

"How am I not what I appear to be?"

"Do go away. Work, call your head-shrinking man. Something."

Emma sighed and left him alone, not sure if she felt better or worse after their talk. Luckily, one of her clients fancied herself in a crisis and called, insisting her life would end if she didn't acquire a certain set of china before next Friday. Emma would have liked to tell her a thing or two about crises, but instead took her order, and had just finished calling it in when Anthony appeared.

"Come on," he urged, holding out his hand.

"What?"

"Jim's computer guru's here."

"So?" Emma said. She wasn't ready to be around Anthony yet, but he was crackling again.

Emma took his hand and he pulled her from the chair. "It's rude to spy on people, you know?"

"Who do you think you're foolin' with that?"

"You are unbelievable," Emma muttered, wrenching her hand away to straighten her suit jacket. But she was already heading for the stairs, and Anthony nudged her impatiently from behind even though she was practically running.

They screeched to a halt at the top of the steps, and Emma could hardly believe her eyes. She wasn't sure what she'd expected Jim's guru to look like, but this definitely wasn't it.

The woman's huge brown eyes were staring at Jim in subdued impatience as he read over her shoulder. He brushed a handful of very black, very long, curly hair out of his way, and the woman's face pinched into a pretty frown.

Emma looked at Anthony and he winked.

The computer guru stood, her head barely reaching Jim's shoulder. Emma stepped forward and introduced herself to Melinda Eliot.

Jim started to say something and Melinda told him to hush. Emma froze, caught with that horrified feeling people get when they're about to burst out laughing in church.

"You'll want to see the suspect's reply," Melinda said.

Emma,

Don't worry—I'm smart enough to do what must be done. You just step aside, sweetheart. This has nothing to do with you. Let the men handle this.

Emma stopped reading, her mouth opening in outrage. Anthony's hand settled at the small of her back, his fingers slipping beneath her jacket to touch her bare skin. The skittering sensations darting through her stomach added fuel to her comment. "The *nerve!* Sweetheart? Let the *men* handle this?"

"It gets worse," Jim said.

And Anthony, I won't have you tainting Emma with your sickness. You're filth. A bastard of society who should have been culled at birth. You pollute everyone around you with your greed and lies, and your very life violates all that is holy. If you touch her I'll cut your hands off. Breathe on her and I'll carve your lungs out.

Emma was right. I should have killed you when I had a chance. Next time I won't let the angels of mercy still my hand.

Doppelgänger

Emma looked up at Anthony and felt her insides crawl up her throat. Smoky brown eyes stared back as Jim said, "Looks like a direct hit with the smart comment. And I love how he's all of a sudden getting a God complex. Driving me nuts with the costume changes."

It was all Emma could do not to scream at Jim. This wasn't a psychological study. Dop was threatening to kill Anthony, Jim's best friend. How could he be so clinical?

Before she could say a word, Jim added, "I'm not too

happy about your performance this morning. If he saw it, your next message may not be so tame."

Tame? If this was tame, what were the other e-mails like? And what had they done? If Dop had seen what happened this morning...

Oh, God. Don't even think it.

She didn't have to say it, either. Anthony's brows drew together and he rubbed her back while asking Jim, "Are you planning a reply this time?"

"Already done. Nothing inflammatory. Just another gentle poke about loyalties. He wants Emma on his side, against you. And us. Stupid to say what he did, but that was probably his arrogance talking. Guess he'll let us know if he was there this morning."

There was a brief exchange about a virus Melinda had attached to Jim's reply. He wanted an explanation on how it worked, but Melinda refused to explain, saying only that it wasn't a normal, attachment-type virus and should yield results quickly if Dop didn't unplug from the phone jack after picking up the message.

Her goodbyes were short but kind, and Jim followed her down the stairs, still demanding explanations.

Emma began, "Anthony, I—"

"Don't." He shook his head. "It's all right."

"No, it's not. We need to get out of here. After what we did this morning he'll kill you."

Anthony settled his hands on her waist, his brown eyes calm. "Jim won't let anything happen to us."

"But—"

"No. It's okay. We're gonna be okay. I promise."

Emma sighed out of sheer frustration. Why was he pretending to be calm? He wasn't calm. She *knew* he wasn't calm. She could feel the anger in him as if it was flowing through his hands straight to her spine.

It was his turn to sigh. "Emma, don't let Dop get to you. Don't let Jim get to you, either. He's a good guy. Just takes some getting used to."

Anthony leaned down to kiss her cheek, and the smell of him made Emma close her eyes. While the feel of his mouth lingered on her skin, he said, "I need to go make dinner."

Once again, neither of them moved, and Emma stared at his mouth. They were alone and they both knew it. If she didn't get out of here, heaven only knew what might happen.

"I," she replied, pointing over her shoulder, "need to go figure out the mess from yesterday's registers."

And the wretch gave a quiet laugh. "Good idea, Emma."

She fled to her office, landing breathless behind her desk. The mess. Think about the mess.

The register receipts during the FBI's questioning were hopelessly fouled up, not that Emma blamed her employees. She was fouled up right now, too. The sooner she got her life back to normal, the better she'd feel. And that life did not include Anthony Bracco, no matter how badly she wanted him. Not even a short, purely physical affair was allowed. She had responsibilities and nothing could stand in the way.

Suddenly very glad her home was overrun with strangers who wouldn't give them a second's peace all night, Emma allowed herself a few minutes to stew about Dop's reply.

Let the men handle this.

If there weren't men involved, there wouldn't be anything to handle!

Emma hoped Melinda's virus would work. And soon.

Chapter 6

Emma worked until the smell of olive oil and garlic became too hard to ignore. Stopping only long enough to take off her heels, she padded barefoot into the kitchen.

Anthony was facing the stove, an unguarded pot of something that smelled like heaven on the island counter's burner. Emma reached for the lid and then yelped as Anthony's hand shot out to catch her wrist.

''No peeking,'' he scolded.

''What are you making? It smells fantastic.''

''Patience, Emma. The pasta needs a few minutes yet.''

He still had her wrist, and Emma abruptly remembered why she hadn't wanted to come up here.

Anthony grumbled and let her go so he could shake the sauté pan. ''Get out unless you mean to scratch.''

Emma knew she shouldn't, but slipped behind him to do it anyway, Anthony batting down her other hand when she tried to rest it on his ribs as she had yesterday.

''Don't,'' he warned. ''You'll get burned. Maybe Charles should banish you from the kitchen, too.''

"I can't believe he told you the enameling story. It wasn't a big deal, really. Nothing a fire extinguisher couldn't handle."

Anthony whimpered when she ran her nails over his shoulder blade. "That's not how he tells it," he argued.

"Yes, well, Charles has a different spin on most everything. But I see you three hit it off."

"He's a fascinating person. What I wouldn't give to read his autobiography."

"If he ever writes one I get first dibs. Shoulder better?"

"Yes, thanks. Now why don't you go change out of that suit? By the time you're done, dinner will be ready."

"You're getting awfully bossy," Emma complained, surprised that she was honestly annoyed.

On second thought she wasn't surprised at all. There was an intimacy to this situation she didn't like. The rare phenomenon of a home-cooked meal aside, she didn't want to get used to this playful easiness between them. She'd fallen for it once before.

"I'm entitled," Anthony replied. "Go."

"It's my kitchen."

Anthony turned suddenly and Emma found herself two inches from his chin. Moving deliberately, he put a hand on the counter beside her and leaned forward.

Emma bent backward, meaning to sidle out of the way, but his other arm quickly barred her escape.

His eyes swept from hers to her mouth, then lower, and back again, tilting his head into perfect position for a deep, endless kiss. Emma's lips parted, responding even though she didn't want to.

But then Anthony retreated with the loaf of French bread he'd grabbed off the counter behind her back.

Well, she thought, he did tell you to leave. But you had to argue.

"Okay, I deserved that," she admitted.

He faked her out with a lunge and she fled, both of them laughing, although Emma couldn't figure out why.

Dinner was much more relaxed than last night. Jim, Hornsby and Layne kept up a sporadic flow of Bureau-speak, but Emma was too busy eating to listen. Anthony watched, tolerantly amused, as she polished off a heaping plate of chicken marinara along with salad and a huge piece of bread.

He leaned over to say, "I take it you'd forgotten what real food tastes like."

She nodded, swallowing. "Yes, but this is better than real food."

"The walleye was good. Too bad you didn't eat it."

"Would you quit? I wasn't in the mood for dinner last night."

"What were you in the mood for?" he asked, a decidedly wicked grin lighting up his eyes.

"Walked right into that one, didn't I?"

"Smack into it." He turned toward Jim. "Any word from Melinda?"

"Nope. Dop hasn't picked up the reply yet."

"How will she know when he picks it up?"

"Don't ask me." Jim shrugged. "We probably don't wanna know."

Emma was so stuffed she could hardly move when Anthony shooed her from the dining room with an order to relax. On her way to the design office, Jim stopped her to introduce the two male agents who'd be taking over while he and Walter left to work on another case.

Layne had disappeared into one of the guest rooms, and Emma seized the opportunity to sneak a peek at her e-mail, only to find that every single archived message from Dop had been removed. Sighing, she answered important correspondence and then went to work on a design.

By nine o'clock she'd returned to her habitual bundle-of-nerves state. Why wasn't Dop picking up that e-mail? Would anyone tell them if he had? She should have called Dillon. Was it too late?

At least Anthony wasn't hovering.

No sooner had the thought occurred to her than footsteps approached and he came in to sit beside her.

"What's wrong?" Emma asked. He looked pale.

"Nothing. Came in to beg a scratch."

Emma obliged, examining him closely. Something was wrong and she was learning to fear the word *nothing* exiting Anthony's mouth. It usually meant something really awful was about to happen, and this time she'd like a little warning.

He stretched forward, propping his elbows on the desk as she scratched. "Are you all right?" she queried.

"Yes, I'm fine. Just sick of being cooped up."

"Would it kill you to tell me the truth once in a while?"

He turned his head to look at her, his eyes wary. "I had a call from a client and I'm ticked off I couldn't leave to take care of the problem."

Emma stopped scratching to cross her arms over her chest. "A client? I thought you weren't working."

"Don't get nervous, Emma. I don't work. Not for pay, anyway. If you can believe it, I consult for a nonprofit, small business support group."

"Nonprofit? You're kidding, right?"

"No, I'm not kidding. Call it penance, but instead of using my dubious talent to spot problems and tear apart big companies, I use it on small ones to patch them up before someone like me can sink the ship."

Concealing her surprise, Emma asked, "What was the problem?"

He told her, and it did sound like a major disaster in the making. It was interesting to see him so frustrated over someone else's affairs. And it looked as though he'd found his dream job. He could snoop, scheme and meddle all he liked, and they'd thank him for it.

When she jumped in with a suggestion, she expected him to brush it off. But he didn't. Instead he thought aloud, expanding the idea miles ahead, impressing her with efficient, flawless logic. "That might work," he said finally. "Thanks."

She huffed out a laugh and said, "It was nothing, trust me."

Anthony pulled out his cellphone and started to dial. Out of respect for his client, Emma turned away and fiddled with the complicated process of combining math and art into an intricate series of bezels that would someday be a pendant.

Within moments of Anthony hanging up she was under siege. He asked question after question, and she explained how she always got her ideas from flowers, but smoothed over the painstaking process that would eventually yield a permanent copy in gemstones and metal.

"You really do like the jewelry biz, don't you?" she asked.

"Yes, although I can't claim to know as much as I'd like. But what really appeals is the veneer you all put on it. So formal and glamorous, but underneath you're as cutthroat as the rest of us."

Emma laughed and shook her head. "Of course you'd love that, wouldn't you? Are you saying you actually like the store, or was your takeover attempt just the never-ending pursuit of profit?"

"That was definitely part of it. Once I started looking into this place I was amazed how secure an investment your beloved shiny things are. Honestly, I took one look at your quarterlies and thought I was in the wrong business. And no one could help but be impressed by the loyalty your clientele shows."

"Wonderful, aren't they? We weren't sure they'd go for Beautiful Things, though. Brady didn't believe we'd sell a single piece," Emma said.

"Well, he was wrong. And I'm sure he's been fed a daily dose of crow ever since."

Emma wrinkled her nose. "Not true. I don't think I've ever brought it up, actually."

"Humph. Come to think of it, when you forget how much you hate me you're almost likable."

"I hate what you did, not you. Business is business, right?"

His expression incredulous, Anthony rumbled with low laughter. "Standing half-naked in front of your bed was business? I don't think so, Emma. You're damned lucky I wasn't a complete monster. Anyone else might not have left without following through."

Emma blinked at him. There must have been some level of trust between them because never once had it occurred to her that he might have hurt her physically. "I wasn't thinking. I was angry. I mean *seeing red* angry. And I have a tendency to…"

"Overreact? Go for the jugular? Do stupid things when angry?" he suggested.

"All of the above?"

"Oh, my Lord. She admits it."

His eyes were filled with laughter and Emma knew she was being made fun of. Had she not spent most of her life feeling like an idiot after blowing up over some small thing, she might have resented it. "Can't say I'm not honest."

"No, I can't. But can I ask you a question without you reading all sorts of sinister meanings into it?"

"This is me we're talking about. I doubt it. Highly."

He grunted a laugh, then sobered. "I overheard something today and I was concerned. Do Brady and Charles get along?"

Emma's eyes narrowed. "What happened?"

"I walked in on them having words about someone named Tanya."

Squeezing her eyes shut, Emma said, "Tanya is Brady's wife, and let me guess what you heard. Brady complained about being so far behind and Charles reciprocated about Brady's family life."

"Yup. Got it in one."

"Why were you concerned?"

"Brady was pretty upset, and I think if I hadn't shown up when I did it might have gotten a lot worse. I was just curious whether you knew how bad it gets down there."

"Not to that extent, no, I didn't. But rest assured I'll be putting a stop to it first thing in the morning."

"Uh," Anthony said, "I wouldn't recommend that. It's just a power struggle, and you might be better off leaving it alone."

"Doubtful. Charles has been acting really weird lately and Brady is just... Well, never mind. You don't need to hear all my—"

"Hold it," Anthony interrupted. "Why did you do that?"

"Do what?"

"Doesn't anyone ever listen when you talk?"

Emma raised an eyebrow, jarred by the question. Before she could deflect it, he clarified, "I'm not talking about business. I mean other things. The things that bother you. Worries."

"Look, no offense, but I don't exactly feel comfortable telling you anything."

"I can understand that, I guess. But pretend I'm not me and just talk for once. If we're penned up together we might as well help each other through this."

For some unknown reason, her temper rocketed into the red.

No, not unknown. She was falling for it again. Hook, line and sinker. Damn him. He looked so innocent, but there was always something up his sleeve. She needed to get out of here. Now.

And she almost knocked him out of his chair on the way out.

"Hey!" Anthony called, diving after her in pursuit. "What the— Emma, stop!"

She could feel him coming after her and every instinct sent her hurling forward, away from the threat. All she wanted was to get away from him, and if he didn't give her time to reason this out he'd regret it.

But he was coming after her, and as she hurried past Layne's room, the two agents poked their heads out into the hallway.

"Everything okay?" one of them asked.

Anthony stopped to say something and Emma went through the front door like a shot, turning left and sprinting up the stairs to the roof. She needed to be alone. There were too many people in her space. And with Anthony crowding her she couldn't think.

Once outside in the cloying humidity, Emma grew even angrier. It was late. It should have been cooler. Everything had to be as extreme as possible, when all she wanted was a little peace.

Gravel crunched under her feet as she made for the greenhouse on the far side of the roof. It had always been her hiding place, and she hoped she'd moved fast enough that Anthony wouldn't be able to find her.

As she approached the half glass, half concrete structure, she spotted a blue card hanging inside a pane. That meant Charles had been up to water today. It also meant she'd forgotten about the flowers for two whole days.

Even madder now, Emma quickened her steps, but she never made it to the door. She heard the stairwell door open and more crunching as Anthony ran after her.

"Would you stop?" he called.

Emma spun around. "No. You stop. I need some space."

"Tough. I'm not leaving until you explain what happened down there."

"Why? So you can feel better?"

"Do you hear yourself?" he asked, now close enough to pin her in place with two steady hands. "I didn't do anything wrong. All I did was bring up an obviously sore subject. I'm sorry, but this takes overreaction to an all new level."

"You know what? Don't do this. I don't want your help and I don't want to help you, either. And I certainly don't want you injecting your opinion all over the place. What goes on here is *my* business, not yours."

"Spare me, Emma. You think I'm after the store again, don't you?"

"You're damn right I do," she retorted, yanking herself free.

"Do you think I'm incurably stupid?" he charged. "I may have kidded you about it yesterday, but I learned my lesson. So now when I'm trying to warn you about something as a courtesy, I get my head bitten off."

"I'm not one of your clients, so keep the courtesies," Emma told him, turning, only to be yanked back into place.

"Don't you turn your back on me," he said. "While we're at it, what right do you have to be angry? You won. You killed the giant. If anyone should be angry around here it's me."

"Why? Because you keep getting exactly what you deserve? It's not my fault you had to be just like Daddy Dearest."

Anthony's eyes flared with anger and Emma took a quick step backward when he said, "You need to keep your mouth shut about things you don't understand."

Now that he was losing it, Emma felt the fear give way to defiance, and taunted, "Oh, but I do understand it now. Without Daddy's power behind you, you're *nothing*."

Anthony stopped and erupted into laughter. "You need to get some new material. And just remember it was *you* who brought up daddies. If you'd had one, maybe you wouldn't be such a witch."

"What are you...I had a—"

"You had a what? A father? Yeah, right, Emma. More like a dependant. Or don't you talk about the fact that he dumped the store in your lap when you were sixteen? My father might be a workaholic sperm donor, but at least he worked. Yours used you as a crutch. And right now it looks like *crutch* is a little more damaging than *burden*."

"You don't know *anything* about my father, so don't you dare say one more word."

"No way. You started this. Now you're gonna finish it."

"I didn't start this. You did, with your pathetic mind games."

"Oh, yes. Let's compare those," he suggested, leaning about a millimeter from her nose. "I offered you an apology yesterday and you stomped all over it. A few minutes ago, I trusted you enough to confide my business problem, and when I tried to return the favor, this is what happened. So as long as you're in the jugular-tearing mood, let's talk about the fact that you still want me and I still want you. Only to you, I'm nothing more than a piece of meat to chew on and then throw to the wolves once you're satisfied."

By the time he'd finished Emma was staring, wide-eyed and frozen. All of it was true, and if she tried to argue she'd feel even worse than she already did. Sighing, she asked, "What difference does it make? I'm sorry if I make you feel that way. I really am. But you can't expect me to see you as anything more than that. I don't want to feel whatever it is between us, anyway."

"I don't understand. Am I such a threat to you?"

Emma blew out a breath. "Look, I can't explain it without coming off like… I really don't want to talk about this."

"Then don't. Just listen. Okay?"

She nodded, groaning at herself for being on the edge of tears. She couldn't let him do this to her again. Her future was mapped out perfectly, and this interlude was looming like a police roadblock.

"Can you at least look at me when I'm talking to you?"

Biting the inside of her cheek, Emma looked up. But where she expected to see disapproving anger, she saw only a placid pair of smoky brown eyes.

"I don't want anything from you," he said quietly. "Except to get to know you again. As people. Not as whatever we were back then. I admit I've never had very good judgment where you're concerned, but I'm trying. And maybe it's okay that you rake me over the coals once in a while. I probably need it. But you don't have to be so defensive."

He paused, and Emma nodded a begrudging acknowledgment.

Then he continued, "Consider it an experiment. After Dop is caught and I'm out of your hair, there won't be anyone around who knows you leaned on someone. It's relatively painless, I promise. And then when you do actually care about someone you'll know how to act."

A laugh escaped before she could stop it. He had a way of putting things that made her feel an absolute fool, but it did feel good to laugh at herself. And how could he make everything okay again? Lord, if she could trust him as far as she could throw him she might have to keep him around for the occasional reality check.

He said, "You know, it's really hard to think pure thoughts when you look at me like that."

Emma straightened, embarrassed that she'd shown her feelings. But her nerves sparked to life, and she found herself anxious for him to act on that tone of voice.

"Too late now," he said, lowering his head to brush the lightest of kisses across her lips.

Her eyes closed as the soft caress raised goose bumps on her arms.

He did it again, this time leaving a warm wetness on her lip with his tongue.

Knowing it was unspeakably selfish, Emma balled a fist in his hair and pulled him down to her. She wanted what they'd had this morning, a scorching, decadent moment of openly wanting and touching without caring what might happen afterward.

And she bit his bottom lip for yesterday's close encounter, drawing a growl from Anthony. He dug both his hands into her hair, holding her still as he deepened the kiss even further, until Emma was fighting for air. After dragging in a breath, she said, "Please. The greenhouse—"

"No," he answered against her neck, his voice a harsh

rasp. "Are you crazy? You know what will happen if we go in there."

"That's why I want to—"

He took her mouth again and they drank from each other, Emma desperately trying to convince him they needed release from this exquisite tension.

When he let her breathe again she said, "Okay, we won't—"

"Yes, we will. And unless you keep condoms in there we're in trouble," he said against her lips, sending messages hot as molten gold to the tight knot of desire forming in her belly.

"But I could—"

"Emma!" Anthony groaned, lifting his head. "Good Lord. I'm not a plaything. Not that I hate the idea, mind you, but I don't want to leave with more regrets than necessary."

Emma nodded again. It wasn't exactly a rejection, but it still hurt. Later on, when she could think clearly, she was sure she'd be ashamed of herself, but right now all she wanted was to make sure he didn't leave until she'd found out whether the sex lived up to the chemistry.

They both jumped at a sharp percussive sound, and the very next second the roof was flooded with light. Blinding light. And a deafening shriek as the alarm wailed to life.

Shocked and frozen in place by confusion, Emma gasped in pain as Anthony's arms tightened like a vice.

"Get in the greenhouse," he shouted.

"No! I need to go downstairs and shut off the—"

"I said *get in the greenhouse!*" This time his voice was a demonic roar.

When he suddenly loosened his hold, Emma stumbled. Seizing the opportunity, she got one hand on the ground for leverage and shot past him toward the door. She didn't need protection. She needed to shut off the alarm.

Idiot agents, she thought, running. When you've got three

million dollars of inventory sitting around you don't advertise problems with your security system.

But she wasn't fast enough. Anthony had swooped like a hawk for its prey, catching the back of her shirt. She was yanked clean off the ground by the strength of his one hand, and hung there, dangling.

The cotton tore and Emma grabbed his leg. He juggled her and caught her up under his arm. By the time he reached the greenhouse she felt as if she were broken in half.

Once he put her down Emma shouted, "What's wrong with you? It's just Hornsby—"

"Hornsby's not here. It's Dop. He shot at the door."

Emma's eyes rounded as she remembered the pop she'd heard before the lights came on. Her indignation over the rough handling was pulverized by sheer terror. They needed to get under cover. Now.

The second the door was open she pushed Anthony in, only to be swung off her feet once more and shoved into the narrow aisle between the flower beds. Anthony backed out the door, closing it behind him.

A second later, Emma heard the emergency bolt shoot home.

She couldn't get out. Anthony had just locked her in. Alone.

Hurling herself at the door, she screamed his name.

Panicked and furious, Emma tried to peer through the thick glass pane beside the door, but it had steamed over in the cooling night air. She raised her forearm to wipe it off so she could see what Anthony was doing, then stopped herself.

Dop had a gun. She'd be giving him a nice clean target. And then she'd be no help to anyone.

Emma cursed viciously, spinning like a caged wolf, desperate for a way out. A stab of primal fear ripped through her chest. She couldn't see anything. Dop could be right outside the door by now.

What the hell was Anthony thinking, locking her in? If

Dop wanted to kill her in the most agonizing way possible, all he had to do was shoot and she'd be shredded by broken glass.

Cursing the protective male instinct, Emma raced for the cement-walled office at the back. As soon as she entered the door the air-conditioning hit her like an icy shower, pumping her adrenaline into overdrive.

The air conditioner was in a window high up on one wall, but if she could get the unit out she should be able to squeeze through. Scrambling onto the desk, Emma shoved and pulled, trying to work it loose.

It didn't budge. Damn thing was bolted in. Emma wanted to kick the wall but her foot got tangled in something.

The telephone cord.

"Oh, for God's sake," she groaned through gritted teeth.

Dropping into a crouch, she untangled her foot and hopped to the floor. The buttons on the phone seemed extremely small. Emma howled in frustration, redialing twice before entering the right design office extension.

And then she waited. Two rings. Three. The sound of her heart thrashing in her chest almost drowned them out.

"Pick up the phone!" Emma screeched at no one, the hairs on her neck beginning to tingle. As if she was being watched.

She hardly dared turn around. It was no use listening for anyone. Nothing was audible over the sound of the alarm.

Do it. Turn around. If Dop was behind her she wanted to see his face before punching it in.

Summoning her courage, Emma turned. And saw no one.

"When I get my hands on that man I'm gonna rip him in half," Emma threatened aloud, the volume of her voice rivaling the alarm.

The phone was still ringing, and the longer she waited the angrier she got. Why had he tricked her into the greenhouse? What did he plan on doing? Taking off after Dop like the big moronic hero that always gets killed?

Emma called Anthony a very bad name, then started as a voice shouted into her ear.

"Layne! Is that you?"

"Yes. Where are you?"

"Anthony locked me in the greenhouse!"

"What?"

"He locked me—"

"I heard you. Are you okay?"

"No! Dop could be right outside!"

"You're safer up there, Emma. Now where did Anthony go? I haven't heard him come down and no one's seen him."

Emma felt a wave of nausea. "Oh, my God, Layne. He's out there alone on the roof."

The phone fell from Emma's hand, cracking against the desk and tumbling to the floor as she raced back toward the door.

Her imagination had summoned an image of Anthony lying on the roof. Cut. His hands. His chest. Bleeding. His life leaking out and staining the gravel. Oozing through the stones like lava.

Weapon. She needed a weapon.

Snagging a trowel, Emma tucked it into the back of her jeans. There was a cement block in her line of sight and she picked it up as though it weighed no more than a feather.

Just as Anthony had yanked a five-foot-ten squirming blonde off her feet.

Adrenaline.

Emma hurled the brick at the widest, closest pane of glass.

A shower of deadly shards exploded out of the frame, and Emma waited only long enough for a long, jagged spike to fall away before making her way out, glass crunching beneath her feet.

Frantically scanning the roof, she saw no one. Nothing.

Her mind churned out possible flight options until she finally recalled the one-story drop to the roof next door.

Racing forward, she leaned over the ledge. Still nothing. Turning for the stairs, Emma fled as if all the demons in hell were nipping at her heels.

Somehow she managed to enter the right code on the roof access door, then clapped her hands over her ears as the blaring alarm in the cement stairway tore through her. It was so loud it was painful.

But all she could think about was finding Anthony.

Five flights of stairs passed by her in a blur and Emma hit the ground floor running.

The trowel dug into her back and she snatched it from her jeans, holding it like a dagger. For the second time that day she went out the street door with her heart in her throat.

Chapter 7

A hand hit her chest and shoved her back. Emma screamed, a full-throated release of terror.

"What the—" Jim yelled, doing a double take and snatching the trowel. "Quiet! Get inside and kill the alarm. Now!"

"What are you doing here? And where's Anthony?"

"Just kill the alarm! He can't hear!"

Panting and shaking now with an overdose of adrenaline, Emma turned and stabbed the shutdown code into the panel. Silence fell, but her head still buzzed from the noise. Rubbing her ears, she moved to the door, where Jim barred her way.

She asked, "What's going on? Where's Anthony?"

"Get back inside."

"No! Why won't you tell me what's happening?"

And then Emma spotted Anthony standing in the middle of the street, shouting into his phone and scanning the upper floors of nearby buildings. His body language was pure frustrated aggression as he stalked back and forth, yelling.

Ears still ringing, Emma couldn't make out a word. Jim was making "keep going" gestures while staring at his watch.

"Oh, my God," Emma breathed. "Is he talking to Dop?"

Jim gave a quick nod, then made a "zip it" gesture. Emma obeyed, straining her ears to hear Anthony. The few words she made out turned her to stone.

Anthony was challenging Dop to show himself.

This was the old Anthony, full of so much arrogance and bravado it shot from him like sparks. Of all the moments for that specter to rear its ugly head. He'd get himself killed!

Going with her gut, Emma waited until Jim's attention was back on his watch. Then she flattened herself to the doorjamb and slipped behind him onto the sidewalk, reaching the curb in time to hear Anthony growl, "Come down here and say that to my face."

He was still looking up, searching, one arm flung wide. "Shoot me, you coward. And you'd better not miss because I'm coming for you, and when I find you… Oh man. You really are crazy, aren't you? You touch one hair on her head—"

Anthony stiffened, then turned to Emma with a murderous look. He dropped his arm, shaking his head. She realized now that Dop could see them both from his hiding spot, and Jim must be waiting for either a cellphone trace or for someone to reach Dop.

Emma locked eyes with Anthony, no words necessary. Coming onto the street might have been a deadly mistake.

But she wasn't afraid. Either Dop was a lousy shot or he didn't want them dead. He could have killed them easily while they were headed for the greenhouse. But they were still alive.

Jim snarled her name as Emma stepped toward Anthony, her hand held out for the phone. Anthony's eyes burned into hers, silently willing her to get back inside.

The next second he swore viciously and pulled the phone from his ear, flipping it shut against his thigh.

And then Jim ordered, "Get her out of here *now.* Take your car, go straight to Beta. Hornsby will intercept. Move it."

Anthony obeyed immediately, grabbing her arm and hauling her down the ramp to the parking garage. It was dark, and Emma was certain Dop would attack any second as Anthony dragged her a mercifully short distance to a black SUV. He jammed the key into the lock, the muscle in his jaw clenching wildly.

Chilly fingers of lingering panic streaked down her back as Anthony shoved her into the car before she had a chance to say one word. Holding her breath, Emma struggled with the lock on his door, sure she'd hear a gunshot before he could get inside.

Thirty seconds later they were racing down the street. Nonsensical questions poured from her mouth, but Anthony said nothing, his hands so tight on the wheel that every vein and tendon stood out like steel girders.

Finally, right in the middle of a question, he exploded. "Why the *hell* did you leave the greenhouse?"

"Wha— Me? Why did you lock me in? I could have been killed! And you, you stupid jerk. Taking off after him like some macho testosterone junkie."

Anthony blew out a sigh of long-suffering frustration and argued, "Damn it, Emma. I put you in the greenhouse for your own safety. What'd you do? Chew your way out?"

"Ugh. You are such a—"

"Close your mouth. We can scream and yell when we get home."

"Home? Where are we going?"

"Emma, I can't drive a stick shift with one hand over your mouth. If you speak again before we get to my house I will not be responsible for my actions."

Thinking hateful thoughts about Anthony and men in general, Emma flounced back in her seat. Words boiled on her tongue and she almost screamed when he ordered, "Get your seat belt on."

Stoplights were completely disregarded as they made their way west at impressive speed, and Emma groaned when they shot past a police car. Its lights came on for only a moment, then shut off again as an SUV with a blue light spinning on the dash peeled around a corner and gained ground.

"Walter?" Emma asked.

"I hope so," Anthony said. His phone rang, and without preamble he answered, "Thanks. Is the system running yet?"

Emma watched pools of shadow sweep from Anthony's eyes to his cheeks in the play of passing lights. And then the image she'd had of him bleeding on the roof filled her mind. Nothing would ever be the same again. Plans for the future seemed trite now that she'd seen, if only for a few seconds, what life would be like without him around to hate anymore.

"All right," he said, "But I hope you know the rearm codes. No one's bothered to tell me how to get into my own house yet."

He hung up and wove his way onto Ashland Avenue. If he lived around here, Emma could understand why they were installing a new system. The old houses were timelessly beautiful but very close together, and for all anyone knew Dop could be living right next door. At the store they'd already had a hundred thousand dollars in security equipment to keep him out.

Anthony pulled into a driveway beside a red brick Georgian, but before she'd caught half a glimpse they were in the garage.

Coming down off the adrenaline now, Emma shivered but hurried out as Anthony moved a set of golf clubs to accommodate Walter's vehicle.

No one said a word until Emma had been propelled through a covered walkway to a split-rock porch, then into a kitchen. The smell of cinnamon was the first thing she noticed, but as the lights came on she thought she'd stepped back a century. Or two. There was a wide fireplace in one wall and the lighting reminded her of the antiquated brass fixtures at the store.

New appliances were the only jarring note, but it was a lovely room. Homey. A bizarre, calming contrast to their moods. The only thing that fit their emotions was the brand-new security panel beside the door.

Walter and Anthony conferred, then Anthony asked, "Can you remember that?"

Emma quit perusing with a start. "Me? Remember what?"

"The codes. If you're here you need to know them all."

They spent the next two minutes on mnemonics, while avoiding each other's eyes. They'd just narrowly escaped disaster and no one was calm enough yet to discuss what had happened or what came next.

Finally, Walter put his hands in his pockets. "Okay, first things first." He pointed at Emma. "She's gonna crash. Pale. Goose bumps, too. Warm bath, brandy and definitely a new shirt. Layne and Jim will get here soon and we don't have much time. No phone calls. Not even cell. Clear?"

Feeling like furniture, Emma was bullied through the kitchen into a narrow hall, up a steep staircase and into a room at the end of a long hallway. She looked around at dark-colored decor and richly textured wood while Anthony dug through a dresser, coming up with a pair of navy flannel pajamas with drawstring pants.

The air between them was black with hostility and Emma knew if she said one word they'd be screaming in seconds. All she wanted was to escape into the tub, where she could get warm and try to relax.

Anthony led her across the hall to another room with walnut furniture, the walls a faint peach. Emma stared. It was definitely not what she'd expected.

He tossed the clothes on the bed and pointed to a door. "You should find everything you need in there. Don't be long."

His brusque tone goaded her into asking, "Why are you so mad at me?"

It came out sounding more pathetic than she'd like, but did nothing to soften his reply. "That has to rank among the dumbest questions ever asked."

"Why? Because I can't read your mind?"

Anthony covered his eyes for a moment, pinching his eyebrows together. "Don't start this. Hornsby and I have work to do."

"Uh, just you and Walter? In case you hadn't noticed, I'm involved in this situation, too."

"No, you're not. You've already proved you can't be trusted to make rational decisions."

"Rational decisions? You're the one who—"

"Don't you dare act insulted." He cut her off. "Did you even stop to think what might have happened if Dop really had been on that roof? Did you think you stood a chance against him? Trust me when I say you don't."

Emma blinked. No, she hadn't considered for one second what might have happened. The only thing on her mind had been that bloody image of him. A hot, powerful rush of anger hit her and she retorted, "You *died* three weeks ago. What was I supposed to do? Sit there and let him kill you again?"

And back came the old Anthony, hands held out in defiant arrogance. "Do I look dead to you, Emma? Did I feel dead to you before the alarm went off? You need to learn your limitations before you get us all killed."

"Learn my limitations? In case you've forgotten I've lived alone in downtown St. Paul since I was sixteen years old. I've somehow managed to survive an attempted robbery at the store and an attempted mugging. Attempted. So I'm not some poor pitiful female who can't take care of herself."

"Neither am I!" Anthony roared.

Emma deflated as the wounded-ego alert went off. Would she never see the day when she didn't have to take a back seat to a man's feelings? His poor, precious ego got bruised and she was supposed to come over all contrite and repentant. Well screw that. "You know, I think I've had about enough for one day."

"Perfect. Once again, make a lot of noise, then back down when the conversation gets a little too close to the truth."

"What's that supposed to mean?"

"Go stew in the bathtub. Maybe you'll figure it out."

"Don't you dare walk away from me," Emma warned.

Anthony stopped near the door. "I'm walking. What are you gonna do about it?"

Emma marched over and closed it with a thump. If they'd been at her place she'd have cracked the door frame. Hands on hips, she waited.

It was Anthony's turn to sigh. "That's it? A door slam?"

"What did you want?"

"I want you to grow up and stop acting like a stubborn princess. You can't outsmart Dop and you're not bulletproof. So stop with the outraged pride routine and let the rest of us handle this."

"Let the *men* handle this, you mean."

Anthony closed his eyes and shook his head. After a grunt of disgust, he said, "That's not what I meant and you know it. But if that's the game you want to play, bring it on."

Fed up, not knowing which Anthony she was fighting, Emma went for the throat. "Can you decide what kind of man you are? Quick like? Because this waffling is getting on my nerves."

Anthony's reaction was too fast to avoid. Emma was suddenly pinned to the door by a much stronger body, his hands hemming her in. "Since when do you care what kind of man I am?"

A stubbled cheek was against her neck, a mouth burning her skin. She tried to say something, only making it more convenient for a kiss that seared her to the bone with raw hunger.

His words thundered in her head as she gave in, the first truly honest thing she'd done in two days. He was right. Up until he threw her into the greenhouse Emma had wanted only one thing from Anthony Bracco. Sex. No sentiment. No responsibility.

But sentiment had taken a giant leap forward, and like it or not, she was addicted to the knowns and unknowns of this man. Right now nothing was more important than what happened to him. Or with him.

Fear, anger and desire clashed into a conflicted mess, but with his hands on her, all she could do was hang on and pray he understood why it was so hard for her to say she was sorry.

Those hands left the door to rake up her shirt and close over her breasts. At Emma's throaty gasp he tore his mouth away, and she stared into flinty eyes that drank in whatever showed on her face. The feeling of complete helplessness in his arms was all new—and all welcome.

And it felt as if he saved them both when he raised a hand to her cheek. This time when he lowered his head the kiss was slow and gentle. Dangerously so. It felt very much like an eloquently phrased apology, and she responded with total submission.

They both jumped when Walter rapped his knuckles on the door. "Thought I heard yelling. Everything okay in there?"

Anthony pulled her away from the door, answering in a husky rasp, "Yeah. I'll be down in a minute."

"Okay. Layne called—they'll be here in half an hour, and we have a lot of ground to cover before then."

Walter's footsteps were incredibly loud as he walked away, leaving Emma staring at Anthony with no idea what came next.

"Have your bath now," he murmured. "But don't be long."

Emma watched him, feeling as if she should say something in reply. But they'd just developed a higher level of communication. She didn't know how it was possible to feel comfortable with him in that moment, but she'd never felt calmer in her life.

When he'd gone she soaked in the tub and came to two decisions. The first was a no-brainer. As soon as she could use the phone she'd call Brady and officially close the store. For a split second she thought about sneaking the call, but now that she understood why Anthony had been so angry she wouldn't cross that line. All she'd done so far in this investigation was make everyone's lives hell, and it was definitely time to slow down and think before she acted.

That comeuppance brought a second decision: to proceed with caution where Anthony was concerned. Emma had no idea when, why or how she'd turned into such a selfish, inconsiderate monster, but she decided to spend the next few days unraveling that painful truth.

Too bad she couldn't call Dr. Dillon. If he'd picked up on it, why hadn't he said anything?

Emma squeezed her eyes shut, cringing. Who did she think she was? Jim, Layne and Walter were working eighteen-hour days to end this thing, and she should be kissing their feet, not forcing them to deal with her.

And Anthony… It was a miracle he hadn't fought back before now. Her feelings for him had changed from distrust and dislike into something she didn't yet understand, but her feelings weren't the only ones that mattered.

Before the alarm went off tonight he'd said more than once that he'd be leaving when Dop was caught. She had no idea what his plans were and she had no right to ask. She'd destroyed his life once already and there was no guarantee she wouldn't do it again if she got scared.

With an unknown future gaping before her, Emma got out of the tub and went downstairs to take her well-deserved lumps.

Jim and Layne looked fit to kill, but when they realized Emma had no intention of defending herself, an electric unease began to ripple through the room. Emma didn't know why. She'd have thought they'd be relieved.

They did look relieved when she met Jim's refusal to close the store with a sigh. She simply curled up under Anthony's arm, absorbing his warmth and keeping her legal arguments to herself. There were too many egos at play in this equation already, and she'd live to fight another day.

Anthony didn't escape the agents' scolding, either. He grumbled a few times but otherwise stayed silent as Jim, Walter and Layne went over what had happened and picked apart the things that went wrong and the things that went right. The first category took much longer than the second. So far the only thing they couldn't complain about was Walter's expertise with the alarm system.

Bored with the recap of something she'd replayed in her mind a hundred times, Emma drifted, lulled by Anthony's thumb rubbing her arm.

Emma finally fell asleep during a ballistics discussion, and Anthony decided it was time she got some sleep. He walked her upstairs, wondering what she'd have to say once they were alone again.

Nothing, as it turned out, and their good-night kiss was, for them, very chaste.

On the way down, Anthony wondered why Jim and Hornsby had come back to the store tonight.

Back in his study, it didn't take him long to find out. Three somber faces greeted him with the news that two more e-mails from Dop had arrived: one intercepted by Melinda that afternoon, the other just an hour ago.

The agents waited silently while Anthony read them. It almost killed him to finish the first one, and the second was so bad he couldn't make it to the end.

The gloves had officially come off. Dop knew he was losing the battle for Emma's loyalty and there was now a clear threat on her life. Anthony sat back to brood as the agents drew conclusions.

"I hate to point this out," Jim said. "But Melinda's certain Dop's using some kind of electronic device to alter his voice. And there's only one reason he might do that."

"I'd recognize it," Anthony said.

"Right, and you'd think he'd be anxious to get Emma on the line, but when she reached for your phone, Dop hung up. Can't help wondering if maybe that device wasn't enough for Emma. Speech patterns or something could have given him away."

"What about her therapist?" Walter asked. "She's on the phone with him constantly."

Jim shook his head. "Dr. Dillon's in good standing with the APA. Left a thriving practice out West to go solo up here. We called two references right away on Monday and he checks out."

Layne sighed. "*He* might check out but it's time to face facts, guys. We've been had. We need to shift gears and look behind Emma for a suspect."

"Huh?" Anthony asked.

"Well, we've wasted an awful lot of time on those employee files instead of looking at Emma. What I'm saying is, maybe Dop didn't drag Emma into this to torture you. Maybe he dragged *you* into this to torture *her.*"

All three men gave her hateful looks. Dop had been yanking their chains since day one and nothing would surprise Anthony less than to find out Layne was correct.

"So let's start with the basics," Layne said. "Who stands to benefit if something happens to Emma?"

Anthony listened to them index everyone from Vivian, Emma's stepmother, to Charles, while trying to get his head around the fact that Emma might be the real reason he had an X on his back.

Part of him wanted to be angry. *Really* angry, and an impotent fury spun in his gut. For the last three weeks he'd believed he deserved all this. That he deserved every second of Dop. And now they were saying his past might not have anything to do with it.

How was he not supposed to be mad? But then again, what was more guilt after two years of sheer self-induced hell? Nothing Dop did could make it any worse.

Nothing except hurt Emma.

Jim said, "It's no use speculating on financial benefit until we've seen her will. And we can't overlook a revenge motive, either. Or obsession. She's notorious for giving men the cold shoulder, and the fact that Dop didn't take potshots at them on the roof makes me wonder."

"Yeah," Walter said. "They were sitting ducks. He probably shot at the door so the alarm would trigger the lights. Then he could see what was happening."

Layne and Jim both nodded, and Layne said, "That would explain the tone of Dop's second e-mail. A very ill-disguised blind rage and jealousy. But what I don't understand is why Dop didn't take a shot at Anthony when he was in the street. Emma wasn't anywhere nearby for most of it."

"Same reason he didn't kill me in the first place," Anthony said. "He marked me but he didn't kill me then, either."

Jim groaned. "God, I hate this guy. What the hell does he want?"

"I'm sure he'll let us know soon enough," Layne said.

A round of dirty looks ensued but then Walter asked in an apologetic voice, "Is it just me, or does anybody else spot the problem with digging into Emma's life?"

Jim groaned again. "Oh, man. How can we ask questions without her flying off the handle? She's not stupid. Far from it. She'll know why we're asking and she'll freak."

"And if she freaks on us within earshot of Dop, we'll lose him," Walter added.

"Or worse," Jim said. "Dop could be an employee or client. There might be something she hasn't told us because she doesn't think it's important, and what if someone does or says something that makes a connection with her? If she figures out who Dop is before we do, that temper of hers could get her killed.''

Anthony squeezed his eyes shut. After what Emma had done tonight there was no denying that Jim had a point. A very valid, fatal one. ''We've got to send her away. Sneak her out somehow.''

''We can't,'' Layne said. ''None of this would have happened tonight if you two hadn't gone out on that roof. There's nowhere safer than her apartment. Nowhere.''

''What about here?'' Anthony asked.

''No,'' Walter told him. ''It's too risky. Even with the security system, there are too many entry points. Our odds are better at the store.''

''Yeah, but if Dop's an employee or client—''

''We don't know that yet,'' Layne said. ''And Walter is correct. Our odds of protecting her from *one person,* surrounded by a store full of people who love her, are far better than here where we can only afford two agents at most. I'm sorry, Anthony. Tomorrow morning we go back.''

Walter asked, ''But how are we gonna handle Emma?''

''You can stop being so afraid of her,'' Layne said.

Anthony's brows went up as Layne went on. ''I've been talking to the employees and that temper you all fear is a bluff.''

''Bluff?'' Anthony repeated. Sure hadn't seemed like a bluff to him.

Layne gave him a sympathetic look. ''It's a simple cycle, really. How much do you know about her father?''

''That he was clinically depressed and dumped everything on her.''

''Correct. But Marshall Toliver did more than that. He taught her that emotions hurt. He got upset with her when she displayed too much emotion, so Emma learned to read the warning signs and adjust herself accordingly. That way, she wouldn't hurt him.''

Anthony looked at Jim, who cringed and scratched his cheek as Layne went on. ''But she also learned that when her father's neglect hurt too badly, throwing a tantrum got his attention, if only briefly. So naturally, that developed into any kind of stress or emotional pain automatically triggering her temper. I'll bet Anthony can attest to that cycle."

He nodded, even though it ticked him off Layne could spend two days here and understand Emma better than he did.

"And while we're at it," Layne said, "we need to talk about Brady."

"Why?" Jim asked. "Do you suspect him?"

"Not seriously, no, although Melinda needs to check into his computer activity lately. What I'm worried about mainly is her stress load, and Brady and Emma are very much at odds over something. Their interactions could get rather tense the closer we get to that Red Cross auction."

"What are they fighting about?" Anthony asked.

Layne said, "Business. Brady knows she won't back down, no matter how much she loves him. They grew up together but he's in trouble at home and Emma is no fool. She doesn't want to let him go, yet she knows she might have to for his own good."

"All right. So what's the purpose of all this?" Jim asked.

"The temper puts her in danger because she attacks first, thinks later. We can control that if we minimize her stress."

Jim asked, "I don't suppose you have some devious plan in mind where we can do more than troubleshoot her stress load?"

"Well, Charles told me something we may find useful," Layne said, trying to sound innocent but failing. "He likened Emma to a spider. We envision all these horrible things happening if we get too close, but that spider's more afraid of us than we are of the spider."

"That sounds like Charles," Anthony muttered. "But aside from giving us the creepy crawlies, what's the point?"

Layne said, "She may have a nasty temper, but self-protection isn't the only reason she reads people. The woman is as curious as twenty cats, and the quickest way to earn her trust is to show her who you are. If she gets upset about something, we talk to her. Open up as a person, not an agent. Include her the way we include Anthony, because he's trusted. Manipulative as hell, but harmless, and it'll work. I guarantee it."

"*How?*" Jim demanded.

"She'll *trust* us, Jim. She'll turn a blind eye to whatever we're doing because she won't want to see it in the first place. Her little denial problem is our best friend right now and—"

"Oh, that's healthy," Anthony scoffed. "Reward the denial and she'll keep ignoring the fact someone wants to kill her."

"It's a choice, Anthony. I like Emma. She's a character. And I'd far rather make her happy, and get to know her, than continue butting heads with that temper."

"I still think it's dangerous."

"Have some faith in her, Anthony. You saw what happened when we got here tonight. We were angry, and afraid she'd go off. So what did Emma do? She went to sleep. Didn't listen to a word we said. If we stop being so damned afraid of her and approach her differently, she'll start listening."

Finally, Jim and Layne left, and Anthony got ready for bed, his head so full he knew he'd never relax until he'd had time to sort out what he'd heard.

Ten minutes of pacing didn't help.

Slipping silently across the hall to the guest room, he was relieved to find Emma asleep. Her hair was splayed on a pillow, glowing in the dim moonlight, and her constantly worried look was gone. He wished she could look that peaceful all the time.

He touched her hair, thinking about what Layne had said. She'd put those words to things he knew but couldn't explain to himself, and it hurt, hearing what Emma had been through.

They had so much in common it was uncanny. He knew

exactly how she'd felt, being invisible to her father until she acted out on the pain.

But Emma hadn't left a path of destruction in her wake like he had. Quite the contrary. Instead of tearing things apart, Emma held them together with all her might.

The loyalty Emma's clients and employees showed was testimony, and he used to believe her returned loyalty was a marketing ploy. He knew better now. Those people were the only family she had left, and she loved them in an Emma kind of way.

Anthony reached an arm around to scratch the scar, wishing there were some way to convince Layne, Jim and Walter not to use Emma's quirks against her. It wasn't fair.

And what if it didn't work? Even if it did, they were still taking a dangerous risk, not telling Emma that Dop might be one of those people she clung to so tightly.

He hated that decision. If something happened, she'd be caught completely off guard.

He'd have to stick close, and ask Charles to do the same while Emma was at work. Cover the bases so someone was always with her. And sooner or later, one of them needed to explain what they'd done with Emma's material auction.

It would have to be him, and the sooner the better, no matter what Jim and Layne said about her stress load. Keeping that secret was more hazardous than telling Emma the truth. The longer they kept it from her, the more land mines they buried for themselves.

He'd have to tell her when the time was right. Afterward, his only hope of staying in her life was the attraction.

Anthony allowed a little hope that she felt more for him than the chemistry. But even if she did, there was no guarantee he wouldn't foul it up. He wasn't what he'd call stable. At least not like Charles. Charles could handle anything because he was totally at peace with himself and his life, and that's why Emma loved him. He gave her the stability she'd never had.

Anthony wished he had that kind of peace. He was trying to achieve it but hadn't managed it yet. Not even close.

And at the moment it felt like he'd never get there without Emma. He loved her and they belonged together. He was slowly regaining her trust, but that trust would take some serious blows when he fessed up to everything.

Maybe he'd start small and tell her what really happened two years ago. See how that went. If he made it through unscathed, he'd tell her about the materials auction.

But Anthony had noticed he wasn't the only one keeping secrets. Emma went of her way to keep the deal with that jewelry merchandiser under the rug. She'd even knocked over Brady's water glass when Brady tried to bring it up at dinner that first night. And earlier, when he'd grilled her about the store, she hadn't said a word.

Why? Was there something about it she didn't want the FBI to know, or was she trying to keep his nose out of her business?

Well, he'd keep out of it. And protect her any way he could while scaring up the courage to come clean.

Right. She'd go to work and leave him no perfect opportunity to confess. And he'd need one, because owning up to all this would take a lot of guts.

Sitting here worrying wouldn't help. Morning would come and these good intentions would fall to the wayside once he got caught up in the tornado Emma called a life. He knew it.

However, morning wasn't quite here yet.

Anthony circled the bed, moving cautiously not to wake her. As he slipped in close behind her, Emma made a soft mewing sound, and when he smoothed her hair from her face, she took a deep, shuddering breath.

He waited for her to settle again before pushing his luck and wrapping one arm around her waist, then fell instantly still as her arm covered his, tucking his hand beneath her ribs.

She wasn't awake. At least not awake enough to care that

he was there, and for one blinding instant he was so overcome with jealousy he couldn't breathe. Was she used to this? According to Charles, no one had ever spent the night in her apartment. But what if Charles was wrong?

They might have a suspect they didn't know about. Or what if Charles was covering up for a lover—because he was the lover?

None of your business if he is, Anthony told himself, but smirked at the idea of Charles, a sixty-year-old man with a beautiful, loving wife, eight kids and four grandchildren, having an affair with Emma. She didn't see him in that light and the suspicion was nothing more than jealousy.

Batting down the caveman instincts, Anthony listened to her shallow breaths. In his mind he told her everything. Or started to. He hadn't made it to the bad parts before sleep claimed him.

Chapter 8

Emma woke to sunlight streaming through an unfamiliar window. There was no moment of confusion. She knew exactly where she was. The evidence was hard to miss, warm and solid behind her, deeply asleep.

Wondering when he'd come in, Emma lay very still. He needed the sleep and it was nice to have him so close. Okay, so one of them had to be unconscious to maintain the cease-fire, but she'd take what she could get.

She stared at a patch of sun on the silver carpet. It had to be almost nine o'clock. For the first time in as long as she could remember, she hoped everything was all right at the store, but didn't really care. No need to worry. Charles, Brady and all the other employees would be defiantly manning their posts.

Jim must have spread an antiseptic version of the truth about what had happened last night or someone would have called by now.

On that thought, Emma felt a slight headache materialize.

Telling herself it was the aftereffect of brandy and adrenaline, she went back to sleep.

The feel of Anthony's knee pushing her leg forward and an arm tightening around her ribs woke Emma again some time later. His chest filled with a deep breath and she moaned a sleepy protest as he rolled to sink his face into her hair. She didn't want to get up. She didn't want him to leave, either.

"Mornin'," he grumbled into her neck.

The vibration of his voice washed down her spine, spilling warm liquid sensations in all the right places. Their legs were tangled together, soft cotton pajama bottoms against her bare skin. No, she definitely didn't want him to leave.

He asked what time it was but she was too comfortable to look. Anthony lifted his head, then Emma felt his stomach tighten in convulsive laughter. "What?" she asked.

"It's ten o'clock."

"So?"

"Please don't tell me you're grumpy in the morning."

"I'm not," Emma stated. "I just don't want to get up."

"Too bad. We have to go back to the store."

"Why? So we can get shot at again?"

"Grumpy *and* cynical."

Emma whimpered and meant to roll over, but the whimper turned into a laughing groan of pain as she moved the arm tucked under the pillow.

Anthony sat up. "What's wrong?"

Carefully easing her arm down so she could roll onto her back, Emma opened her eyes to see Anthony grinning.

"Jerk. It's not funny."

"Guess that'll teach you to throw cement blocks."

She wrinkled her nose at him. He looked gorgeous, even with his hair standing on end. Dark, scruffy cheeks were still creased into a grin, and Emma would have touched them if she'd dared move her arm again. What she really wanted to do was beg for a back rub, but she knew where that would lead.

"Scratch and I won't make fun of you," Anthony said.

Emma sighed but scratched anyway, surprised that the scar didn't bother her anymore. But it reminded her that she'd forgotten to do something before bed last night.

She told him, "Good thing you're sitting down because I have something to say. Two things, actually. One, thank you for throwing me in the greenhouse. Two, I'm sorry you had to."

Looking over his shoulder, Anthony raised a brow at her, and she gave him a sheepish, guilty look in return. It was no one's fault but her own if he didn't trust what he was hearing after two days of constant sniping.

But he said, "Well, then, you're welcome. Two, you're forgiven so long as you promise you'll never scare me like that again."

"Only if you promise not to go after Dop again. If you had any idea what went through my head in that greenhouse, you'd think twice. Deal?"

"Deal. How bad is your arm?"

"I'll live," Emma told him, slightly amazed she'd lived through an actual apology. But she was starting to get nervous about this cocoon of gentleness they'd created. Inside it they were matter-of-fact about the strangest things. Like wanting each other. Like openly admitting that they cared what happened to each other, when a week ago they couldn't have cared less. Plus it was open season on their personality flaws, and Emma couldn't imagine ever talking with anyone but Anthony that way.

She'd miss this when the case was closed and he left.

Don't think about that. She had time yet and he had spent the night with her—sort of. Taking a left-handed approach to find out why, she said, "I suppose you thought I'd try to sneak back to the store last night."

Anthony leaned back, propping himself on an elbow. Close up she could see the fine lines around his eyes. She'd probably never understand why the sight made her realize she loved him. But in the moment, she moved straight past fear to resignation. He wasn't the same person he'd been, and she would be careful. He couldn't break her heart again if she didn't let him.

"No, you were out cold," he answered, and started to laugh. "Actually, I figured you'd shove me onto the floor when you were ready to leave."

Anthony met her haughty look with a tolerant grin. She was fishing for the reason he'd spent the night in her bed. Falling asleep had been a mistake, but a profitable one. Sure looked to him as if there were a *lot* more to her feelings than chemistry.

Reminding him quickly that she was one seriously difficult woman, Emma turned blunt. "I suppose you won't tell me why you ended up in here last night."

How to lie his way out of this one? Deciding not to bother, he answered, "I ended up in here because I wanted to."

The look he received was vintage Emma. Nice try, buddy. Thinking it was a good thing he lived for a challenge, he watched her formulate a reply.

There she was, dressed in his pajama shirt and very little else, green eyes sparkling like the gems she loved so much. Very tempting, and he was already picturing the possibilities.

His eyebrows drew together as he watched her do the oddest thing. Her lashes lowered for a second and a faint smile played on her lips. Like it was a big sacrifice, but she'd decided not to say something heinous.

Now there's progress, he thought, draping his arm over her again and feeling her warmth through the shirt. She smelled like flowers. Something heady in full bloom.

Their mouths were a millimeter apart when the phone on the nightstand rang. Emma jumped and Anthony stole one greedy taste before answering.

Eyes locked with hers, he said, "What?" into the phone.

Jim responded, "Did I interrupt something?"

"Almost. But not quite."

"Well, you can forget it now, my friend. Let me talk to Emma."

Anthony asked why and was told, "Hey, Layne and I already flipped coins and you lost. I get to tell her this one."

"Like I'd trust you to flip fair. Besides, you owe me."

Emma gave him a quizzical look as Jim said, "Will you ever forget about that damn sidewalk thing? I didn't tell you because I wanted Dop to get your natural reaction."

"Yes, too bad your henchmen aren't as twisted as you. Now what's the story?"

"Oh, all right," Jim said, relenting. "Brady just called. Seems the insurance company's finally coming across with that auction lot. Brinks truck due to arrive at one o'clock."

"Definitely worth a flip. We'll be down in a minute."

He didn't give Jim a chance to comment before hanging up.

"What's going on?" Emma asked.

"Good news."

"They caught him?"

"No, but this might make up for it. We have to be back at the shop by one because your auction lot's coming today."

Her eyes lit up like the Vegas strip and she dazzled him with the smile he remembered from those first few days together.

But her words brought him to a halt.

"This is going to be such a good day."

He'd expected anything from a snooty "it's about time" to a leaping fit of triumphant happiness. Instead he was getting a quiet glow of pure joy. Didn't she ever get boring?

But the joy was fleeting and he watched it leak slowly away. "What's wrong?" he asked.

"Nothing. It's just that I already had a billion things to do today, and great as this is, it's a complication."

Now she was speaking a language he could understand. "What billion things did you need to do?"

She raised her eyebrows. ''Have you seen my desk lately? I got part of the mess from the registers dealt with yesterday, but I haven't even made a dent in getting it re-entered into the computer. Not to mention the backlog of bookwork from Beautiful Things and a gem tracking system to implement and—''

''Slow down,'' he said. ''Ever heard the word *delegation?*''

''Yes, and I'm quite good at it,'' she sniffed, giving him an arch look. ''The problem is we desperately need another bookkeeper and until I find a decent one, I'm stuck with the extra work.''

''Not a crisis. I happen to know a skilled number cruncher who has nothing better to do today.''

Her mouth opened, no doubt to tell him he was off his nut if he thought she'd let him near her books, but again she changed course. ''You'd do that?''

''Emma, I will be your slave for life if you give me something productive to do today.''

She laughed. ''Been bored, have we?''

''Painfully. But this way everybody wins. Maybe by the time they nail Dop we can have you caught up.''

''Let me get this straight. You actually *want* to do book work?''

Anthony laughed at her scandalized expression. ''Hey. You've got your shiny things, I've got my numbers.''

''You have issues.''

Still laughing, he dragged his cheek across hers, illiciting a giggling complaint. She shoved him, then broke into a groaned giggle from her sore muscles. When he bit her neck she went for his ribs, finding the ticklish spot dead-on.

Emma incinerated all his good intentions with the feel of her hands on his skin. Now his goal was to sink himself deeply inside her and feel that passionate body explode in pleasure.

She was looking up at him, smiling, but her eyes smoldered with the same need he felt. It might be horrible timing but Anthony started unbuttoning her shirt, watching for a stop sign he knew would never appear.

Emma, of course, helped with the buttons. He'd been half-aroused already, but blood raced straight to his groin as she wiggled closer to rub a long, supple thigh against him.

"Emma..." he cautioned, then felt air leak from his lungs as she undid the last button. Flannel was pushed away, baring a lush pink nipple on a rounded curve of pale skin. Beautiful.

He explored her with his mouth, baring another silken breast and almost roaring in frustration when she writhed beneath him. A war was going on in his head, one side amazed that he could make her this wild, the other reminding him frantically that Jim never knocked before entering a room.

All the while, she urged him ruthlessly on. "Anthony, please. I want to feel you. Go lock the door. I'll be quick. Please... Just take—"

To stop her mouth, he kissed her. She had no idea. After two years of enforced celibacy it would be *very* quick. And if she didn't stop talking, round one would be over before anybody took anything.

"No more," he told her in a breathy growl.

"But you're leaving when Dop is caught and—"

They both groaned in frustration when the phone rang again. Anthony snatched it off the hook, and this time his "What?" was nowhere near polite.

How could she believe he was going anywhere once Dop was caught? Was that what she wanted?

"I thought you said you'd be down in a minute," Jim replied.

"I will be. Emma's sore from the brick toss, so she'll be soaking for a while. I'm about to hit the showers. Want to interrupt me in there, too?"

"Well, excuse the hell out of me—" Jim was saying as the receiver slammed down.

"All right," Anthony sighed. "Jim's getting impatient. Your torture privileges have expired."

"Torture? You want—"

"Yes, I do," Anthony interrupted. "But this isn't the right time. We shouldn't do this until we know where we stand."

"Then tell me what I need to know!"

"You're the one who needs to do the telling," he said, pretty certain he'd be struck dead by lightning for that lie. "Go soak. I'll find you a shirt and some ibuprofen. They'll be out here when you're done."

She stared as he got out of bed, and he could feel her eyes on him all the way to the door. Without looking back, he went to his room knowing he'd just screwed up.

So much for good intentions. He was supposed to confess, not indulge.

What a mess. He might well be in love with her but he was still afraid of her. Confessing was too scary, banking everything on someone who might not be able to handle what she heard.

And Emma didn't need him running away every time he got scared.

Forty-five minutes later, after he'd had time to mellow a bit and talk to Jim, Emma appeared in the kitchen doorway, swimming in one of his polo shirts and the jeans she'd had on last night. Her hair was loose and hung in a damp shining mass down her back.

At her hesitation, Jim and Layne greeted her as if she was an old, dear friend. Emma eyed them warily for a moment, but then came in to grab a cup of coffee.

It looked as though their "new-approach" plan would work. And he'd obviously been forgiven for walking out on her earlier. She pulled her chair closer to his before sitting down.

Jim had an agenda, and he didn't waste any time getting started. Charles had given him a copy of Emma's will and they planned to slowly work their way through the beneficiaries. He said, "I'm sure Anthony told you Brady called and he wasn't very thrilled about all the action last night. Does he resent our presence that much or is something else going on?"

Emma shrugged. "I'm sorry if he was rude, but it has nothing to do with you. His attitude's been rotten for a while now."

"Rotten in what way?" Anthony asked.

"He's mad at me for something, is all."

"Why's he mad at you?"

"It's just business, and it'll blow over. Seeing that material delivery in the vault should do the trick. Either he'll quit or I'll fire him."

All three of them chorused, "Fire him?"

Anthony could see her battling distrust already. She didn't like them asking about Brady.

But she said, "He's been getting job offers from some pretty big names, and I think we've outgrown each other, if you know what I mean."

"No, I don't know what you mean," Layne said.

"He's always been there for me. Through everything. And he's the first to admit I've returned the favor. But things have changed. It started with the design business and got worse when he married Tanya. In case you haven't heard the rumors, she hates me. I don't blame her, either. Brady spends way too much time at work and that makes the store sort of like the other woman. It's not that we don't want or need him there. But some things are more important."

Anthony wanted to roll his eyes. Emma was the last person who should accuse anyone of putting work above all else. And now he was wondering if he hadn't developed one of Layne's so-called patterns himself. He cared about Emma. He'd cared about his father, too. And they both cared about business more than they cared about him.

"You think he should accept one of those offers," Jim said.

"Maybe. I don't know. I'd hate to see him go, but..." Emma trailed off in a shrug.

"May I ask you a very sensitive question?" Layne inquired smoothly.

"May I give you a very insensitive answer?"

Layne chuckled. "We understand he's the main beneficiary of your estate. What will you do if he leaves?"

Why was she asking that? Emma's expression echoed his own confusion and Layne needed to do something or Emma would clam up soon.

Layne made the instant save. "I'm sorry. I grew up with lawyers and I know how messy these things can get."

Anthony almost started laughing when Emma asked, "You grew up with lawyers?"

At Layne's nod, Emma visibly relaxed and said, "Then you can imagine the look on my lawyer's face when I told him that even if Brady leaves, he'll still get my life insurance. I know it's strange, but I do owe him something after all we've been through. Charles will get the store, though."

"How much is your life insurance?" Jim asked.

"Four million," Emma said, giving Jim a long look. "What's going on here? Why are you so interested in Brady?"

"Relax, Emma," Jim said. "I'm an FBI agent. Nosiness comes with the territory. If you think you hate it, talk to my ex-wife."

"Why doesn't anyone ever tell me anything?" Emma complained. "I didn't know you were married."

Anthony had to rub his eyes to hide a smile. Emma was proving every word Layne had said last night, and Jim had just met his match in the nosiness department.

But Jim must have decided not to push their luck because he changed the subject. "Oh, news from Melinda. Dop picked up our reply and the virus is digging into his system. However, as feared, he unplugs from the phone jack when he shuts down so it's not talking to Melinda yet. But when he plugs in again, things should start rolling."

Anthony rested his arm across the back of Emma's chair and she laid her hand on his thigh, actually listening as Jim continued. "And I have something to show you which may or may not be good news. Depends on your perspective, I guess."

Jim pulled a rolled-up newspaper section from his back pocket and slapped it on the table. Emma took her hand away, leaving Anthony's leg ice-cold while she flattened out the paper.

There was no missing the item Jim meant them to see. A color photo, six inches square, graced the all-too-popular "Get a Load of This" gossip column.

Right there for the world to see were he and Emma in a clinch outside the coffee shop. The photographer couldn't have gotten a more inflammatory shot if he'd tried. Emma was twined around him like ivy and, God help him, but seeing her so abandoned set him on fire all over again.

The article was less sensational but the hint of Dop's hand in it quickly cooled him off.

> St. Paul—Formerly missing corporate acquisition vampire Anthony Bracco and bauble empress Emma Toliver caught in the act Tuesday morning by an anonymous source. Rumor has it the pair was reunited under duress and their personalities don't mesh quite as well as their... Well, you've seen the picture. Enough said. Watch for more developments as more information becomes available.

"Anonymous source?" Emma said. "This was taken at eye level from across the street. He was close. No one saw anything?"

"No," Jim told her. "You two drew quite a crowd with that kiss. He must have been in it. I'm sorry, I'm sure this is the last thing either of you needed right now. But we've spoken to the reporter, and believe it or not, she's cooperating."

"She'd better," Emma said. "I sold her a cocktail ring at cost two weeks ago."

"Do you think she'd plant a story for you?" Jim asked.

"Now hold on," Layne broke in. "We'll handle that after we've had some time to decide whether Dop did this for attention or if he's just taking another swipe. Of course, if you'd rather we let it go—"

"No!" Emma interrupted. "Go after him with both barrels. If you don't, I'm calling that reporter and telling her the truth because I can't take much more of this."

Her chair screeched on tile as she got up, one hand over her mouth. Everyone else held their breath and prayed she wouldn't explode.

She didn't, but Jim and Layne disappeared, anyway, and Anthony knew he was expected to clean up their mess. Pulling a reluctant Emma into his arms, he asked, "It's not that bad, is it? People have short memories. I'm sure you'll get a few questions, but I doubt anyone has the guts to ask if you've lost your mind and taken up with me again."

Softening a bit, Emma scolded, "Please don't talk that way about yourself. Yes, people will ask questions, but your family's going to see that and I'll die of embarrassment tomorrow night. Other than that, no, it's not that bad."

Seeing the almighty Emma embarrassed, Anthony couldn't help but laugh. "Trust me, Emma. Mom and Geoff have seen worse."

"Yeah, well, as if they didn't already hate me for ruining your life, now I'm mauling you in living color."

Cringing this time, he corrected, "Emma, they don't hate you. Much as it pains me to admit it, they were and always have been on your side."

"You're joking."

"I'm afraid not. Long story. And I'll tell you just as soon as I recover from knowing Dop got that close."

"Tell me now."

"No." he said. There wasn't enough time to start now. "I'm starving and we should go so we have time for lunch before your precious babies arrive."

"I hate it when you guys put me off. And speaking of which, why didn't you tell me Jim was married?"

"Not a real popular topic. His marriage was a disaster from the word go," he said. "Now go sit down somewhere and relax. I need to grab my tux for the auction."

"You're going?" she asked, and if he wasn't mistaken there was a hint of relief in her voice.

"We all are. Along with about two hundred security guards."

She rolled her eyes but sat down to finish her coffee. Stopping at the door, Anthony watched her shove the newspaper to the other side of the table.

After he'd packed another bag, he stood in the middle of his room, staring at the nightstand.

Chin in hand, he let the guilt set in. It was no easier to justify what they were doing to her now than it had been last night, and he stood there, knowing that participation mangled his rules.

But it had worked like a charm so far. Emma had been so interested in personal things Jim and Layne had said that she'd forgotten the questions they'd asked about Brady.

Opening up to her had been easy for them. They didn't have confessions to make that would send Emma through the roof.

He had to get it over with, and he'd have ample opportunity tonight unless Dop pulled something. The only problem was, Anthony wouldn't place bets on his ability to walk out on her a second time if she wanted to do more than talk.

Right now he felt like a character in a cartoon with an angel on one shoulder, a devil on the other. The angel was saying he had to tell her everything, and the devil was mocking him. No man in his right mind would turn Emma down, even if that man was sealing his own coffin in the process.

The nightstand loomed. In the shallow drawer was the solution to the impending dilemma. But the angel was right. If he had protection handy as a safety net, it would make it easy to say yes instead of telling her what he'd done. Gave him an excuse to do what he wanted when he knew it was wrong. For both of them.

"Aw, hell," he muttered, reaching for the drawer.

Chapter 9

With an hour remaining before the auction lot was due, Anthony observed Emma in her packed dining room. Five other agents were on duty now and everyone was carefully tiptoeing around their hostess.

They needn't have bothered with the kid gloves. Emma was wholly preoccupied with the clock, barely paying attention to Jim and Layne as they discussed a press statement.

"It doesn't really matter what we print," Layne said. "But it would be a good idea to dispel what the reporter said about duress. Someone else will get curious and we'll be under media siege with the accompanying flood of gawkers and crazies. So maybe we should find a new angle."

"Like what?" Emma asked, surprising Anthony. Her eyes were still on the clock, but apparently she was listening, after all.

Jim and Layne started a volley of psychobabble about how Dop might react to different explanations. Emma started fidgeting again, chewing at a thumbnail.

Grinning sympathetically, Anthony reached out and threaded his fingers through hers. "Relax, Emma. It'll be here soon."

"Yeah, I just—" Emma began, then nearly choked as Jim said something about an engagement announcement.

Both of them told him to shove that idea, but when Anthony turned back to Emma she'd flushed crimson.

"Are you okay?" he asked.

"Um…not really, no."

"What's wrong?"

"Forget it. I'm too embarrassed to ask now."

He laughed. This was priceless. "Come on. Ask."

"I never even bothered to ask if you had a girlfriend," Emma said, then grimaced.

"You think anyone would put up with me?"

"Good point."

"Witch."

"Jerk. What are we going to print?" she asked.

"That's up to you, I guess. Whatever you say goes."

Emma's eyes took on that quality of a cat who'd just spotted prey. "Why don't we take full advantage of this statement? Say you're a consultant now. You came home to help me because I'm up to my neck running two businesses, and something big's about to happen with Beautiful Things."

"Now you're talking." He smiled. "Free advertising. So what am I? Lackey? Overqualified bookkeeper? General manager?"

"Hmm…general manager. For real or just for show?" she asked.

"Excuse me?"

"I really do need a general manager."

"No way, Emma. Forget it."

"Why not? You said you'd help," Emma reminded him, turning sideways in her chair and leaning forward.

"I did and I will. But only until you're caught up."

"Yeah, and then I'll just get behind again. What am I supposed to do then?"

"Hire a general manager. And quit looking at me like that."

"What? My guilt trip's not working?"

"Not even a little. Behave yourself, woman."

"You're *this* close to caving in, aren't you?"

"Quit it. Much as I admire shameless opportunism, you can't win this one."

"We'll see. You know you love this place."

"Emma..." Anthony warned, staring at her mouth. But then he realized the room had fallen silent, every eye on them. And once he saw how he and Emma were sitting it wasn't a surprise. She was practically in his lap.

Anthony's cellphone picked that convenient moment to ring, and seeing the caller's name on the display, he left Emma to explain while he stepped out.

Halfway to his room he said, "Hi, Mom."

"Don't you *Hi Mom* me, young man. Can you explain why I have to hear from Jim that Dop took a shot at—"

"Hold on," Anthony interrupted, closing his door. "I meant to call but I haven't had time."

His mother cleared her throat meaningfully and said, "If the paper's anything to go by I would imagine you haven't."

"Oh, God. Can we not talk about this, please?"

"Fat chance. Does this mean I'll finally have a grandchild, or do I need to adopt a normal son?"

"Better start filing with agencies."

"Ugh. You're impossible."

"That seems to be the general consensus," Anthony agreed.

"Imagine that. I suppose Emma's half-dead of embarrassment over the picture."

"Pretty much. You won't be too awful tomorrow, will you?"

"Watch it. I'm still your mother. And considering I just

had to explain the picture to Maxim, you should be a little nicer.''

Anthony sank down on the bed. ''What does he want now?''

''Anthony, he's your father. What do you think he wants?''

''Ammunition.''

''That's a fine thing to say,'' Sophia chided. ''He resigned from his own company and moved back here to be closer to you. What more proof do you need?''

''A signed affidavit saying the other shoe's not about to drop.''

''Did I raise you to be this way? He's trying.''

''How can you defend him?'' Anthony asked, feeling all the old anger boiling to the surface again. To hear his mother extolling Maxim Bracco's virtue was bending reality.

''I'm not defending him,'' Sophia soothed. ''I'm merely stating the truth. Frankly, I can't believe it myself, but I think he may have actually loved the last bimbo who dumped him. Celia, or whoever she was.''

''Well, that's too bad, isn't it?'' Anthony grumbled.

''It's not his fault you were too dense to know how you felt about Emma. That whole thing was your own doing from start to finish. Something I'm sure you haven't told her yet.''

''What she already knows is damning enough.''

''She may not get as mad as you think, honey. In fact, all things considered, she probably won't care. Besides, you can consider it practice for explaining what you and Charles—''

Anthony heaved a sigh of relief as someone knocked. He sped through a goodbye and opened the door.

Emma came in, asking instantly, ''What's wrong?''

''Nothing. Just got off the phone with my mother.''

Emma groaned. ''How mad is she?''

''I thought we covered this. Time to go down?''

"Almost. But if you've forgiven me for the bulldozer tactics and still want to help with the bookkeeping, we should talk first."

Anthony followed her into the design office, admiring the ratty jeans and light pink tank top she'd donned for the foray into the vault. On the way down the stairs she asked, "Can I con you into another favor?"

"Stupid question."

She smiled. "I need to get that greenhouse pane repaired. It's too hot outside to leave it broken. There's a glass guy who owes me big time, so if I give you the number will you call him?"

"Okay," he said, standing by as Emma unlocked a fireproof cabinet to reveal a platoon of huge index card cases.

"Here." She tossed him a key ring. "You might need these if you have trouble with account information. Just make sure you lock it afterward."

She came out with a card. "Here's the glass guy's number."

"Please don't tell me you keep a card with everyone's name and profession on it," Anthony pleaded. There was curious, and there was compulsive.

"Name, address, phone numbers, profession, anniversary, birthday, wife, husband, sisters, brothers, children, grandchildren, favorite stones and metals, china and silver patterns if applicable. Everything they've ever purchased. Some cards even have notes on what they like to talk about."

He couldn't help it; he burst out laughing. "This is the most anal retentive thing I have ever seen in my life."

"Yes, well, the Toliver compulsions gave us our reputation, and I would be lost without these cards. They're like time capsules, really. Some are more than a hundred years old. Here," she said, pulling out an example.

Anthony took it, a five-by-seven index card with a smaller one stapled to the front. The original was brown with age and covered with tiny, spidery blue handwriting. Whoever

Ephraim Staten was, he'd married Eugenia on June 9 1877. Eugenia preferred colored stones to diamonds and leaned heavily toward white gold. Her birth date was listed, as well as those of several children and grandchildren, each with a reference number to his or her own card.

"This is amazing," Anthony said. "You shouldn't hide these, Emma. I'll bet they would mean something to the families."

Emma breathed out a laugh. "Ephraim's granddaughter is one of my best customers—Ginny Lewis. She offered me two thousand dollars for that card but I distracted her with an orchid bracelet. Come to think of it, that was right before you showed up Monday morning."

"Small world," he said.

"Indeed. Anyway, you may not need them but just in case, here they are. If you can't find something you need, yell."

"So Brady's okay with me doing this?"

"Why wouldn't he be?" Emma asked, closing the cabinet.

"Did you tell him?"

"No, but as far as I know I'm still the boss around here."

Anthony refrained from comment. For the next half hour she walked him through the computer system, but more touching went on than explaining.

And then Emma suddenly jumped off his lap. "Hurry up. They're here."

Laughing, Anthony asked, "How do you know?"

"I've been listening to that truck pull up for twenty-six years. Come on," she ordered, grabbing his hand.

"I can wait until tonight."

Emma responded by planting her heels and yanking him from the chair. "Don't be such a party pooper."

He had a hard time keeping up as Emma dragged him down four flights of stairs to the loading dock, where Charles, Brady, Jim and Hornsby were already waiting.

Emma's arm was still sore so Anthony made her stay out

of the way as the men helped the Brinks drivers unload huge armored carriers. He'd known the lot was large, but the size and number of containers was impressive. With all this, Emma would be rolling in product.

He supposed now, watching her and Charles, that it had all been worth it. Emma was glowing. Luminous. But she was the consummate professional, referencing identification numbers from the insurance company's ledger before signing off on containers.

Then began the laborious process of getting the crates up to the vault in the workroom. Even with dollies and the freight elevator, all five men had to work together.

As they heaved and grunted, Anthony watched Brady like a hawk. The man's gaze clung to Emma, and Anthony wasn't the only one who noticed. Jim was the next to see it and his eyes changed into the flat, ancient-looking orbs of a lawman.

It took Hornsby longer to catch on, but as soon as he did, he pulled his gun from an ankle holster and tucked it into his pants, in plain view. Anthony tried not to smirk as Jim followed Hornsby's example.

Through it all, Charles helped quietly, giving Anthony the occasional sidelong stare. It had to be obvious what both Brady and Charles were thinking. Every vengeful instinct was kicking in. Not only was Anthony's scar burning, but every time he saw Brady's eyes on that tank top on Emma, he wanted to haul him outside and punch his lights out.

Left with no option but to endure, Anthony considered pulling Emma aside and telling her to go easy. Brady was spoiling for that argument she'd warned them about, and Jim might make things worse if he tried to remove one of them from the situation.

The agents stepped out on the premise of checking in with security, but they were really going to check the Bureau's records on the man coming to repair the greenhouse. Once they were gone, Anthony perched on a safe as the inspection began. Now alerted to the subcurrents of the people before him, he observed the dynamics.

Emma had devised a system for how the stones would be stored and tracked during the cutting and setting processes. The three of them talked it through, Charles showing that he'd played a big part in setting it up, and understood how it would work.

Brady was like a petulant child, throwing up every possible problem they might have and bemoaning the extra work.

Remembering his own corporate experience, Anthony sneered. Anyone at Bracco Inc. who had spoken to him the way Brady spoke to Emma would have been thrown out with a severance check rammed down his or her throat.

Yet Emma handled it well, probably so used to it she no longer noticed. Most of what Brady said was ignored. Everything else was countered with a solid, patient argument.

Hearing the amount and nature of the work to be done before they could begin producing pieces again, Anthony realized just how much help Emma would need. Charles was doing what he could, but Brady would obviously do nothing without whining. She really did need a general manager to watch over the store, and he understood that Emma had only been half joking at lunchtime. Or maybe she hadn't been joking at all.

Much as he'd love to jump at her offer, Anthony knew it was the wrong thing to do. He couldn't run the business and love Emma at the same time without getting the two hopelessly tangled and confused.

On the other hand, the thought of someone else becoming her general manager made him ill. He knew he'd always regret turning down an opportunity to be in her life simply because he was too afraid of screwing up. And so far he wasn't doing too hot in that arena.

That was the only thing he missed about his former life.

Purely win or lose, no acceptance or rejection taken personally.

"Hey. Hello," Emma said, waving a hand in front of his face. "You're a million miles away. What's wrong?"

"Nothing. Just thinking."

Emma gave him a probing look. "I hate it when you say nothing."

Someone outside the vault called for Charles, and Brady followed him out. Anthony watched, wondering why Brady felt it necessary to find out who wanted Charles and why. "Yes, well. I suppose I'd better get to work."

"Don't leave," she said. "Don't you even want to see them?"

"You're like a little kid with your shiny things."

"I know. I'm thinking about tossing a bunch of the faceted ones on the floor and rolling around in them for a while."

He laughed, realizing she probably wasn't kidding this time, either. "Can I watch?"

The look she gave him sent a hot rush of blood through his veins. Everyone and everything else was forgotten as Emma nudged between his knees to twine her arms around his neck and kiss him so hard he almost fell off the safe. It was over in an instant, but Anthony wouldn't be standing up anytime soon unless he wanted everyone to see how she affected him. And as Emma backed away, Anthony prayed Brady wouldn't return for a while. The thin tank top wasn't hiding his effect on her very well, either.

"Thank you for helping," she said.

He nodded, locking eyes with her. "There's no one in the apartment. Let's go up and you can thank me properly."

Man, he was hopeless.

Her eyes narrowed a bit. "Don't tease. Need I remind you who backed out this morning? You were right, you know. I'd hate us both afterward."

"How long would it take you to forgive us?"

"Anthony..."

"Hey, I was perfectly well behaved until you kissed me."

"What? So now we're keeping a self-control tally?"

"Might as well. Something to pass the time until I figure out how you operate."

"If you figure it out, tell me and we'll both know."

Anthony feigned shock, his eyes laughing. "I picked a fight and you let it go."

"I did, didn't I? Hmm. Maybe because bickering with you is starting to feel too much like foreplay."

"In that case—"

"Hush your mouth, Bracco," Emma scolded.

She couldn't help laughing as she laid a finger across his lips. He looked as if he was ready to come off that safe and give her an education in foreplay.

Unfortunately, Brady chose that moment to return, and didn't approve of what he'd walked in on. Emma didn't care what Brady thought. She'd had enough of him already to last a few months.

Charles came in a moment later, and Emma turned back to Anthony, finding him staring at Brady with about as much enthusiasm as she felt. She picked up Anthony's hand and asked, "Will you stay while we admire our precious babies?"

"No. I'd love to but I need to get started on my project."

He squeezed her hand and stopped to whisper something to Charles on his way out. Since when were they on whispering terms?

Emma shrugged it off. Charles was a force in and of himself, and somehow it made her feel better that he and Anthony got along. My, how things have changed, she thought.

Three hours passed while she, Brady and Charles examined the uncut gemstone blocks, pleasantly surprised by some, satisfied with most.

She still couldn't believe they'd gotten that auction lot. Half the industry must be asleep at the wheel if they'd landed something worth this much with their modest upper limit.

Charles was finally called away again by a part-timer who needed help getting the back off an heirloom earring someone had stepped on.

Emma hoped Brady would follow, but he didn't. And wasted no time in asking, "What the hell's going on around here?"

She sighed. "You'll have to be more specific."

"You know exactly what I'm talking about, Emma. A week ago, you'd have killed Bracco on sight, and now he's doing our books."

"Look, I know it must seem strange to you, but is it too hard to believe that I forgave him?"

"Since when do you forgive anybody anything?"

Emma abandoned a brick of jasper. She'd known this moment was coming but it still made her feel sick. "Since when do I have anything to forgive?"

"Oh, that's right," Brady answered with ugly sarcasm, "Bracco and I are the only ones who've ever made you angry."

"Yes, you did make me angry last week. Selling the necklace I meant to put up for the Red Cross auction was pretty low."

"I told you that was an accident. You never talk to me anymore, so how was I supposed to know?"

Sighing, Emma said, "It was clearly marked and now I have to… Just forget it. I know the label came off, but you're the one who's been angry lately, not me. I've asked you why a hundred times and it always dissolves into this."

"What, now you're mad because I'm mad?"

"Huh?" Emma balked and tried again. "Until you tell me what's bothering you, I can't do anything about it."

"What's bothering me is you don't listen to me anymore. All you care about is that Neville jewelry deal. Couldn't care less how anyone else feels, and it's almost like you *want* me to accept all those job offers I keep getting."

"You know what, Brady? Maybe I do want you to accept one of those offers. Tanya hates you working here and maybe it would be best if you went somewhere else."

"Are you firing me?" Brady asked, taking a step toward her.

Not once had Emma ever felt threatened by Brady Wilson, but she did now as she noted his fury. If he thought she'd back down he was crazy. No matter what she did or how hard she tried there was no pleasing him, and after all the uncomfortable truths she'd faced in the last two days, one more wouldn't hurt.

"Give me one good reason why I shouldn't," she said. "If anyone else had racked up that many complaints I'd have fired them long ago. But I've kept my mouth shut because I love you. If the situation was reversed, what would you do?"

"What the hell is *wrong with you?*" Brady shouted. "You're honestly going to fire me over that stupid deal?"

"Okay, that's enough," Emma shouted back. "Go home. I have enough to worry about without you screaming at me. And don't come back until you've calmed down."

"Hey," Jim called from the door. "Everything all right?"

His eyes were like laser beams, scanning Emma first, then zooming in on Brady.

"Everything's fine," Brady snapped.

Jim stepped inside. "I believe Emma asked you to leave."

"Jim—" Emma began.

She was interrupted by Brady saying, "No. When you've got your head on straight, we'll try to talk."

Emma stared in amazement as he stormed out. Jim gestured to someone outside the vault, in a silent message even Emma could understand as "get him out the door."

Stomach roiling from the insanity of the last few minutes, Emma put a hand over her mouth and nose, wishing she hadn't eaten lunch. Complete and utter disbelief enveloped her, and when Jim came up beside her she flinched.

"Emma," he soothed, concern and confusion permeating his voice. "Are you okay?"

She didn't bother to answer until he said, "Come on. Let me take you upstairs to Anthony."

"No," she said. "I don't know what just happened."

Emma rubbed her forehead, her head suddenly aching. Had she really fired Brady? She didn't think so, but his parting shot about getting her head on straight seemed to hang in the air like a cloud of confusion. He'd started the argument and she'd tried not to respond, and she didn't think she'd taken his bait.

All she'd tried to do was show him things from her point of view, and the next thing she knew he'd made it sound as if she was a heartless, fire-breathing dragon.

The truth was probably somewhere in between, but she couldn't see it at the moment. Maybe Dr. Dillon could help sort it out. He'd said he'd make sure he was available at any hour until Dop was caught, and she hoped to God he meant it.

Jim was no help. He looked just as confused as she felt when he muttered, "You told us this morning it might happen."

"Yes, but I didn't really believe… Oh, God. What have I done?"

"Emma, it'll be okay. I think everyone's hit their stress threshold for the week. Seriously. This place is like a pressure cooker. I know you want to have a look at the stones, but maybe it would be better if you went upstairs to relax."

"I'm fine. Tell me we'll catch Dop. Lie, if necessary."

"I wouldn't be lying if I said we're getting close. Melinda got some activity off her virus a few hours ago, but she's still trying to make sense of it. And Layne's people unearthed another possible suspect. So things are looking up, I promise."

"Has Dop replied to that e-mail yet?"

Jim said, "No, not yet. Hopefully he will and I'll be able to get a better read on where he's taking us. I'd hate to go into tomorrow night with no idea what to expect."

Emma felt tears gathering in her throat. "Please don't tell me I can't go to the fund-raiser."

"No, I know it's important, Em. Hey. Come back into the vault with me for a second. I gotta let you in on a secret."

What now? Following him warily, Emma inched the heavy door almost closed behind them as Jim asked, "Okay, you know that Anthony and his dad don't get along, right?"

"No, but I do now."

"Why are you looking at me like that?"

"I'm sick of no one telling me anything until it's critical."

Jim snorted a laugh. "This isn't critical. For us, anyway. It's just that Maxim's been added to the guest list. Anthony doesn't know and Sophia won't let me tell him."

"What fresh hell is this?" Emma sighed. She didn't need yet another thing to worry about, and it certainly didn't sound as though Anthony would enjoy seeing his father. "Maybe we should call your ex-wife and see if she'd like to attend, too."

"Where did that come from?"

"I thought as long as you were in the mood for an ambush, maybe you should count yourself in."

"Let's not get nasty here. I doubt if you'd enjoy Karen's presence any more than I would. And I know Anthony wouldn't. Besides, it's time Anthony gives his old man a break."

"That's Anthony's business, not mine," she said on reflex, but then couldn't hold back. "Why?"

Jim pushed his hands into his pockets and examined his shoes for a moment. "Has Anthony said anything to you about him?"

"Other than calling him a workaholic sperm donor, no."

"You haven't even asked where Anthony's been for two years?"

"No. Why bother? He won't answer unless he wants to."

"True," Jim said. "All I'm asking here is that you be gentle and help him through this somehow. You're probably the only one who can keep him from disappearing again when he sees Maxim."

"Disappearing? Is it really that bad?"

"You know that scene you just had with Brady? Multiply it by about two thousand and make it last for thirty years."

"Okay," Emma sighed. "I'm going to pretend I understand what you mean. Now if you don't mind I'd better get back to work."

"Sure you don't want to go upstairs?"

"I'll go upstairs when I'm good and ready."

"All right, then. But please stay out of trouble."

Half an hour later, curiosity had nearly eaten her alive. Something about the way Jim had said she and Anthony wouldn't enjoy Karen's presence and the ongoing war between Anthony and Maxim was too confusing not to follow up.

After securing the vault, Emma sped up to the third floor and found Anthony hard at work behind her desk.

Seeing him, it hit her all over again how he belonged here. Even after all that had happened it felt as if everything and everyone had just been marking time, awaiting his return.

Struggling to find something intelligent to say, Emma asked, "Did the glass guy come yet?"

His smoky brown eyes looked her over, stirring her blood. "Yes. To say the man 'jumped to' is putting it mildly. Dare I ask what you did for him?"

Emma felt a smile gather around her eyes. If she wasn't mistaken, she was witnessing jealousy. Distracted by a glorious scent, she stepped inside. "What's that smell?"

"I thought a celebration was in order so I got you flowers."

Petulance. This was too much fun. Emma closed the door. On a table behind it was an enormous spray of magnolia blossoms. Don't laugh. Please, please, don't start laughing. It's a very sweet gesture.

Too late. Emma pulled her lips between her teeth and bit down, trying not to giggle at the fat white-and-pink blooms.

"Uh, why are you laughing?" Anthony asked, his hands hovering over the keyboard.

"I'm not. They're lovely," she told him, skirting the desk to peck his cheek. "Thank you."

She yelped as Anthony dumped her into his lap.

"Let me guess," he said. "You're laughing at my memory. I thought magnolias were your favorite."

Feeling suitably guilty, Emma said, "No. I only told you they were my favorite because it was April at the time and they're impossible to get. I just wanted to see if you'd do it."

"Witch. Thank God I had a resourceful secretary."

"Jerk," Emma said, eyes glued to his smile. "How's it going?"

"Fine," he replied, getting ever closer to her mouth. "Funny you didn't mention you were two full months behind. And when were you planning on telling me what happened with Brady?"

"Mmm...I don't want to talk."

Anthony's hand closed over her breast, teasing a taut nipple with his thumb. Her entire body lit up and a slow, warm ache pooled between her thighs. She would have given anything for some privacy, to go upstairs and give Anthony all the pleasure he was giving her until they were both too tired to talk.

"Have you ever slept with him?"

"What?" The question was like an icy hand pressed to the back of her neck. She was out of Anthony's lap before he could stop her, and as Emma stared at him through blazing eyes, she saw not one hint of remorse.

"I'll take that as a no."

''How can you even ask me that?''

''Because you wouldn't tell me otherwise.''

Biting her bottom lip so hard she was sure she'd drawn blood, Emma retorted, ''Well, let's have a rundown of the women you've slept with, shall we? What about Karen?''

''Excuse me?'' Anthony said, his eyes turning cold as flint.

''Did you or did you not sleep with Jim's wife?''

''God, you're vicious. Brady was a legitimate question, all things considered.''

Before she could answer, her legs had carried her up the stairs. She stopped only long enough to grab her cellphone, then went to the roof, slamming the door so hard it hurt her ears.

Chapter 10

The greenhouse was pristine, all traces of broken glass gone as Emma passed through a sea of fragrant color. By the time she reached the office's futon couch, Dr. Dillon was on the line.

Still too angry to talk about Anthony, Emma poured out an account of the fight with Brady, telling Dillon exactly what had been said and asking if she'd done anything wrong. Dillon made her back up to explain the necklace, surprised she hadn't told him.

"I didn't tell you because I completely lost it. And I was embarrassed."

Dillon sighed but didn't say anything for a moment, then murmured, "It's okay, Emma. Just tell me what happened."

She let her head fall back against the couch as she explained that last Tuesday, while she'd been scouting equipment for the empty building next door, Brady had sold the gardenia necklace she'd intended to auction at tomorrow night's Red Cross fund-raiser.

She distinctly remembered marking its box with a huge

red label after arguing with Brady over Neville, the jewelry merchandiser. She didn't want to believe Brady or anyone else had removed the label, but it couldn't have come off on its own. Yet afterward there it sat, on the shelf where the box had been.

"It was an accident," she said. "And it wouldn't be any big deal except I promised the foundation a Beautiful Things necklace. On one hand that's a good thing, because necklaces are all I have left. But on the other, those necklaces are the lily, which I can't sell because of the patent, and a rose necklace I don't want to sell because it means something to me. But, thanks to Brady, I have no choice, so the rose one is going on the block."

"I can see why you'd be upset with him," the doctor said. "And in all honesty I think you handled the argument better than I might have myself. But why don't you tell me what really sent you fleeing to the greenhouse."

Emma wrinkled her nose, annoyed that she was so transparent. She told him what Anthony had asked, miffed when the doctor said she'd overreacted. Of course, she hadn't told Dillon she'd been in Anthony's lap at the time but somehow she didn't think that would matter. A simple "no" wouldn't have killed her.

And as predicted, Dillon returned to the lust issue, bringing up the biological and evolutionary differences between the sexes. His point was that survival-of-the-species instincts made it much easier for males to distinguish physical attraction from love than their female counterparts.

Emma had heard it from him and the Learning Channel a hundred times, and he did have a point, she supposed. But whether she liked it or not, there was something stronger between her and Anthony than biological urges. Had she been able to explain it, she would have.

So she let Dillon say his piece, as she thought about Charles. Charles always said things happened for a reason, and maybe the gardenia necklace had been sold to finally end the tension with Brady. Things would be better for everyone if he left. Him most of all.

Dillon said something about Anthony leaving after Dop was caught, and she cringed, imagining what the doctor would say if she confessed she thought she was in love with Anthony. He'd ask, "What makes you think that?" and she'd have to explain the lines around Anthony's eyes.

Dillon would make sympathetic noises while thinking she never listened to a word he said.

When the session ended, Emma clipped the phone to her pocket and crossed to the stereo. It was surrounded by three tall bookcases full of CDs and books, plus pictures she hid from prying eyes. Her parents, the stepmothers, close friends, Charles's huge family, Brady and Tanya... Emma looked at them all, knowing tomorrow night would bring an end to an era, when Beautiful Things would overshadow Toliver's Treasures.

She was proud of her success. The label was the first thing she hadn't had handed to her in life, but as her time at the store grew more limited she would miss the historic feel of the place. Once in a while she needed that sensation—generations of long-dead Tolivers holding her hand as she survived one more day of their legacy.

Emma smiled at a picture of her mother and herself sitting on the oak stairs. It was taken on Meredith's thirtieth birthday, about four months before she'd died. Emma was in her lap wearing a big silly grin. And if you looked hard enough, right by her mother's feet there was a faint mark in the oak where Emma had crashed her trike.

"I was such a brat," Emma muttered. She'd gotten away with murder at the store. The love of shiny things had started young, and Emma's favorite place was the workroom, where she could use all five senses to absorb the process.

Even as she stood in the greenhouse she could smell sharp acids, hear the buzzing whine of the diamond wheel, feel the texture of an empty gold setting. Of course, back then, tasting anything got her booted out of the workroom instantly. But the sight of all those shining, glorious pieces would forever be enough motivation for her designing.

She'd had other quirks that got her in trouble. Not only did she like to touch the shiny things, she liked to swipe them and secrete the unfinished pieces and unset stones up here among her mother's beloved flowers.

Smiling ruefully, Emma put in an Otis Redding CD and passed the time convincing herself she wasn't mad at Anthony. It wasn't as if his past didn't give her qualms. And she supposed he did have a right to know if she'd slept with Brady, since Brady might be around for a while. Might.

Dinnertime had come and gone while she was on the phone, but she felt no desire to go downstairs until it started to get dark. No way was she staying up here as the cooling glass fogged over.

Emma found the apartment door wide open, and as she entered, she stopped at the sound of voices in the den.

"...can't let her stay up there thinking all night," Jim said.

Anthony argued, "And can't you see she's had enough? This was supposed to be a good day, but what does she get? A bunch of mind games. It's not fair and I refuse to participate anymore."

"You will if Layne has anything to say about it."

Emma stepped back onto the landing and raised her eyebrows, wondering what power Layne had over Anthony. What next?

"Yeah, well, Layne's not here, is she?" Anthony challenged.

"No, she's not. But that doesn't mean I won't show Emma yesterday's e-mails if worse comes to worst."

Yesterday's e-mails? Why, that lying—

"Do it and I'll break every bone in your body," Anthony said.

Jim snorted. "I'd like to see you try."

There was a brief silence and then Jim said, "On second thought, why don't we just—"

"No. No more scheming. I'm going up there to apologize, like I should have done hours ago."

"Apologize? After she asked if you'd slept with my ex-wife?"

"After what you said this morning can you blame her? Maybe you should turn that psychology crap on yourself for once," Anthony argued. "You said defensiveness marks guilt or fear. No clearer case than this, is there? Karen made a pass at me. Big deal. Was it my fault? No. But you still think it's your fault. Well, guess what, Jim? It was Karen's fault. So the next time you feel an urge to advise me on women, take a deep breath and fight it."

Emma grimaced while another silence descended. She heard them walk out into the hall, and then Jim called, "You're right, Emma. He's a jerk. But you both win. No more games."

Sighing, Emma stepped through the door.

"Be quieter next time," Jim told her.

Anthony watched him walk away. "Welcome to manipulation central. How may we manipulate you this evening?" he announced, turning to Emma. "Well then. I guess the secret's out."

"Which secret would that be?" she responded. "That Jim likes to manipulate people or that I got two e-mails yesterday?"

She was still wondering about Layne, but put it aside when Anthony said, "Trust me, Emma. You don't want to see them. I almost threw up and I'm not the one with the weak stomach."

Jim's cellphone rang and the two of them did their best not to make eye contact. Unable to take this distance between them another second, Emma said, "Anthony, I'm sorry. I had no right to say what I did about Karen."

"And I had no right to ask you about Brady. We're even."

Liar. "Are we?" she asked. If Layne was holding something over his head, Emma would do them both a favor and make him tell. Then there really would be an end to the mind games.

Anthony tipped his head, crossing his arms over his chest as he leaned against the wall. His white button-down shirt was untucked from jeans, and the high-tops were untied, as always. Why couldn't the man tie his shoes? And how was she supposed to trust him when there always seemed to be another secret lurking around?

"What do you mean?" he asked. "Are we really even?"

She nodded, and he added, "You heard that bit about Layne?"

"Yeah."

"All right. No, we're not even. But—"

"Bracco! Get in here," Jim yelled, with enough force to send them rushing for the design office.

Jim was on both his cellphone and the phone on her desk, talking to two people at once. He told them to hang on and said to Anthony, "Read this. What does he mean?"

Anthony went behind the desk, but when Emma tried to follow he and Jim barked, "Get back!"

While Anthony read whatever was on the screen, Jim looked up at her for a moment, his eyes dropping again in embarrassment. Emma wondered what it must be like for him to live with that between him and his best friend. Part of her had to admire him for what he'd done. He might be manipulative, but he'd just apologized in his own weird way at his own expense. He'd made darn good and sure Emma knew about the mind games and what had really happened with Karen. They both knew Anthony wouldn't have told her on his own. He could barely be bothered to share his own details. No way would he spill someone else's.

"Emma, come here a sec," Anthony prompted. "I know I've heard this somewhere but I can't place it."

On the screen was an e-mail message formed like a poem, and Emma immediately recognized it as lyrics. "Bleed it out—bleed it out of my soul" was the line that stuck.

"It's a song," she said.

"That son of a..." Anthony growled, snatching the phone clipped to her pants pocket. "Is Hornsby still at my house?" he asked Jim.

"I don't know. Why?"

Anthony dialed and then said, "Hey, Walt. I need you to do me a favor. Go into my study."

He looked as though he might explode and Emma rubbed his back, watching him as he said, "Open the center drawer of my desk. There should be a key ring in with the pens. Got it? Okay, turn and face the cabinet. Yeah, the wood thing under the window. The key's got a red dot. Open the cabinet and tell me what you see."

There was a pause and then he barked something in Italian—a bad word Emma knew from a high school friend—and she frowned.

"Sorry," he muttered, putting his arm around her waist before turning his attention back to the phone. "It wasn't empty before the attack. So this means you guys missed something. If Dop took that stuff, he's got about three boxes of files, and my journals, too. What? No, okay. You head out."

"What's going on?" Emma asked as he hung up.

"Soon as Jim's gone, you and I will be having a very, very long talk."

Emma raised her eyebrows. "Where's Jim going?"

Jim answered. "Melinda's virus just nailed Dop. Computer registration info, a credit card number and a billing address. Digital trace confirms his connection to the Internet is coming from that address, so our crew is getting ready for a raid."

"So this could be over tonight?"

Anthony nodded, pulling her out of the way as Jim hung up both phones. "Okay," Jim said. "Here's the deal. You have two men downstairs watching the perimeter, so you're free to move around. But make sure this place is locked up tight at all times because there's no guarantee he won't go mobile with his equipment. I'll call as soon as we know something."

Already on his way out the door, he checked his shoulder holster for his gun, and Emma and Anthony said in unison, "Please be careful." He waved, breaking into a run.

Left alone, they continued to stare after him. Emma had mixed feelings. If Jim and crew ended this tonight she'd give every member of the Bureau one serious discount for the rest of her life. However, if it ended, Anthony would be leaving. But not yet.

"Hungry?" he asked. "You missed dinner."

Fifteen minutes later they were in the greenhouse office, making a picnic of the cheesecake Anthony's housekeeper had delivered earlier. The futon had been laid flat and an ice bucket holding two water bottles and a magnum of champagne sat nearby in case they had cause to celebrate.

Anthony watched her take a bite. "How can you eat that? It's so sweet it makes my teeth hurt."

"Hush," she said. "Now, what are we talking about?"

"Well..." He blew out a breath. "Let me put something on the stereo and I'll get it over with."

He got up to survey the CD collection and smiled. "Led Zeppelin? You keep the boring stuff downstairs for a reason?"

"It's too distracting when I'm trying to work."

"Ah. So the real Emma hides up here."

"I guess so." She shrugged.

Anthony put it on and turned the volume down, stopping to laugh at something. "What?" she asked.

"Is that you?" He held up the picture of her and her mother and she nodded. He said, "Pigtails and cute as hell."

"I was a heathen."

"Was?"

"Knock it off. And quit stalling."

"Okay," he sighed, stretching out on the futon. "I should have told you this a long time ago, but now that it appears

Dop's made off with some sensitive materials, I'd rather you hear this from me than from him."

"Sensitive materials?"

"You heard me on the phone. There were a bunch of files in that cabinet concerning some of my more controversial business dealings, including information about your store. Tax records, that kind of thing. It looks like Dop took them the night I got cut. Jim never found any evidence that he'd been inside, and since I was laid up for a week, it got missed."

"Anthony," Emma fumed.

"Don't get mad yet." He held up a hand. "That's nothing. Anyway, it wasn't until you said 'song' that I figured out why the bleeding thing sounded so familiar. I'd written about that song a couple weeks before I descended on you. That's how I knew he'd somehow gotten his hands on my files and journals."

"You wrote about that song? About the bleeding thing?"

"Yeah, well, it sounds melodramatic now, but that song reminded me of my father. Things were rough between us back then and there were times when I couldn't stand knowing we had the same blood in our veins."

Emma grimaced, praying Maxim wouldn't show up tomorrow night.

"Told you it was melodramatic," Anthony grumbled. "At any rate, here's the part you'll be mad about. Ready?"

Thinking she already knew what was coming, Emma was wholly surprised when he asked, "You know how people commit suicide by pulling a gun on the police? That's basically what I did. Career suicide by kick-starting the infamous Emma temper."

"What?" she squawked.

He sighed. "I was stuck. I wanted out of Bracco but I knew my father would make it impossible to leave. My only option was to do something so awful the stockholders would force the board to fire me. So I went looking for the biggest public relations blunder of all time and found you."

Was she hallucinating? "Excuse me?"

"Let me finish before you kill me. Yes, I did everything you accused me of that night, but I had an ulterior motive. And it all went basically according to plan, except for one thing. You didn't raise unholy hell like you were supposed to, so the stockholders didn't get the full brunt of what I'd done right away."

"Right away?" Emma echoed. She could feel a flush creeping across her skin, but she grabbed hold of her temper with an iron fist. He was finally coming out with what Layne was holding over his head, and if Emma blew up now he'd never talk again.

"Yeah, I… Well, when you didn't go to the media, I did."

"You. Were the one who went to the media," Emma repeated, feeling like a dim-witted parrot. But the things they'd said about him in the press had to be incredibly painful, both the truth and the lies. Why had he done that to himself? And to her?

The full import of what he'd done hit home, and Emma could do nothing but stare. Maxim Bracco hadn't cut his son loose. Anthony had done it himself. He'd wanted out of his own life so badly he'd been willing to destroy himself in the process. Why?

"What's the rest of the story?" Emma asked.

Giving her a long look, Anthony played with a futon button. "It's personal."

"So were the things they said about me in the papers. Tell me how you made the jump from getting what you wanted to disappearing for two years?"

He squeezed his eyes shut. "I suppose I owe you that much. I…God. I'm really bad at talking about this." He paused for a moment, then continued. "My parents broke up because Maxim rarely remembered he had a family. Then he screwed her in the divorce, so she moved here from Chicago, went to nursing school and worked herself half to death raising me without any help from him. And you know how I was back then. I figured I had a score to settle with the old bastard."

Anthony stopped to gauge her reaction. She tried to keep her face impassive, but it wasn't easy.

Starting again, he said, "I figured the only way to pay him back for what he'd done to Mom was to take the only thing he cared about away from him. So for six years I worked with him, overshadowing him every way I could. And just when I had the board in my pocket and Maxim by the throat, I decided it wasn't worth it. It was hurting Mom more than it was hurting him. But then I discovered getting out wasn't as easy as getting in, so I went after the store. You got caught in the middle. I know an apology isn't worth much, but I am sorry, Emma. For everything."

Emma said nothing, letting it sink in. She understood him now, and while she didn't approve of his motives or methods, it hurt her to know he'd grown up with that much pain and anger.

Shaking her head, Emma knew there was more he hadn't said. "What did your mother have to say about all this?"

"Not much. She'd written me off when I went to work for Dad, and when she heard what I'd done to you I was officially uninvited to her wedding."

"Oh, Anthony," Emma sighed.

"Don't you dare get all female sympathetic, Emma."

"I'm not. But that's awful."

"Not really. Actually it was the best thing that could have happened. Geoff stepped in and we got everything worked out."

Now more worried about tomorrow night than ever, Emma asked, "And where do things stand with Maxim?"

"I don't know. I haven't talked to him for almost two years."

"But you talked to him after you got fired?"

"Yep. He wouldn't leave me alone. Every day there was some new scheme. A new company, more perks—it was pathetic. And obviously I wasn't too receptive," he said, sitting up. "I knew he'd never quit, so I left St. Paul. Disappeared to keep him away from me. And as far as I know, no one's had any contact with him until Mom called him about Dop."

Oh, man. Tomorrow could be a disaster. Emma had no way of knowing what would happen when Anthony saw his father. And why was Maxim coming? Was there another scheme in the works or had he realized how close he'd come to losing his son?

Thinking first, she asked, "Did he come to the hospital?"

"Why?" Anthony asked, spearing her with his eyes.

Emma turned her hands up. "It's just a question."

"No it isn't. You're being way too calm about this. Are you missing the point here? I *changed my mind* that night, Emma. Once you brought up marriage I fully intended to go through with it and take controlling interest. So if things hadn't gone the way they did, you wouldn't be here anymore. Your clients would have torn me to shreds, but I'd still have gotten what I came for. And I'd have used you as my staunchest defender to keep this place afloat after the Bracco fallout. Then I'd have gotten rid of you somehow."

"Nice honesty, but none of that matters, Anthony. It didn't happen that way. Now answer the question. Did he come see you in the hospital or not?"

"Yes, he did. But I was too whacked on meds to know he was there. Which was probably a good thing."

"Anthony—"

"Emma, look. I know you don't understand, but I'm not like you. I can't just…forget what he did to my mother."

"And you."

"I can take care of myself," he grumbled.

"Uh-huh. But your mother's forgiven him. She's moved on, and from what I've seen of her and Geoff, she's happy. And you obviously care about Geoff, so it all worked out, right? Now, why are you still mad at Maxim?"

"It's not that I'm mad. I don't trust him. There's always some new plan around the corner, and now that he's resigned from Bracco Inc. I'm waiting for him to turn up expecting something. Pretty much the same way you feel about me."

Ignoring his last comment, Emma felt a spurt of anger douse any remaining excitement for tomorrow night. She was awed by the changes in Anthony and couldn't even imagine the work it must have taken him to get from where he'd been to where he was now.

Why would his family jeopardize those changes by bringing Maxim to the auction? After everything they'd been through, Emma found it very hard to believe Sophia would do this without a darn good reason. Maxim might not have anything up his sleeve this time, so it might be wiser to keep her mouth shut and her eyes open.

"You can always say no," Emma told him.

Anthony sneered at her, and afraid he'd quit talking, she asked, "So where were you and what did you do for two years?"

"I was up in Brainerd and I fished."

"Fished?"

"Yes. You know that thing with the hook and slimy bait?"

"Smart aleck." She grinned. "Do you have a house up there?"

"I bought a lake property around the same time that I bought the Ashland house."

"A property with a house?"

He laughed and she stared. She couldn't help it. He was so gorgeous when he laughed it stole her breath.

"You'll love this," he said. "The only thing on the property was a two-room hunting shack, and I lived there until the lake house was built."

"You? Lived in a shack?"

He grinned. "Yeah. A little far removed from the penthouse, but waiting for the house was worth it. Built part of it myself. You'll have to come up sometime and see it."

Did he mean that or was he being polite now that he'd

made his confession? Time would tell. But at least it explained his scarred, callused hands. "You're going back up there when this is over?"

Both of them glanced at the silent cellphone, but then Anthony said, "I don't know. I don't have to be in town to do the consulting thing, but it's nice to be home again."

"You don't miss the quiet?"

"Only when you're yelling at me— Ow. No pinching."

"Jerk."

"I know. I deserve it, witch."

"So you just fished?"

"In between bouts of self-torture, yes. I spent a lot of time thinking about what you asked me on Monday. What I'd do differently if I could go back and do it over again."

"Did you ever come up with an answer?"

"Yes and no. After I realized the amount of damage I'd done I felt guilty as all hell. I'm having a war with my father and everyone gets annihilated except him. The man's got more lives than a cat, I swear. At any rate, there were times when I..."

"What?"

"Promise me first you won't scream."

"Depends on what you're about to say."

"Fair enough. I did call the store four months ago. I asked for you but got Charles because you were out."

Emma tried to keep a straight face but couldn't manage it. "Boy, can you imagine that conversation if you'd reached me?"

"Honestly? No. I can't. What would you have said?"

"I probably would have been too shocked to say a word."

"A speechless Emma. What a moment!" He winked. "But there's something I've been meaning to ask. I always pictured you gloating once I got fired. I gather that wasn't the case, and I can't help wondering if I wounded more than your pride."

"It's kind of late to ask that now, isn't it?" Emma asked,

her heart and stomach turning over simultaneously. How could she answer that? If she told the truth he'd think he owed her, and that was the last thing she wanted. Then again, considering his offer to do the bookkeeping, she'd better not take anything for granted.

"Emma?" he prompted.

"I've got a question first," she ordered. "If Dop hadn't happened, would you still be helping with my books?"

Looking confused, he said, "I don't get what you're asking."

"I don't want you thinking you owe me."

"Emma, look at me. Look at me," he repeated, a gentle hand helping her obey. His eyes weren't gentle as he said, "I know every second I've been here you've been waiting for me to slip back into character. It won't happen, and I think by now we both know I would have found my way back here somehow, Dop or no Dop. So if you think it won't matter if you lie to me right now, believe me. It matters."

For a moment she didn't understand, but the look on his face was explanation enough. His eyes were nearly black and he stared with an intensity that erased two years of swallowed anger.

Oh, my God. If he'd looked at her like that even once back then she'd have handed him her entire life on a platter from her own silver department.

But now, knowing how much he'd held back this week, Emma donned a pensive expression. She scooped up a big fingerful of the cheesecake's strawberry topping and slapped it onto his forehead.

Anthony closed his eyes, his whole body shaking with silent laughter, but didn't stop her as she smeared it down his nose. He sputtered a laugh as she continued over his mouth to end with a flourish at his collar.

His eyes opened. "Are you finished?"

Smiling with a look of bright, satisfied innocence, Emma nodded.

"Feel better now?" he asked.

Smiling wider, she nodded again, but her eyes grew round when he gathered a huge glob for himself.

"All right," Anthony said, painting a line across her right cheek. "That's for the evil black dress."

Emma squeezed her eyes shut, trying desperately not to laugh. She didn't even try to stop him; it was way too enlightening to hear what he was mad about.

Painting her left cheek, he said, "This is for punching me." And at her neck. "This is for being such an iceberg. And this last one is for not trying to find me even once in the last two years."

Chapter 11

Emma opened her eyes but squeezed them shut again, howling with laughter as he smeared his hand from her nose to her jeans. She fell over backward and he followed, rubbing the strawberries on his forehead into her neck.

"Still have that dress?" he asked, making her gasp as his mouth closed on the juncture of neck and shoulder.

Shaking her head, Emma managed a breathless "I burned it. But we won't be needing it."

"Mmm. Wouldn't stay on long, anyway."

They hurried downstairs to her bathroom sink. Anthony vetoed Emma's shower plans and raked her shirt off before saying, "We won't be able to hear the phone if Jim calls. Later. Twice."

"Promise?"

He dipped his head to lick away a strawberry that had fallen between her breasts, shooting hot and cold tingles across her skin. Goose bumps. The man gave her goose bumps.

The sight of his dark hair shining in the light and the wiry feel of it between her fingers was all it took. He was vitally alive and she was hopelessly in love with him.

Dr. Dillon was very wrong. This wasn't survival of the species. This was two people who were meant to be together.

She fumbled with buttons as Anthony worked his way up to her neck and followed his mouth with a hot, wet washcloth. Emma could barely think as the soft cotton rubbed her clean. Anthony deliberately took his time, stripping off her bra and starting on her breasts. Flames roared from tight nipples straight to her thighs, and Emma did away with her jeans as fast as shaking hands would allow.

He was thoroughly enjoying himself, looking at her with hazy eyes. If he didn't stop soon she'd be screaming.

"Anthony, we have all night for that. Don't make me wait."

The washcloth dropped to the floor and Emma found herself on the cold marble countertop a second later. Anthony pulled her legs apart, his mouth burning hers with an urgency that made her melt. She didn't know how they could feel this way after all they'd put each other through, but there was no way she could live without him.

Forget Neville. Forget the deal, forget everything that would steal one second of her time with Anthony.

Her feet now locked behind his back, Emma could feel the heat of his erection through way too many layers of fabric.

"Bed," she ordered as soon as he let her breathe again, and she hung on, delighting in the feel of his rough throat against her swollen lips as he carried her next door.

Anthony put her down long enough to get his shirt off, and they tumbled onto the bed. In the soft golden light his skin was pure bronze, and Emma tasted it while wrestling with his button fly.

She felt totally out of control but she wouldn't have it any other way. This was how he'd always made her feel and she loved him for it. Well, when she wasn't furious with him. But he was always pushing for more. Rushing her toward something, and making love would be no different.

And while she was finally getting her chance to touch him, the truth arrived. Things always happened for a reason. Maybe they'd had to hurt each other to get to this rare place where she could see both the good and bad in him and know it was safe to love him, anyway.

But it wasn't a one-way street. Anthony showed her things about herself that weren't too wonderful, either. She was already well acquainted with those things, but he had a sense of humor about them. Bickering was simply their means of keeping each other honest.

She found the trail of hair leading into his boxers and he complained gruffly, "Emma, please. Have a little mercy."

She barely heard him and quickly found herself on her back, and arms pinned to the bed by one firm hand. "Wait," he commanded, then took his cellphone from his pocket and laid it beside them, next pulling out a condom. She didn't care that he'd come equipped, only that he hurry, and she was more hindrance than help as he made sure they were safe. Then she settled back into the pillows, the feel of scratchy legs against smooth ones maddening as his hands explored.

"Anthony?"

He whispered "What?" into her navel, raising another rash of goose bumps and a hot blush.

"Please."

She heard him breathe something in Italian before his fingers captured the lace at her hip. He kissed her through the silk, bringing her very near the end before they'd really begun.

With torturously slow hands, Anthony dragged the fabric away, searing a line down her inner thigh with his cheek. Emma inhaled sharply and a finger covered her mouth.

"Shhh. We don't know where those agents are," he warned.

Letting out a quiet peal of wicked laughter, she opened

her mouth to catch his fingertip between her teeth, sucking the end.

"You..." he started to say, then stared down at Emma with his whole heart in his eyes.

She blinked. Nothing held a candle to this.

Emma memorized every bit of that moment, the first time Anthony Bracco said I love you.

She tried to echo his look and it must have worked. The grin she'd never forgotten appeared just a second before he took her mouth.

Unbelievable. She loved him. And he loved her even more for knowing how he felt without him having to say a word. Over and over in his mind he told her he loved her as she wrapped her legs around him again, drawing him against her.

"Emma, I—"

And then she stopped him from actually saying the words, with a gentle squeeze of her legs. She was so warm and tight he couldn't think at all then, and sank the rest of the way in one barely controlled motion.

Emma arched beneath him, crushing her breasts into his chest. It had never been like this for him. Ever. Normally he'd be thinking *do it and get out as fast as you can.*

But if Emma wanted to get rid of him she'd have to kick him out. She owned him. She always had. There would never come a day he wouldn't want her, and he realized now that he'd been wrong the other night. They already had peace together, even surrounded by this Dop madness. Upstairs, he'd told her things he'd never told anyone, but she hadn't bitten his head off after all.

She seconded that emotion in her own contrary way, nipping at his neck and whispering promises that set him on fire.

He grabbed her hips and thrust deeper and deeper until he could feel her heating and tightening around him. But just when she was right on the edge he slowed down to make her hold out a little longer.

Laughing guiltily at her impatient complaints, he wrapped his arms around her and plunged on at a reckless pace. Emma's hand slid down his back, but before she made it very far he covered her mouth with his, to capture the breath of passion as the first waves hit. Her internal muscles pulled at him and he couldn't wait any longer. With one last, powerful thrust he exploded in release.

She didn't let him rest long, and he made good on his shower promise before Emma finally fell asleep, utterly exhausted. Her head was on his chest and he stroked her hair, staying awake long afterward, tired but overcome with a bad feeling.

Anthony knew what would happen when Jim called to say they hadn't caught Dop. Reality would set in, and faced with another day of waiting, Emma would go to work and pretend none of this was happening again.

He didn't care if Layne said rewarding the denial was a choice. Didn't mean it was a good choice. When Emma threw herself into work, it was as good as saying it was better to be there than with him.

How would he deal with that? He loved her. And he couldn't hold them together alone.

Adding to Anthony's worries, Charles had said some things today that stirred up mixed feelings. On the positive side, he'd said it wasn't easy to earn a spot in Emma's heart, but once that spot existed it was there forever.

On the negative side, he'd also said, ''Emma wants what Emma wants and if something does not fit her picture, she simply ignores it.'' Basically the same thing Layne had said. Half the FBI could attest to that, too, while they were tiptoeing around the store, praying she'd continue to pretend they weren't there.

It wasn't that anyone thought Emma unbalanced. They were being careful so she wouldn't get upset. And in her own way she was the strongest person he knew, but that strength required preparation for the reality of tomorrow night. Security would be extremely tight, and it wasn't just the FBI they'd be dealing with. Hotel security and a private security company had been enlisted for extra help.

Those people wouldn't tiptoe around Emma. After two nights of skirmishes, Dop would be on the rampage, and the security guards would be touchy. If something happened, Anthony would be the one she resented for it.

What a mess. There was no way he could dodge all these bullets. And he must like to live dangerously because he'd had the perfect opportunity to finish the confessions and talk through the security issues while they'd been upstairs in the greenhouse.

Emma couldn't have made it any easier. She'd taken the Bracco confession without so much as a blink, and instead of coming clean about what he and Charles had done, he'd made love with her. It didn't take much thought to realize that wasn't a very smart move.

All right. New rule. No more of this until he'd told her everything,

Anthony kissed the top of Emma's head, breathing in the smell of her. If the world came apart tomorrow, he wanted to remember this moment.

In the morning, the sound of her voice woke him. She was hissing at someone in the hall. ''I don't care what time it is. Let the man sleep.''

Hurrying out of bed, Anthony whipped the door open. Emma yelped as he dragged her inside, then she wrinkled her nose and laughed. Grateful no one else had been near by the door, he remembered his clothes were still strewn between the bathroom and bed.

He didn't give her a chance to say anything before kissing her good-morning, and Emma twined her arms around his neck. The feel of that body, separated from him by only a thin layer of silk, was almost enough to make him forget his new rule.

She, of course, was edging him toward bed, so he stole a breath. "What do they want?"

"To tell you Dop got away, but they got your journals and files back."

At his look she said, "Yeah, that's basically what I said, too. Who cares, right? Bit of a problem, though. The information Melinda got last night was all based on a social security number that was stolen from someone who'd died. The owners of the office building had that same information, so they still don't know who Dop is. Otherwise, they don't know if he bolted because he knew they were coming or what."

"Perfect."

"Mmm...you're gorgeous," Emma said, kissing his neck. "But Charles will be here any minute with my lily and I need to find my good loupe."

"Well, hold on a second."

His hands fell to his sides as Emma started lifting jewelry-box lids. "There it is," she announced. "Okay. What were you going to say?"

Anthony sank down on the bed. She was totally preoccupied. Definitely not the time to tell her what he and Charles had done, especially when Charles was on his way here. "Nothing."

"Gotta go," she said. "I'll be in the vault if you need me."

"Emma." He held up his hands. "Wait for me."

"Uh, actually, if my setting design didn't work you might not want to be within fifty yards because I'll blow a gasket like you've never seen. But don't worry. I called Dr. Dillon and he's making a house call later."

He raised his eyebrows. Well, then. Just when he'd forgotten how unpredictable Emma could be, here she was surprising him again. Dillon was a good idea. Jim wouldn't let him in the building without talking to him first, and knowing him and Layne, they'd have him go to work on Emma about tonight. Hugely relieved, he said, "All right. But like it or not I'll be down in a minute."

Emma kissed him and walked out, perfectly calm and collected. After finding his jeans, Anthony sneaked across the hall and got ready quickly, still pulling on a shoe as he hopped into the hallway.

Jim was on him instantly. "We need to talk."

"Not now."

"Anthony—"

"I said *not now*. I'll be back in a while."

"But—" Jim broke off with a curse as Anthony took the steps down to the second floor four at a time. Reaching the vault, he was brought to a halt by Charles's outstretched hand. Emma was bent over a black velvet case, holding the loupe to her eye. Charles was beaming like a supermodel, but when Anthony opened his mouth to ask if the necklace worked, Charles shushed him.

Left to wait, Anthony peered at the necklace, his eyes widening. If he didn't know better he'd swear he was looking at a real stargazer lily. It looked exactly as if someone had twined the stem and bloom around the mold. The petals were a delicate translucent pinkish-white, the throats a myriad of specks, colors and textures. Even the stamens were perfect, spilling out of the flower in vivid gold.

Jade, he figured, for most of it. But as he edged closer he could see opal and enameling, and some kind of pinkish stone he couldn't identify. The stem was a curved spray of green gems complete with spear-shaped leaves. Could be emeralds, but they looked too clear.

But it would have to latch somehow and spoil the realistic effect. Thinking it was beautiful anyway, Anthony watched as Emma lifted the piece to inspect the platinum setting. He'd seen a lot of jewelry come off a lot of necks in his day, and this piece looked nothing like any he'd ever seen. There were sections of mesh dotted with triangles of the nearly white metal, and tiny ladders of yellow gold.

Emma probed sections with her fingernail for an eternity, and if she didn't say something soon, he'd lose it.

Eventually Emma announced, "It's perfect."

Charles said nothing and both men followed Emma to a mirror, where she stood with stubbornness radiating from every pore. And Anthony couldn't help but smile when Charles finally cried, "Would you give me that accursed thing?"

Emma handed it to him and ordered Anthony, "Hair."

She swept it up and Anthony held it in place while Charles wound the piece around her neck. The stem end perched just above her left collarbone, then twined around to the bloom that rested a little off center, halfway between Emma's left breast and her throat. There was no clasp in sight.

Charles backed away and Anthony's hand jumped to catch the necklace before it could collapse and slide down into her dress.

But it didn't move. Not one inch. It sat there, defying the laws of physics, and Anthony raised his eyes to Emma's.

Brow furrowed, stared at the necklace in the mirror. They all stood frozen, waiting for it to slip even slightly out of position.

It didn't. And then Emma started moving, so Anthony stepped away. No matter what she did the lily stayed defiantly in place.

"It is no use," Charles told her, grinning. "It worked."

"No adhesive you're not telling me about?" she demanded.

"Nothing. Just a perfectly designed and weighted piece. What can I say to you? You have achieved the impossible."

Her hands fell to her sides and she breathed, "Oh my *God.*"

Charles's grinned widened, and as Emma stared at the necklace in the mirror again, he turned to Anthony and winked.

The very next moment Emma was hugging Charles so

tightly the poor man looked as if he couldn't breathe. But he was laughing, saying, "I knew it would work. You are the best designer I have ever worked with."

"It's perfect, Charles. Absolutely perfect. Without you this would never have happened. You know that."

"It was my pleasure and honor. Now, I wish I could stay to gloat, but if I am to make the auction I must work."

Emma kissed him on the cheek before he left, and then she stood there, looking slightly lost. "I don't believe it."

Anthony had no idea what to say. This was so totally out of his realm he felt as if a million miles lay between them. The last several minutes had shown him Emma had a life mapped out before her that he played no part in.

"Say something," she squeaked, her eyes dewy.

"I—I can't. I'm stunned."

"So am I. I can't believe it worked."

"Emma, this is huge."

"I know. I guess I didn't let myself believe it would work, and now that it has, I… What am I supposed to do?"

"File your patent?" he suggested.

Emma sighed and pulled the necklace off, dropping it into the case with a singular lack of care.

Anthony crossed his arms over his chest. "Care to tell me what's wrong?"

"Remember last night when you told me about your dad? How once you had him by the throat you decided it wasn't worth it?"

"Yes, but what's that got to do with anything?"

"Well," she said, "that's exactly how I feel right now. Neville's offering me the kind of deal a designer can only dream about, and now that I've got it I'm not sure I want the consequences. I've got one master goldsmith and a dozen part-timers who can barely handle the simpler pieces, and now I have to get a patent in the works. Even if I wanted to start producing pieces, I don't have the resources."

"So find them. If you choose to do it, you'll do it."

"What if I don't want to? What if I just wanted to see if I could? Am I obligated now?"

Anthony whistled in surprise. "I can't answer that. But it's not like you have to decide this instant."

"Yes, I do. Neville will take one look at this thing and start asking questions. He wants what we were doing before. The florals. But this is..."

"Then don't wear the lily, Emma. Show me the piece he wants."

For some reason her eyes grew mistier and she bit her bottom lip. Wondering what on earth was going on, he waited while Emma opened a cabinet and pulled out another necklace box.

When she lifted the lid, he was no less surprised than when the lily had clung to her neck. Inside the case was a necklace just as beautiful, but conventional, if only in the sense that it circled the neck and latched. But again it was so realistic he felt that if he touched it his hand would come away smelling of rose petals.

All he felt capable of saying was, "It's beautiful, Emma. I can see why he'd be interested. What's the problem?"

"I backed myself into a corner." She sighed, then asked, "If I tell you something, can you listen without doing that whole guy thing where you have to fix the problem?"

"I'll try."

"Good enough. Okay. When we first started Beautiful Things, modern designs were selling the best. But I wanted to do flowers. Not just two-dimensional, impressionistic flowers. It's hard to explain."

"No it's not. They're the real thing, only permanent," Anthony told her. "Permanent Beautiful Things."

Emma's eyes flitted up to meet his, and what he saw then was a four-year-old child who'd lived through losing her mother, then had lost three more mothers thanks to her father's instability. Nothing and no one lasted. Except Charles. And the store.

"I never thought of it that way before. But you're right.

Anyway, when they started selling I felt like I'd created a monster. We couldn't keep up. The money was rolling in, but getting quality stones and metals isn't always as easy as it might sound."

Anthony stayed carefully silent.

"So," she continued, "as luck, or fate, might have it, just when I'm in the worst material shortage in history, Neville calls and says he wants to meet, but the only time he had open is tonight, and I told him I couldn't do it because I have a charity thing— Don't look at me like I'm crazy. The Tolivers have supported the Red Cross forever, and my mother would roll over in her grave if I didn't contribute. So I asked him if he'd rather I come to New York, but he said no, as long as he'd be here, he'd come to the fund-raiser and buy whatever I put up for auction. That way it would be a write-off as well as an acquisition."

"So what's the problem?" Anthony asked.

"The problem is, last week Brady accidentally sold the piece I was supposed to be putting up for auction. Gardenias. It's one of our better designs and it sells like crazy."

"I don't like the way you said 'accidentally', Emma."

"Neither do I. But what's done is done, and the only pieces I have left..."

Man. Emma was so close to tears she couldn't even finish. So he helped. "Are the lily and the roses. And you can't give up the lily until you have the patent. Isn't there anything you can do?"

"Even if we'd gotten the stones before yesterday there wouldn't have been time to complete any of the backlogged pieces, so it doesn't matter."

If there were ever an opportunity to keep his mouth shut, Anthony knew this was it. But he had to know. "If you had the resources, would you pursue the patent?"

"*Resources* isn't the right word," she said, running her finger over one of the jeweled roses. "I can easily give us another influx of cash to get what we need, with my own money. What I really need is *help.* I can't do this alone anymore. All along, the plan was for Brady to run the store while I focused on Beautiful Things, but he never wanted me to go into business with Neville. He'll leave, and this isn't exactly a business you can hand over to a stranger."

"No, I can see that," Anthony agreed, feeling the full brunt of her situation. To know she'd been carrying this alone without saying a word made him feel like hell.

"But," she said with forced brightness, "when things get back to normal we can always make more roses, right?"

He bit the inside of his cheek to keep himself from saying anything. Those roses weren't meant for anyone who didn't carry Toliver blood in her veins. If he'd been thinking, he would have known immediately. One of the pictures upstairs in the greenhouse showed her mother with a garland of roses around her neck. On her wedding day.

The woman he loved was being pulled apart at the seams and there wasn't a single thing he could do about it. Well, there was plenty he could do, but she'd asked him not to.

Anthony knew he needed to stop meddling, and he might have let it go if he hadn't pictured Emma walking down the aisle wearing that necklace.

As she closed the lid on the roses, he felt as if he'd been punched, as if something had been stolen from him personally. No way would he let that necklace go. Not when he had the ability to stop it. And no way was Emma going to slip out of his life a second time.

"Anthony," she said, "please don't take this the wrong way, but I need some time to figure out what to do. Go have lunch or breakfast or whatever, and talk to Jim. He's been patient."

Nodding, he brushed a few hairs off her cheek and kissed her. He needed time to think, too, but Emma claimed all his attention for a few moments.

And then she gave him a smile that didn't quite reach her eyes. "I'm going to the greenhouse, okay?"

"What about lunch?"

"Later. I'm not hungry." Then she added, "Don't worry.

I'll get it figured out and I'll be fine. Maybe Neville won't be interested and it won't be an issue."

"I wish there was something I could do. Are you sure—"

"You *are* doing something," she interrupted. "You're helping me get caught up with that stupid bookkeeping and that helps me more than I can say."

She kissed him again, then said, "Now go play nice with Jim."

They walked up the stairs together, Emma heading up the last flight as he forced himself inside the apartment. He was more worried now than ever, but he relaxed when he found Jim in the den and was introduced to Dr. Dillon, Emma's therapist.

Dillon was about forty, tall and thin, dressed in a somber charcoal linen suit. He had a restful demeanor that Anthony hoped would help Emma make her decision.

"I've brought him up-to-date," Jim said to Anthony, then turned back to Dillon. "So hopefully you'll be able to talk some sense into her. This is a dangerous day and she's got to stop pretending that none of this is happening. We don't have any idea what will happen while we're out of our safety zone and we need Emma focused on keeping safe, not all this other crap that's going on."

Dillon sighed. "You should've called me sooner. I'll do my best, but if you need me tonight, call this number." He handed Jim a card.

The doctor turned to Anthony and shook his hand, a faint smile on his face. Anthony could only imagine what Emma had told him, but the man couldn't say a thing about it. Wishing everyone could be bound by confidentiality laws, Anthony said, "She just went up to the greenhouse."

"Isn't it hot up there?"

"The office is air-conditioned," Jim said. "I'll take you."

To Anthony he said, "I want you to find Charles and get him up here. The three of us need to talk while she's occupied."

Chapter 12

Anthony had Charles waiting in the den when Jim returned. ''Man, it's hot out there,'' he complained, dropping onto the couch. ''All right. So why don't you tell me why you looked gut-kicked when you walked in here earlier.''

Anthony explained about the roses, watching Charles's face as he told Jim what Brady had done. ''He sold the gardenia necklace on purpose, didn't he?'' he asked.

It took awhile, but Charles finally nodded. ''Yes. There is no other way it could have happened. They'd just had an argument, and I watched her put the label on the box. She was very upset. Slapped it on rather forcefully.''

Jim and Anthony looked at each other for a moment before Jim declared, ''This whole case stinks to high heaven. There isn't a single person associated with Emma that has the background we're looking for. No electronics or computer skills, no rap sheet, no nothing. And I'm getting damned sick of chasing my tail here. We've gotta flush this guy out somehow.''

''So we've cleared Brady of suspicion?'' Anthony asked.

"Yes. No. I don't know anymore," Jim said. "Layne needs to get back here before I lose my mind."

He glanced at Charles and muttered, "I'm sorry. I'm sure this is the last thing you needed to hear right now."

"I cannot say it makes me feel better, no. But I can answer a question about the way Brady has been acting."

"Oh?" Jim prompted.

"Emma does not know this. Brady will not tell her because she will erupt. His wife, Tanya, left him three weeks ago. She is pregnant and fed up with him never being home. He is not Dop. He feels guilty swatting flies, for heaven's sake."

"Why won't he tell Emma?" Jim asked. "I mean, I understand why she'd be upset, but angry? What's that about?"

Charles watched them uncomfortably for a moment before he answered, "This is a complicated situation for Brady, made more so by people like yourselves who believe he is in love with Emma. He is not, but he does feel obligated to her. And all the recent fighting stems from this deal with Neville. Brady knows there will be nothing left of her if she goes through with it. We all sympathize that she has worked hard for this and feels very strongly about creating something that has not been given to her, but it is as if she is… What is the word you people use these days?"

"Medicating herself," Jim supplied.

Charles pointed at him. "Yes. That is it exactly. A placebo to fill the hours so she does not have to face what is really wrong with her. Brady has been trying to tell her that for months, but his methods leave something to be desired. I feel for him, though. He loves his wife. But he loves Emma, too, and he cannot leave her behind like this."

Jim said, "Gotta hand it to the guy. Risking life and limb, selling that necklace. Passive aggressive attack. He sold the gardenias so she'd have to back out of the Red Cross auction."

Charles nodded. "Brave, but stupid, I am afraid. I don't

think he understood how serious Emma really was about Neville until yesterday. And after all Brady's attempts, it looks as though Emma still plans to go through with the auction and the deal."

"Okay," Jim sighed. "What a mess. Maybe we don't dislike Brady so much as we thought."

Anthony looked out the window. He'd been dead wrong about Brady. He'd also been dead wrong about Emma. She might not leave destruction in her wake but she was causing damage, if only to herself.

Everything he'd just heard put an entirely new spin on what happened downstairs a few minutes ago. Emma knew full well Neville was a mistake, but things were falling apart around here. Changing. And she'd go through with the deal because she couldn't hold things together anymore.

The Emma he knew was smarter than this. But she was hurting, and didn't understand that she was bringing this on herself.

Well, he sincerely hoped Dillon would help her figure it out, because he'd seen things like this happen a million times in his former life.

Making an emotional decision to go into business with Neville would be the kiss of death for Toliver's Treasures. Anthony might not know much about what went on at the store, but he did know one thing. It thrived because it stayed small, and it was dedicated to its clientele like no business he'd ever seen. And those fiercely loyal clients chose to spend their money here because Emma genuinely cared about them. She spoiled them rotten. If she spread herself too thin and her clients got neglected, there were a hundred other boutiques that would be more than happy to oblige them.

She was self-destructing and didn't even know it. He'd been there. Making decisions that damned near ruined his life just to prove to himself he was better than his father.

Her situation was a little different, and he understood that what happened downstairs hadn't been intentionally orchestrated to reel him in. But the fact remained that if he stayed, he'd take over the store, leaving Emma free to accept Neville's offer.

She'd have exactly what she wanted. Him. But only as an expedient solution to a problem. He'd have nothing. He might have Emma in body but he'd never have her heart, and he didn't want or need anything else.

Anthony continued to stare out the window while Jim told Charles about last night. They knew they had the right man, given that they'd found Anthony's files, journals and pictures. They'd gotten some equipment, but there wasn't a single fingerprint to be found on anything.

There were many things on Jim's nerves, such as the fact that Anthony hadn't received any e-mails until after the attack. Plus the fact that Dop had stolen files full of information he'd poured into the e-mails and phone calls, leaving high odds that Dop had nothing to do with Anthony's past. But if Dop had come from Emma's camp, Jim still couldn't come up with a clear motive or benefit that involved Anthony, other than Layne's proposed "torture" idea.

"Well, I was thinking last night," Anthony said. "You know how a cat kills something and brings it to you and you're supposed to praise him?"

"Interesting," Jim mused. "But why leave you alive? It just doesn't make sense. See what I'm talking about here? Not a bit of this matches the facts. What the heck is this guy waiting for? He could have moved on Emma a long time ago and no one would have known he was coming. And what kind of person leaves not one stinkin' fingerprint? This guy has skills. Charles, is there anyone we're missing? Vivian's husband. Neville, the jewel guy. Peter Carlson. Help me out."

"I am sorry. I cannot read minds."

"You read mine," Anthony grumbled.

"No. I read Emma's. No need to read the same thing twice."

Jim cracked up and said, "I gotta go find me a bad guy."

When he'd gone, Charles said, "You have that look again. The 'I want to meddle' face."

"Charles, we can't let her lose that rose necklace."

"What do you have in mind?"

"Emma, I'm happy for you. Proud of you, even. But you have to be realistic," said Dr. Dillon, setting his hands in his lap.

"I asked for help," Emma said. "Not realism."

Dr. Dillon sighed and Emma chewed her bottom lip. Damn, this was hard. They'd only had one face-to-face session, and somehow baring your soul was a lot easier over the phone.

He said, "If you have your mind made up, then—"

"But I *don't* have my mind made up. You don't understand. I really don't know what to do about Neville. If I go through with the deal I won't have any time for Anthony. Oh, why does everything have to be so complicated?"

"Because you're making it complicated, Emma. If you truly love him and he truly loves you, none of this will matter. Tell me. Why do you love him?"

Emma blinked at the doctor. "I don't know if I can explain."

"Try."

"He... He's perfect for me. He's smart, he's funny, he listens and he laughs at me when I'm being a nut. Charles says things happen for a reason, and I know you don't really believe it, but I do. Anthony and I make perfect sense. Especially after what happened two years ago. It's like it was always meant to be, but he had to change first."

The doctor nodded. "And why do you think he loves you?"

Rubbing her forehead, she said, "If I could answer that I wouldn't be asking you for help."

"Okay. Let me tell you this. Whenever I do couples counseling I look at behavior patterns, and I think I understand why you're so afraid. You don't believe his changes are strong enough to withstand the demands of your life. Now, while it's a *good* thing he likes this place, it's also confusing. He'll want some control, and he'll deserve that."

"Yes, he will."

"But you won't be good at giving it to him," Dillon said. "So far in your life you've had to answer to precious few people, and no one has the power to hurt you the way Anthony does. And he'll push because that's who he is. You'll get mad. When you get mad, he'll run. When he runs, you'll get even madder. An endless, vicious cycle unless one of you learns to control their behavior pattern. And right now, frankly, I don't see that happening."

Emma paused to think about Dillon's words. They were too true. Anthony was always pushing her, and heaven knows she pushed right back. Unless they struck some sort of balance, they hadn't a prayer of making things work.

"You're right," she finally said. "I don't want to lose him, but this is forever we're talking about. I feel like I'm being forced to make a decision before I'm ready, and I'd hate to give up the Neville deal for something that's not a sure thing."

"Nothing is a sure thing," Dr. Dillon said. "But it sounds to me as if you've already made a decision."

"What?"

"Emma, don't burn the bridge with Neville. Not until you know for sure where Anthony stands."

"But he said the same thing you're trying to—"

"No. You have to think about *why* he said it. He has his own motives. I don't. And that's something you have to think long and hard about before tonight."

"You're right," she sighed. "And you're running late. I'm sorry. I didn't mean to keep you this long."

"You won't get off quite that easy. As long as we're asking why, let's think about that speech you gave Anthony. You've had your doubts all along about Neville, and to me it sounds as if you were asking Anthony to make the decision for you."

Emma let her head fall into her hands. She had been. No doubt about it. One minute she was yelling at Anthony because he was sticking his nose into everything and the next she was practically begging him for advice. Some balance they had going.

"He won't, Emma. He can't. And it's not right for you to make him. Not when you don't know yourself whether what you're feeling is real or just physical."

Oh, now that was the limit. "I wish you'd stop saying that. It's not like that. It was, but not anymore."

"Are you sure?"

She sighed again while Dillon glanced at his watch. He said, "I have to go. If you need me, just call."

They stood, and just like last time, Dillon gave her a hug. "It'll be okay," he said. "You'll make the right decision."

She raised her eyebrows dubiously and walked him out.

They left for the fund-raiser later than planned because Emma was a wreck. And not one of them could blame her. She kept looking at them all, trying to read them, and their nerves were so electric Anthony was sure someone's hair would start on fire.

As they walked into the Whitney's fifth floor ballroom, he scanned the room, not liking the *L* shape. He couldn't see the entire space at once, and that probably accounted for the thick wallpaper of tuxedoed security guards.

Trying to relax, Anthony watched Emma. He'd almost thrown her back in her room when she emerged in that dress. It was silk, the palest green, with straps looking to have the tensile strength of a spider's web. Oh, but it didn't end there. Her hair was neatly coiled atop her head so it wouldn't interfere with the lily, leaving nothing to interfere with a bare back, either.

To his eyes, the lily wasn't the only thing defying physics. Those ridiculous straps were the only things holding up the front of her dress as she clutched the box holding the rose necklace.

And he was trying not to jump to any conclusions. Just because she'd worn the lily and brought the roses didn't mean she'd decided to go through with the Neville deal. He'd have to wait and see what happened.

He had a bad feeling, though. It was the first time in days he'd felt like running. Only this time he'd be taking Emma with him.

And then he heard a familiar laugh and felt Emma tense up.

"There you are!" his mother's voice chirped.

Emma smiled mechanically and Anthony's eyebrows raised as his Mom ignored him completely to kiss Emma on both cheeks. "I'm so glad you could come," Sophia said warmly, and he relaxed a bit more as Emma's smile turned genuine.

Geoff nudged him with his elbow. "Hey."

"Hey, Geoff," Anthony said. "How've you been?"

"Same as always. You?"

"Can't complain."

"You'd be crazy if you did," Geoff told him, stepping forward as his wife introduced him to Emma.

Anthony couldn't help a surge of pride as Emma proceeded to charm his parents' socks off. He didn't know how she did it. His mom was grinning like a fool and even the normally staid Geoff was making fatherly noises as Emma smiled away, saying that she was fine and everything was going to be all right.

Watching Emma, he almost believed it himself.

"Honey," his mother said finally, pushing up on her toes to kiss his cheek. "Forgive me but I have to do some hustling for the hospital. We're all at the same table so we'll see you in a few. And Emma, please make my boy be sociable for once."

Emma laughed. "You don't ask much."

Sophia chuckled knowingly, rubbed Emma's arm and wandered off with Geoff.

"Sorry," Anthony grumbled.

"Don't be. She's wonderful." Emma smiled. The quality of it raised a red flag, and she seemed to be scanning the room with an almost predatory intensity. Who was she looking for—Neville?

Then she said, "Let's go hand this over."

The trip to the stage was very educational for Anthony. There wasn't a single person Emma didn't know in this town, and every last one had seen their picture in the paper. He was razzed a few times by people they both knew, and even had his hand patted by Ginny Lewis, whose card he'd seen at the store. Ginny clucked like a hen but Emma obviously adored the woman.

But the strangest thing was Emma herself, walking half a step behind him, holding his arm. She couldn't have sent a clearer message if she'd grabbed a bullhorn and announced she belonged to him. And judging by some of the looks they received, no one would dare ask anytime soon about the general manager statement Layne had planted in the paper that morning.

By the time the roses were handed over, Anthony's head was spinning.

And all too soon he was introduced to Neville. Right away, suspicion grabbed Anthony by the throat. Neville was at least six-five, young and definitely had an eye for Emma.

But Anthony put a quick damper on the suspicion. Jim said everyone in this room had been checked out down to the color underwear they wore and, given the situation, he needed to check himself. There was a difference between suspicion and dislike.

Anthony was introduced as her general manager and Neville remarked, "Really? I wasn't aware you had one."

"It's only been a few weeks," she said.

"Champagne?" Anthony offered. Best to give her some space.

"Thank you," she said, kissing him.

Well, he thought, that ought to give Neville something to think about. About halfway to the bar he spotted Layne and

Charles, and he hurried in their direction. As he neared, they stepped into the foyer, Layne gesturing for him to hurry.

"Are we all set?" Anthony asked.

"Yes, but it wasn't easy," Layne said. "And it's going to cost you. The auctioneer did not come cheap."

"Who cares about money?"

Anthony slipped away to the bar, then delivered Neville's and Emma's champagne before excusing himself. He roamed, talking to people he hadn't seen for a while, until he accidentally backed into someone and, turning to apologize, found himself face-to-face with his father.

Anthony stared, frozen where he stood. As always, he had the sensation of looking in the mirror. Maxim had a few more gray hairs than the last time he'd seen him, but otherwise nothing had changed.

"Hope I didn't surprise you. Your mother invited me."

"What are you doing here?" Anthony managed to ask.

"Well, I couldn't show up at Emma's, could I? I just wanted to talk to you. To see for myself that you're all right."

"Since when—"

Suddenly Emma was at his elbow, cutting him off. "Hi," she said, hand extended. "I'm Emma Toliver. You must be Maxim."

Anthony ground his teeth. She looked ready to go a few rounds. Maxim shook her hand, returning her inspection, but Anthony could see him waffling already. "A pleasure."

"What brings you here tonight?" she asked. Anthony's hands had gone cold, and when he placed one at the small of her back she glanced at him with eyes sharp as a blade.

"You two," Maxim answered.

"Oh?" she replied with a healthy trace of haughtiness. Anthony needed to end this before she clawed his dad's eyes out. Much as he appreciated the support, the last thing anyone needed right now was a scene.

Maxim didn't help. "You've obviously read the *Art of*

War. Will you offer me a chance to save face, or will you go directly for the kill?''

Without missing a beat, Emma told him, ''Guess you'll have to wait and see, won't you?''

''Emma…'' Anthony called her off, and when that didn't break the stare-down, he said, ''Honey?''

She finally turned icy green eyes to his, and he suggested, ''Why don't you go find Mom and Geoff?''

''I'll do that.''

''Hey,'' he said when she started to turn back to his father. Catching her chin, he brought her close, kissing her before whispering in her ear, ''Thank you, but I'll handle this. Play nice with Mom.''

Emma's back was ramrod straight as she walked away, to be quickly nabbed by Sophia. They disappeared into the foyer, leaving him to roam through this nightmare alone. But it wasn't himself he was worried about. It was Emma. She was in rare form tonight.

''She's lovely,'' his father observed. ''But it would have been nice if Sophia'd warned me about your bodyguard.''

''That's enough.''

''You're reading me wrong, son. I'd say having someone like Emma on your side wasn't altogether a bad thing. You can be sure I won't be allowed to screw up.''

Anthony sighed, the collar of his shirt feeling unnaturally tight as he indexed all the exits from the building. If it weren't for Emma, he'd already be gone.

''So we're taking sides? Drawing battle lines?'' Anthony asked.

Maxim nodded to a quiet corner and as they started walking, he said, ''I know I have a lot to answer for, but I didn't come here to make trouble. You won't take my calls, you moved from hotel to hotel so I couldn't find you. Wasn't quitting my own company enough? What else can I do?''

''You can stop lying. I'm sure that decision had more to do with Celia kicking you out than anything else.''

''All right,'' he admitted. ''There's some truth to that. I

screwed up. I've spent my entire life screwing up. And I almost screwed you up, too. It's a blessing you had the sense to turn out like your mother."

Anthony had no idea what to say. Never once in his entire life had he ever heard Maxim admit he'd been wrong. Especially not in a personal context.

"All I'm asking from you is one more chance. I know I'm to blame for this whole stalker thing, luring you into Bracco the way I did. If I hadn't turned you into me, you never would have attracted that kind of attention."

"I'm responsible for my own actions," Anthony replied. "If you're feeling guilty, don't waste the energy."

He needed out of here. This was too much to handle in one night, and if his father didn't let him leave soon he might crack up long before Emma did.

"I don't know what to say other than I'm sorry," Maxim said. "If I apologize to Emma will you lighten up?"

"Maybe," Anthony answered. "But she won't make it easy."

"I would expect not. However, if she's still speaking to you it says rather a lot about her powers of forgiveness."

He grunted. "I'd better go save Mom."

Maxim didn't follow, and before Anthony made it too far he spotted Brady. He had half a mind to make peace with him but he needed to get back to Emma.

Dinner was painfully uncomfortable for everyone involved. His mother chatted with her two husbands, while Jim, Layne, Brady and Charles kept utterly silent. Emma was jumpy but at least she'd stopped sparring with Maxim.

Things only got worse once the auction started, and as the items sold one by one, Emma edged closer and closer to Anthony until they were practically sharing a chair.

His phone rang, but as the rose necklace was about to go on the block he ignored it, putting a tight, protective arm around Emma.

She shook. Neville did his best but couldn't figure out who he was bidding against. Emma was turning green now, and when Neville gave up at twenty-five thousand, she sighed, "What a disaster."

As the applause erupted, the smile on her face looked painful.

"It's all right, Emma," Anthony said, testing her power to read him. But she was too upset to see it.

"Did you see who won?" she asked.

"No." And that was the extent of the conversation until the auction ended. Others at the table got up to mill around as the orchestra set up, and he felt Emma relax when Brady left.

Anthony asked, "Would you like to go home?"

"I don't think we can. You'll have to ask Layne."

"Emma," he repeated, "do you want to stay or do you want to go home?"

She put her hand on his leg and smiled halfheartedly. "You're sweet, but I can't leave until I've talked to Neville. He probably thinks I'm the rudest person on earth. I handed him my champagne glass when I saw your dad."

Anthony glanced over at Neville's table, doing a double take when he spotted Layne sitting next to the man, sparkling with laughter. At least they were covering their angles.

It was getting late by the time all three of his parents had returned to the table.

"Dance with me?" Emma asked.

He did, although he would have liked to question his folks. They had a lot of explaining to do. But as he took Emma in his arms, memories of last night's passion made him forget everything else for a while as she clung to him, still shaking.

This can't go on forever, he thought. Her body was cracking even if her head wasn't, but it wouldn't be long before something bad happened. She turned her face into his neck and said, "Anthony, I have a confession to make."

"Hmm?"

"I knew Maxim would be here. I should have told you,

and I'm sorry, but I wanted to give him the benefit of the doubt.''

All things considered, namely his mother's powers of persuasion, Anthony just shook his head. ''Emma, it's not your fault. Even if you'd told me, there wasn't anything to be done about it.''

''You're not mad?''

''That would be just a tad hypocritical, don't you think?''

He felt her smile against him and his whole body ached to be back at her apartment, alone with her. But that would never happen until he'd taken care of business.

Gesturing to Jim behind Emma's back, he pointed toward the balcony just a moment before she asked, ''Will you stay with me this time while I talk to Neville?''

''Of course. But come outside first. There's something I need to know before we do this.''

Carefully keeping Emma in front of him, he swept past Jim on the way out, and the handoff was very slick. One-handed, Anthony tucked the box into the back of his pants.

Outside, Emma grabbed the railing and pulled off one shoe.

''Feet hurt?'' he asked, holding out his arm so she could hang on while removing the other.

''Yes. They're killing me.''

''Marry me.''

Emma stood up slowly. ''What did you just say?''

Even in the dim, orange-hued light he could see her blanche. ''I just asked you to marry me.''

She set her shoes on a wrought-iron table. ''Why would you do something like that?''

''You know why, Emma,'' he told her quietly, settling his hands on her waist. ''Can I have a preliminary answer before I decide whether I really want to continue this conversation?''

Green eyes stared in disbelief for a moment, but he could feel her waist constrict in a laugh. And then another. She shook her head. ''Only you would propose to a woman while she's taking off her shoes. Preliminary answer? Maybe.''

''Okay. I can work with that,'' he responded, taking a deep breath before going on. ''Why do you think I called the store? It seemed the only way to get you out of my head was to remind myself how awful you could be.''

''Oh, that's flattering. Thanks.''

''No comments from the peanut gallery, please. It only took me about ten seconds on Monday to realize what I was too stupid to see two years ago.'' He paused for another deep breath. ''I love you, Emma.''

Emma put her arms around him, and before she could happen across the box, he pulled it out and held it up. She stared at it for what seemed like an hour before asking, ''What have you done?''

''I bought the necklace.''

She sighed at the oversimplified answer. ''How?''

''Not important. But I should tell you this first. You know how Charles is always saying things happen for a reason?''

''Yes,'' she said, drawing the word out dubiously.

''When you showed me this necklace earlier, I recognized where the idea came from and I know why it's so important to you. Can't get married without it, and I don't want you to. I don't want our daughters getting married without it, either.''

Emma pried her eyes off the box to stare at him, hints of confusion and distrust chasing each other over her features. But there was something else there, too, which didn't prepare him for her cold reply. ''So you think our daughters are getting married wearing that necklace.''

''Can you stop *doing that to me?*'' he pleaded. ''Why can't you just say what you think instead of throwing everything I say back into my face?''

She stepped back from him and answered, ''Because I don't know what to say! You know I love you, but trust me, it isn't easy. Every time I turn around you're doing something that makes me want to scream.''

"I didn't mean to hurt you with the auction. Either auction," he said, overwhelmed with relief that she'd said she loved him, and hoping to God that they survived the next ten minutes, because he had a lot to say if she'd give him a chance to say it.

"Either auction?" She groaned. "Please, someone tell me this isn't happening. What did you do, Anthony?"

"I need you to understand something before I explain. We never meant for you to find out about this, and you never would have if Dop hadn't shown up."

"Is that supposed to make me feel better? And who's 'we'?"

"Oh Emma, I'm so sorry," he breathed. Anthony couldn't stand this but he absolutely had to get it all out. "I don't know where to start. I did call the shop and I spoke to Charles. For a long time, Emma. Since that day, he's known everything I told you last night. I don't know how he got it out of me, but that's exactly what happened."

"Oh, God," she groaned.

"Just hear me out. I didn't mean to keep talking to him. Honestly. But I did. Not much until you started preparing your bid for the materials auction, and before you blow up, listen to me. He loves you like you're his own daughter, and he knows what kind of pressure you're under. He knew your expendable capital wasn't enough, so he asked me for help, knowing I'd do it. So we padded your upper limit."

By the time he finished, she was clutching her head.

"I would never have done it if there was any chance you'd find out. I knew I was crossing a line, but I felt so guilty I couldn't stand it anymore."

In a voice that froze his spine she said, "That would explain the discrepancy in the insurance appraisal, now wouldn't it? How much do I owe you?"

"No way, Emma. Forget it. You needed that auction lot and what's done is done."

She didn't say anything for a while, just curled her arms around herself and stared at her feet. He was getting ready to panic when she finally asked, "Is that what Layne's been holding over your head this entire time?"

"Yes. My job was to keep you here and keep the store open, business as usual, or she'd tell you. And before you can ask, no, nothing that went on between us had anything to do with her. I love you and I would have done it anyway to keep you here where you're safe."

"Safe? From what? From being hurt? Nice work."

"Emma, please. I've told you everything now, and I hope you aren't mad at Charles. He's been acting weird because he knew about the attack. Jim wouldn't let him tell you, but as soon as Brady described your e-mails to him, he called me. And both he and I feel guilty about the auction, but it was better than standing by, doing nothing while you needed help."

She turned away from him, one hand on her hip, the other rubbing her forehead.

"Emma, say something."

"How *could* you? I don't… How do you expect me to feel?"

"I knew you'd be mad," he sighed, and when he moved to touch her she stepped away. "Emma, what's—"

"No." She cut him off. "Don't say it. Don't you dare say that to me again."

"Say what?"

"What's done is done. Can't change it. Whichever platitude you were going slap on this like a bandage. You've even got me doing it now, and I can't live with dishonesty like this, Anthony. It's over. We can't keep hurting each other and then excuse it away with 'Oh darn, I've done it again. Whoops. No big deal.' I can understand what you did with Charles, maybe, but if you knew I'd be mad, why did you do it again tonight? When is this going to stop? And what am I supposed to tell Neville?" Emma stared at Anthony with a look of barely controlled fury.

"Now hang on a minute, Emma," he said. "This morning you said you couldn't do this without help, and just because you can't get off the fence doesn't mean I'm stuck, too. Okay, so maybe I crossed the line, but I didn't do it to force you into anything."

"The hell you didn't," she said. "You thought you could buy your way in. Again."

He was clenching his teeth so hard he thought his jaw would break. Damn it. Would she ever stop pinning the worst possible motive on things? He didn't want to fight with her, but if she kept this up he'd give her a taste of her own medicine.

And his father chose that moment to come through the door with Trenton Neville. "There they are," Neville said. "I didn't know Maxim was your father. You should have said something. What a small world this is."

"Teeny tiny," Emma muttered, slipping her shoes back on.

Anthony stayed silent as she turned around, so pale her skin looked transparent.

Neville saw the box in Anthony's hand and asked, "Is that the rose necklace?"

Anthony watched the hem of Emma's dress start to shake. What was he supposed to do here?

Grasping at straws, he said, "Yes. There was a mixup with the event coordinator. The wrong piece was delivered, so the company bought it back. Emma meant to tell you beforehand, but my father surprised her and they started chatting. You know how he gets."

"Ah, yes," Neville said. "Well, no harm done. I would have gotten myself in trouble with the IRS eventually, anyhow. But I'd like to talk about production."

"The rose necklace is one of a kind, Neville," Anthony told him. "And we'll patent it, too, if you make it necessary."

"Guess you were right, Max. He fights dirty."

One of Maxim's eyebrows arched. "The jewelry business isn't a cushy place. Stick around long enough and you're bound to get yours sooner or later."

"Truer words were never spoken," Neville said. "What about the lily? What are your plans?"

Anthony looked at Emma for an answer. All he got was a pale, blank expression. And he could feel his father's eyes dissecting him. Why did Maxim have to be out here? He'd known there was trouble and he'd somehow use it against Anthony.

But it was Maxim who said, "I think it's a bit premature for plans. Emma's gone through rather a lot lately, and a charity event is hardly the time or place to discuss these things."

"What is this?" Neville laughed. "A tag team? I can't tell if y'all drive a really hard bargain or if you're trying to edge me out completely."

Maxim laughed in turn. "You can't be edged out of something you never had, Neville. You always get yourself in trouble with that."

"Yes I do, don't I?" Neville answered. "Let's go drink too much Scotch. You," he said to Emma, "may call me anytime you like, and Neville Enterprises will extend the red carpet."

She managed a tight smile as Maxim said, "Give me a moment."

Neville went back inside, and his father asked, "What's going on out here?"

Here we go. Questions from the Antichrist of relationships.

"Nothing," Emma said. "Excuse me." She went inside, out of Anthony's sight, no doubt on purpose.

Two options. Staring at his father, Anthony decided that running had its appeal. The other option was to stop running and start talking.

Brady might have had zero luck getting through to Emma, but Brady had never been in her position. Anthony had. He'd survived the death of his ego and he was better for it. And maybe it really was time someone gave her a dose of her own medicine. Point out some simple truths she'd hate him for, then pray like hell that Charles was right about everything happening for a reason.

Turning to Maxim, Anthony said, ''Go entertain Neville. I'll call you tomorrow.''

''Sure you will.''

''Please don't start with me,'' Anthony warned, holding up a hand. ''I need to take care of this.''

''Go ahead. Good luck. Yell if you want me to call 911.''

Anthony rolled his eyes and took off after Emma.

Chapter 13

Emma found a bathroom far from the ballroom, too numb to do anything but hide. Charles. It was simply inconceivable he'd do something like this behind her back.

She wanted to believe it had been Anthony's idea, but she knew better. There was no way he could have known about the auction if Charles hadn't told.

What a nightmare. Right now she was glad she still had time to decide what to do about Neville. Something to keep her occupied while she spent the rest of her life regretting she'd ever met Anthony Bracco.

Emma sank into a chair and supported her head with cold hands. Unbelievable. Anthony just couldn't help but meddle, and whenever she found herself thinking he couldn't possibly push any further, he proved her wrong. First the debacle two years ago, followed by last night's career suicide confession. And now he'd manipulated the Red Cross auction, which was nothing in comparison to the materials auction.

Charles had played a role in that, and part of her understood why Anthony had done it. Guilt was a powerful force, but no matter the platitudes he offered, Anthony had no right to interfere in Beautiful Things, tainting that one jewel in her crown that she'd worked so hard to earn.

And what stunned her was that he'd known perfectly well she'd be mad, but he'd done it anyway. When would it ever stop?

Dr. Dillon was right about everything. That vicious cycle was already turning and neither Anthony nor she could stop it.

Emma jumped as the bathroom door opened and in came Anthony, locking the door behind him.

Please don't let him do this, she thought. She couldn't take any more. She just wanted to be numb. Big surprise he'd show up to push again.

He dumped her purse on the vanity and asked, "You know what the only difference is between you and me?"

Emma frowned at him as he tugged his bow tie free and sent it and his jacket flying after her purse. "What?"

"You draw blood before you run. But you run, just like me. How many times have you taken off for a bathroom or the greenhouse? That doesn't even begin to cover the times you've simply retreated into happy denial land. And you know what worries me?"

She waited, knowing he'd come out with it. This would be Anthony's attempt at bloodletting before goodbye, and if she could stand it for a few more minutes she'd be okay. He'd leave and it would be over.

"When's it gonna end?" he asked. "When you've driven yourself into exhaustion?"

"Anthony, stop. Dillon said we were awful for each other and he's right. This isn't love. This is… I don't know what it is. A power struggle and plain old lust, I guess. Neither one of us can tell those two apart."

"Stop talking. It's not lust and love you can't tell apart, it's your father and every other man you meet. The bad thing is, a lot of men *are* like your father. They never figure out what's important until it's too late. My father's a prime example. So was I, until I finally figured it out. But because your father never did, you and I will both suffer."

"*Go away!*" Couldn't he see what he was doing? She was trying to save them more pain and he was prolonging it.

"Yell all you like. But I'll *always* love you and nothing you do will ever change that. Me? I get to leave here knowing you only love the parts of me you can deal with. The rest of me doesn't matter as long as I don't interfere with anything important."

She wanted to deny that. Hotly. But she couldn't. "Why are you doing this? If you're leaving, please just go."

"I'm not going anywhere until you understand I've been where you are, Emma. I made some stupid decisions, but you still have a choice. You can take stock and learn what matters before you dive facefirst into hell like I did."

"That won't happen," she said. "Dillon and Charles won't let it. I won't, either."

"Bull. You wanna take advice from someone, take it from me. I'm the one who loves you. And I'm the one who'll have to put up with being treated like I don't matter. How would you like that, Emma? How would you like it if Neville had that rose necklace right now and I let you get away with this crap?"

"Yes, well, apparently it doesn't matter what I'd like. You'll do what you want, anyway."

Anthony turned crimson. "Stop it, Emma. You don't get to blame me for this one. How do you think I feel, knowing what you've got planned for me?"

What? She stared at him and he stared right back. He wasn't about to give up. "What have I got planned for you?"

"You want me to take over the store so you can go into business with Neville. That's some relationship. You'll never have time to feel anything and that's exactly the way you like it."

''That's not—'' She started to argue but couldn't even finish. She was so tired. Of everything.

But Anthony still had a few bullets left. ''Dop can't go on forever, and I'm gone. Neville will be waiting, so the onus is on you.''

''Imagine that. Go,'' she said, the words coming out in a watery gulp. ''Layne can't stop you now, so just go back up north and forget you ever knew me.''

He cursed under his breath and Emma flinched as he pulled her up. ''Haven't you heard a word I've said to you?'' he demanded. ''Dillon's wrong and Charles is right. He told me that once you let someone into your heart, that space is there forever whether you like it or not. But I can only fill one space. I can't make up for everyone who's died or left you holding the bag.''

''I never asked you to—''

''Emma, you would never have to ask and that's the difference between lust and love. I changed. I know how to put you first. Always. But you won't—you can't—do the same for me. *That's* why I'm leaving. You can't give me all of your heart and I can't accept less.''

She understood, and for just a moment she let herself feel the pain. But the numbness was right there to save her, and she said, ''Fine, then go.''

Anthony shook his head and started to say something else, but his cellphone stopped him. He answered, then breathed, ''What? Are they... No. I won't. We'll meet you downstairs.''

Shrugging back into his coat, he said, ''We need to go. *Now.*''

He grabbed her arm and unlocked the door, dragging her after him while she demanded to know why they were leaving.

''I'll tell you on the way,'' he said, pushing through a stairway door and stopping only long enough to bend down to take her shoes off.

"We need to run?" she gasped through a throat tight with fear.

Anthony didn't answer, and Emma was completely out of breath by the time they hit the lobby. They stepped right into a car, Jim barely giving them time to get in before taking off.

Layne was on the phone and her hushed, hurried tone made the hairs on Emma's neck stand up. Something was very wrong, and once again, Anthony didn't want to tell her. She saw him catch Jim's eye in the rearview mirror, and Jim shook his head.

Emma couldn't wait for the mind games to end. "If one of you doesn't tell me what's going on I'll—"

Anthony sighed and took her hand. "While we were on the balcony, Brady and Charles were sent home with one of the agents. The police were called to Brady's address about thirty minutes ago. We don't know what happened yet because it's taken this long for the police to get ahold of our people."

Emma could feel her chest tightening already. If anything had happened to them there would be hell to pay.

"Breathe, Emma. In and out. Slowly. Come on. We need you to hold it together."

Anthony grabbed her, but wasn't fast enough. Emma fainted before she fully hyperventilated.

"How could you send them home with one man?" Anthony demanded, gently maneuvering Emma so she was lying across his lap.

"Anthony, can we not do this now?" Jim argued. "Your parents are meeting us at the hospital and you can hand her over to your mom while we find out exactly what happened. We've pulled everyone available to the scene, so we should know something soon."

"You don't know how bad anyone's been hurt?"

Layne lowered her phone to say, "The agent's still unconscious. One of the EMTs told someone that Charles is all right, but Brady's in pretty bad shape."

"Oh, God," Anthony groaned, and looked down at Emma. She wouldn't be able to handle this.

Emma was still out cold when they reached the hospital, but she started coming to as Anthony carried her inside. His mother flew into action, taking her to a closed-off section of the emergency room, far from the hectic activity.

People were hurrying in every direction and Anthony felt like he was in a war zone. It got worse when Geoff took him into a trauma room where a team swarmed around Brady.

It was bad. Anthony didn't need Geoff's assessment of internal injuries to know that. But Brady would be in Geoff's hands soon and if anyone could save him, Geoff could.

When Geoff left to prepare for Brady's surgery, Anthony slipped next door where Charles was having a minor scalp wound and an x-shaped cut on his left arm cleaned before suturing.

Jim and Layne were already questioning him about why they'd all gotten out of the car. The answer was simple. Brady had finished off the night with a few too many drinks, and Agent Sloan hadn't dared let Brady stumble up the stairs by himself. So he'd made Charles come with them. Dop had been wearing the ski mask again, and the only new bit of information Charles could offer was that Dop had said something about rocks.

"Rocks?" Layne asked.

"I think so. That may not even have been what he said. I had been hit on the head and woke up to find my arm bleeding and Dop standing over Brady..." Charles trailed off, closing his eyes to block out the memory.

Anthony shook his head. Charles was too gentle a soul to handle this. But at least he was physically fine. Mostly.

A moment later Charles was making a joke about Emma's men having matching scars. All things considered, it wasn't funny, but Anthony smiled anyway.

On the other side of the E.R. another crew was working

on Agent Sloan. Dop had attacked from the darkened foyer of Brady's apartment building, and the agent had been wearing a bulletproof vest. Dop's first swipe of the knife had deflected off the vest but connected with his neck and chin, sending him backward down cement stairs. The large veins and arteries had been missed, but the man would need X rays from his fall and surgery to clean and close the wound.

Returning to the doorway of the trauma room, Anthony watched as the team tried to stabilize Brady, thankful that when he himself had been the one on the table, he'd been unconscious before, during, and after all that.

He put his hands in his pockets, not sure if he was ready to save Sophia from Emma. She still had him reeling. He'd truly believed that if they had it out once and for all, everything would be okay. He was the one who never wanted to talk. He'd made the effort, but nothing had changed. If anything, he was more confused than ever.

He knew one thing, though. He wasn't going back to the store. His house was ready now and until Dop was caught, that's where he'd be because Dillon had a point. Sometimes he and Emma were perfect together, but most of the time they were awful. Sooner or later, one of them would go too far.

And it stung, knowing he wasn't innocent. He'd forgotten his own rules, and he'd pushed too hard.

Okay, so maybe Dillon was more right than he'd thought. He didn't care much for Dillon's lust and love crap, however. From what Anthony had seen, all Dillon had accomplished earlier was to make Emma a nervous, confused mess. She should have felt better after that session, not worse.

It bordered on malpractice in Anthony's book, but Emma was out of his hands now.

The only thing that had the power to change his mind was Brady. If he died, Anthony would stay. For a while, at least. He wouldn't be able to live with himself if he left when Emma needed more than Charles. Or Dillon, who obviously didn't know how to help her.

Maxim came up beside him, saying nothing. What was there to say? Life was strange. Here he was, standing with his father, watching the same thing happen to Brady that had happened to him. He felt like the Ghost of Christmas Past.

"Will he make it?" Maxim asked.

"Not sure."

Anthony saw his father's face go white, and understood now why Maxim was here. Guilt, plain and simple. Anthony didn't know yet if he could handle a repentant Maxim. But it looked as though he'd be expected to try.

Maxim said, "You should go help your mother. Emma's not being very cooperative."

"You've been in there and exited alive?"

His father laughed. "Barely. But I suppose I should go pour Neville into a cab. This has been the most memorable business trip of his life."

"He's here?" Anthony asked, surprised for some reason.

"Yep. In the lobby."

"He's been with you all night?"

"Yeah. Why?"

Anthony had a flash of something in his head. "Go put him in a cab. I need to talk to Emma for a minute."

As he hurried through the emergency room, information clicked through his head.

Rocks. Something about rocks. Charles might not be sure that's what he'd heard, but it would be pretty hard to mistake that word for anything else.

Rocks. What rocks?

Anthony stopped dead in his tracks as the proverbial light bulb exploded over his head. They'd been wrong. Completely wrong. No, this wasn't about him. But it might not really be about Emma, either.

Rocks. Stones. A million dollars' worth of cut and uncut, easy-to-transport stones. God only knew what their street value would be. Right under their noses and they'd never given them even a moment of serious consideration.

Dop was sixty miles ahead of them. Changing his guise from one minute to the next. Keeping the FBI scrambling to protect human targets, when the truth might be that all Dop was waiting for was delivery of those stones and an empty building.

And Jim had pulled the last two agents off the store to cover their bases after Dop had attacked Brady and Charles.

The pieces fit, but he still had no idea who it could be. All the employees and a handful of clients who knew those stones had been delivered. Dop might have been watching from the street. But after the fiasco the other night, and Dop disguising his voice, it had to be someone close.

He needed to know who Emma had told about—

Anthony broke into a run. He knew who it was. It had to be Dillon. He fit the physical profile of Anthony's attacker. He'd just seemed so innocuous and nonthreatening they'd overlooked it.

So what if his credentials had checked out? That didn't mean a therapist couldn't sideline as a jewel thief. Or that a jewel thief could set up false credentials to sideline as a therapist.

The bottom line was, no one else would have been privy to that much information about Emma. Or himself. Or the FBI.

And it would explain a lot of Emma's behavior today. God only knew what Dillon had said to her this afternoon. Judging by the belligerent tone of Dop's two last e-mails, they were probably lucky Dillon hadn't killed her on the spot.

Crazy, Anthony thought. This is way too crazy to be true. But if he was right, some demented whack-job had been messing with Emma's head for three months.

Three months. The timing was perfect. Emma had started seeing Dillon two weeks after the trades had announced she'd won the auction. And Dillon had relocated here *after* the announcement.

Really crazy. But he had to make sure. He knew Emma had told him about the materials auction. She told him everything because she trusted that sick son of a bitch.

When Anthony found Emma, she and his mother were sitting side by side on a gurney wearing matching scrubs. Emma was demanding to see Brady and Charles. Sophia was comforting her as best she could.

Anthony asked if they knew where Layne and Jim were.

"No." Emma shook her head. "What did you do with the rose necklace?"

"I gave it to Layne for safekeeping, Emma," he said carefully. "I'll get you the roses, but I need to know if you told Dillon when your auction lot arrived."

Emma gave him a look. "Yes, I told him. Unlike you, I don't keep secrets."

Anthony sighed. He needed to find Jim. Fast. "I'll be right back. You two don't leave this room," he ordered.

He left them there and caught Jim rushing for the door. "Hey!" Anthony called.

"I can't stay. Melinda's got computer activity again."

Computer activity? Why would Dillon do that? To make sure the FBI kept running in circles? "Hang on," Anthony said. "Are you absolutely positive Dillon checks out?

"Why?"

"Listen to me. The auction lot. We got it just a couple weeks before Emma started seeing Dillon. Crazy as this sounds, I think Dillon's going after those stones. Think about it. Rocks?"

Jim stared through him for a moment, then said, "Find Layne and tell her what you just told me. Sorry, but I gotta follow up on the computer activity, even if it's a wild-goose chase. If you don't find her, call me."

Anthony nodded. "Go. But make sure whoever's listening to the phone calls doesn't hang up if Dillon calls Emma."

"Done." Jim said. "Get going."

Anthony went in search of Layne but she was nowhere

to be found. All the other agents were either still at the scene or on the move with Jim.

Okay. Now what? Jim said to call him, but he was busy. And the whole idea was insane anyway.

The store was only five minutes away. If he called the police, they'd take forever to get there. Might as well go scout it out and spare everyone a big drama over nothing.

Anthony hailed a cab and with a little inducement made it in three minutes. And as soon as he saw the control panel through the front window, he knew he'd been right. The alarm was shut off completely.

He pulled out his cellphone and called Jim, explaining where he was and informing him he'd never found Layne.

"I know I shouldn't have come over here, but—"

"Yeah, well, too late. I'm on my way. But you *stay out* of that store, you hear me? Get someplace safe and we'll be there in ten minutes." He hung up.

Taking a deep breath, he caught the sharp tang of gasoline and looked around for the source. Moving a little closer to the front door, the smell was stronger.

Oh, God. Dillon was going to burn out the store.

Knowing he shouldn't, he opened the door, and the smell of gasoline was sickening. He sprinted up the steps, groaning as he saw the century-old oak paneling marred with jagged *X*s. Emma would explode when she saw that.

Anthony rushed into the workroom, and there was Dillon with two enormous duffle bags slung over his shoulders, almost breaking him in half with their weight. The vault's ship-wheel handle had been damaged during his hacking, and a small electronic device hung from yellow and red wires below the digital combination lock.

Dillon's head snapped up in surprise, and all Anthony could think to say was "Put those down."

Dillon's eyebrows raised. "Well, well. Looks like someone around here has a brain after all."

"Sick bastard. Scaring her with the e-mails and pulling her apart with your so-called therapy."

Pulling the bags off his shoulders, Dillon said, "Okay, you got me. But this whole thing is your fault. You weren't supposed to come home that night and when you did I had no choice."

Anthony crossed his arms over his chest. He didn't understand why Dillon wanted to talk, but it would buy time until Jim arrived. "Why the *X*?" he asked.

"Thought it would make a nice calling card. That's what they look for, you know. Far better they were looking for a deranged lunatic than a simple thief."

Anthony rolled his eyes. "Why were you at my house?"

"To see what I could find out about you. Learn how to break the hold you have on Emma."

"Not possible."

"Debatable. And if you'd just stayed gone, none of this would have happened. You screwed the whole thing up. But your journals and my impromptu artwork on your back gave me the perfect method to keep the FBI focused on you instead of Emma."

"Then why did you start e-mailing her? Seems to me you'd have been better off keeping quiet."

"I thought she'd run." Dillon shrugged. "I didn't want her in harm's way when the time came, but Carlson hung on to the stones forever. And then you and your FBI friends showed up. It's your fault I had to get more aggressive."

His fault. Right. He needed more time. Had to keep Dillon talking, but he was getting fidgety.

"How did it start? With the stones or Emma?"

Dillon laughed. "The stones. I'd been watching that auction lot and when she won I started casing this place. And then her. It was so easy, Anthony. The building might be secure, but the computers aren't. I learned everything I needed to know by hacking. The security codes, the vault specs, everything. And then I intercepted her request for a therapist referral. After some more computer magic, next thing I know? I'm her therapist. Red carpet right into her head."

Good God. What had he done to her?

Dillon continued. ''She was only too delighted to do our sessions over the phone. If she'd ever come to the office your friends raided last night that would have been a huge problem.''

Anthony shook his head. ''So you've had the inside track all along, just waiting until the stones arrived. And Emma's told you everything the FBI's been doing this week. Pretty slick.''

''Yes, and her input was very useful in learning how to get the FBI out of the store. Last night's computer games were a test. After that, I knew if I hurt someone they'd pull the last two agents to cover the scene.''

''How could you do that? Charles is the best thing in Emma's life but you carved him up anyway. And Brady's barely hanging on.''

''Charles and Brady were your fault. That was supposed to be you. The only thing I needed was nightfall, and for you to answer your phone at the Whitney. Figured you'd do the macho routine again and I could pick you off in the street. Competition would be eliminated, and I'd have free run of the store for hours. But no. You were too caught up with *my* Emma to answer your damned phone.''

Anthony said, ''Pretty stupid of you not to kill me Tuesday night when you had the chance.''

''No. Not stupid. Careful. I couldn't risk potshots with Emma anywhere near. You saved your own life, throwing her in that greenhouse, you know. One stray bullet and she might have been hurt.''

Anthony stared. ''You think everything else you've done hasn't hurt her? What's wrong with you?''

''I *love* her. I never meant to hurt her but you made me. And I wouldn't need to kill you if you hadn't touched her. But it'll work out. The beauty of it is she'll come to me for comfort. Her design business is ruined without these stones, the store will be burned out, you'll be dead. What else can she do?

Anthony's brain was going full throttle, trying to figure how much time had passed. Dillon was getting more agitated by the second. He might not have much time left before things got out of hand.

He needed leverage. Leverage would be good. Winging it, he said, "You underestimate her, Dillon. She's not as pliable as you think, and we had an interesting talk about you this evening."

Dillon stiffened. Bull's-eye.

"What did she say?"

"After I've walked you outside, I'll tell you."

"Forget it, Bracco. I won't leave without destroying this place. You know that. Now what did she say?"

"I'm not saying a word until you leave. And we don't have much time. The FBI's already on their way here."

"I almost hate to kill you. You're smart and I like that," Dillon said.

"If I let you take the stones *and* tell you what Emma said, will you leave?"

"Stop. You can't win by fooling me, so don't waste our time. If you just let me knock you unconscious you won't feel a thing."

"Bring it on, Dop."

Dillon smiled. "Ooh, ready for round two? You didn't fare too well last time."

"I'm not a violent man. But I'll bet you are. Been to therapy for that? How many shrinks have you seen in your lifetime? Could you see straight through them like Emma does?"

A blatant lie, but Dillon didn't need to know that.

And it backfired. Dillon moved fast. Anthony avoided the first strike and drove his fist into the man's stomach so hard the force lifted him off his feet. A rush of air poured from Dillon's lungs and he stumbled forward, then straightened as though Anthony hadn't touched him.

"Sorry, Anthony," Dillon croaked. "I suppose I should warn you that I was once in the Special Forces."

A fist Anthony couldn't avoid flew forward, smashing into his jaw. His head snapped sideways but he kept his feet. "What's the matter, Dop? Saving it for the feds?"

Anthony swung then, his hand erupting into pain as it connected with Dillon's skull. The man went down hard, his head cracking into the edge of a workbench.

Going for his phone, Anthony knelt down to take a pulse and make sure he hadn't killed him.

Dillon had a strong pulse. And quick reflexes. His hands flew up and chopped Anthony on the sides of the neck.

Stars. Everywhere. He was about to pass out. The phone fell from his hand and Dillon was up, driving a knee into his back.

Anthony vaguely registered the sounds of Dillon fumbling with something. Then the feel of wire biting into his wrists.

"Let's see if you were a good boy and put Emma on speed dial."

Anthony croaked out a curse, and Dillon responded by grinding a knee into his ribs.

"Watch your mouth," Dillon scolded, dragging him off the floor and slamming him into a chair. A bomb blast of pain exploded in Anthony's chest. Still seeing stars, he planted his feet to keep from falling over as the wire sliced into his skin.

The phone beeped and Dillon laughed. "There she is. All right. You have one last chance to tell me what she said."

"It doesn't matter. She won't come. Emma's not stupid."

"She is when it comes to you," Dillon said. "This'll be fun."

The phone beeped again and Anthony kicked at him.

He couldn't block the blow that smashed into his chin and made his ears ring. But he could still hear the phone conversation. "Emma? This is Doctor Dillon. I need you to listen very carefully."

There was a delay before he stated, "He's here with me and very upset. What did you say to him tonight?"

Panic hit Anthony like a freight train. Emma had just asked where he was, but she'd know that if Jim had made it to the hospital. What if he hadn't, and Emma didn't know about Dillon yet? He had to warn her, but his jaw and chest were on fire.

"What?" Dillon cried. "My God, that's horrible! No, he didn't tell me. What happened? Are they okay? Are *you* okay?"

Another pause. "If you're coming home we can meet you there. In fact we could probably beat you there," Dillon said, hitting Anthony in the arm.

Sick son of a bitch. "Emma, don't!" he shouted.

A foot crashed into his ribs and Anthony could hardly breathe as he heard, "Don't talk to me like that, Emma. Tell you what. You bring me the rose necklace and I'll let him live. But just so you'll know I'm serious, let's give you a time limit."

A familiar, blazing pain ripped across Anthony's shoulder as Dillon slashed him with the knife.

"I just cut him, Emma. If you can get here in time without telling the FBI, you might be able to save him. Get the necklace here— What? Why you little—"

The phone smashed into the wall and Dillon howled. Well, that's Emma, Anthony thought, watching with detached interest as the man Emma had relied upon to rid her of the temper kicked chairs over, then turned on him.

"She just killed you," he snarled.

"No, you just killed yourself," Anthony retorted, fighting to stay awake.

"Think you're awfully clever, don't you? It won't work. I know how to talk to Emma. She'll come around. And when she does, you'll find out who she really loves."

"She doesn't love you. She loves me. She'll never want you."

Dillon said, "Time to shut up, Bracco. If you're lucky, you might still be alive to watch me prove you wrong. But if you're right, God help you both."

It took everything Anthony had left to laugh. "You really are an idiot, aren't you?"

The last thing Anthony saw for a while was a fist.

Later—he didn't know how much later—Emma was standing ten feet away, staring at him. Something was different. The roses. They were around her neck, over a familiar sweatshirt. One with a blotch of blue paint on the *U* in University of Illinois at Chicago. Jim's sweatshirt.

Why was she wearing Jim's sweatshirt?

Oh, hell. They'd wired her.

Dillon was to the left, talking.

Anthony shook his head to clear it, wincing at an answering blast of pain. He could only see out of one eye, but he could see Emma. She was green. It wasn't his eyesight. She was terrified.

Dillon didn't notice. "If you'd just listen to me," he was saying. "We need to talk. I didn't mean to—"

Anthony jumped and felt another crushing wave of pain when Emma suddenly barked, "You *idiot!* Why did you have to do that? Now everyone'll know!"

Confusion. Dillon asked, "Why did I do what?"

"Mark up the store! And gasoline? What were you thinking? God! I thought you were smarter than that."

"I am! I am smart!" Dillon protested. "Emma, I love you. Can't we—"

"Shut up," she snapped. "I don't know why I wasted all that time with you. I thought you understood what I wanted. To be free of him. Free of this place. He wouldn't want me if I didn't have it."

Oh, Emma. Did she have any idea what she was saying? He hoped she didn't honestly believe that. That she was only saying it because she was scared.

Dillon pleaded, "I knew you were trying to tell me something, Emma. I did. Please tell me what you want. Whatever it is, I'll give it to you."

Don't. Emma, please don't. She didn't seem to realize how dangerous this guy was. And where the hell was Jim?

Anthony could feel the sticky wetness of blood dripping down his back. Even if he could get the wires off his wrists he wouldn't be able to fight Dillon.

But she knew. She was goading him about intelligence. Like Jim had said.

"I want you to put that knife down before you hurt yourself," Emma soothed.

Dillon faced Anthony, gloating. "I told you. It's me she loves, not you." He turned back to Emma and set the knife down on a workbench.

She was safer. Anthony started to drift but fought the peaceful lure of unconsciousness again.

"You don't care about him at all, do you?" Dillon asked.

"Of course not," Emma said. "I want someone like you. Why do you think I went through therapists like water before I found you? I *need* you. You help me see things I couldn't see before."

Dillon took a few steps and Emma added, "Like that picture in the paper. Disgusting. But you showed me."

A few more steps. Please don't let him get any closer, Anthony prayed.

"I knew you'd see it, Emma. You belong to me, not him."

"I do," she said.

Only a foot away. Emma moving her right arm, wiggling it. Something in her sleeve…Anthony couldn't see what.

"We can go away from here. I'll love you like—"

There was a sharp zapping sound and Dillon jumped.

Then crumpled.

"Shut up, freak," Emma said, stepping over him and dropping the stun gun before rushing to Anthony. She was even more vividly green now, but his eyesight was getting blurry.

Too many punches and too much blood lost, he thought, feeling a buzz in his shoulder as Emma checked the wound. Then she was crouching before him, ordering, "Anthony, talk to me. Come on. Help will be here in a second. Stay awake, okay? You promised we'd be all right. Oh, God—''

Her hand felt like ice on his cheek, and if he'd had enough energy he'd have struck a match to this place himself. Maybe then she'd understand that the store had nothing to do with how he felt about her.

He tried to tell her he loved her but his mouth wouldn't cooperate.

''Anthony, stay awake, please!''

She moved then, tugging the wire off his wrists and pressing something soft against his shoulder.

Noise. Everywhere. Feet on the steps. Jim yelling. Maxim and Geoff yelling louder. And Emma yelling loudest as hands lifted him from the chair.

Chapter 14

Emma stood beside Sophia outside an exam room, listening while Anthony grumbled at the doctor trying to change his shoulder dressing.

It was six o'clock in the morning. Both women were exhausted, but Anthony's complaints were like music to Emma's ears.

Everything was flooding back to her now, from Layne and Jim racing in and scaring them all half to death, to Dillon on the phone. She could barely remember what he'd said. She'd just shut down. The fear, the horror and the helplessness had been so overwhelming she had no idea how she'd survived those agonizing minutes it took to rig her with the microphone, make sure the stun gun was charged and race to the store.

They hadn't been sure what they'd find when they got there, but she'd been okay when Hornsby turned the cameras back on and they saw one of Anthony's hands move. He was unconscious but alive.

And she'd held her breath while agents stole silently

through the loading dock to set up positions before she had to go in.

For a few seconds upstairs, she believed they were too late.

Seeing Anthony bloodied and bruised sent her mind straight out the window. Dillon had been talking but she couldn't even listen. All she could do was stare at the man she loved, who'd been brutalized for no reason other than her, and a few chunks of rock.

Then Anthony woke up and the temper had to be managed. All she was supposed to do was get Dillon to say he'd attacked Brady and Charles. If he got too close she could zap him, but the only thing on her mind had been making him put that knife down before he finally succeeded in killing Anthony.

Zapping that lunatic had felt good, though. She'd never get over the fact she'd paid someone to torment and rob her. How could she have been so blind?

She kept thinking she should have known somehow. That every time Dillon said something that rang false, she should have asked questions. But no. It was much easier to believe Dillon's survival of the species garbage than to listen to her own heart about Anthony.

Anthony, who'd done more in five minutes than years of therapy combined. When he'd said he could only fill one space it was like he'd walked into her heart and turned on the lights.

Getting her head around that concept would take a while, she knew, and she hoped he'd change his mind and stay. If Sophia let her see him, she'd apologize like there was no tomorrow.

Bad timing, however. He was a mess. He'd had fluids, his shoulder was stitched up and he'd been through a round of X rays. His ribs were sore but intact, and his eye and the surrounding bone were unharmed, thank God.

"Men make such crappy patients," Sophia sighed.

Emma managed a smile before Anthony let out a stream of Italian that made Sophia cringe.

"Now I know I didn't teach him that," Sophia sputtered. "When he was a boy I said all the bad things in Italian, thinking he didn't understand. Obviously he did. But he's grown quite the vocabulary since then. Good Lord."

Emma knew Sophia was only talking for the sake of talking. So she said, "If you need to have a nervous breakdown, go ahead. I'll join you as soon as Geoff comes down with more news."

"No. No nervous breakdowns. Brady will be fine. And Mr. Potty Mouth's definitely on the mend. They'll hold him under observation, though, so you can't take him home quite yet."

A cold hand closed over Emma's heart. She didn't have a home until the gasoline was handled. And until she talked to Anthony, she had no idea if he'd stay.

She and Sophia stood in silence while the doctor finished and finally left Anthony in peace.

Sophia said, "You'd better hurry if you want to see him. He'll never sleep if they don't dose him to the gills, and the nurse will be back pretty soon."

Emma took a deep breath, pushed the door open and found Anthony lying on his side, facing away from her. The sound of the door brought forth another spate of Italian.

"I suppose I should be glad I don't understand that," she said.

Anthony tried to sit up, the expletives in good old-fashioned English this time. Wincing, Emma hurried around the bed and helped him sit up.

"Sorry," he grumbled. "Didn't know it was you."

Emma couldn't help but touch him, straightening his hair and examining a face she loved but could only see half of, thanks to the bandage over his eye.

"I just wanted to see… Well, no, you're not all right. Silly thing to say."

Anthony nudged her chin up with a hand, examining her. ''What about you?''

She shrugged. ''Charles went home. He's fine. They say Brady will be fine, too. Did you hear about the baby?''

Nodding, Anthony said, ''You're okay with him leaving?''

''Yes. I'm happy for them. He'll be a good dad. And he won't have any trouble finding a different job.''

''Sounds like you have his life all settled, then.''

Giving him a guilty but reproachful look, Emma chose her words carefully. ''Everyone needs a nudge in the right direction now and then. Sort of like what you did for me earlier tonight. Had I listened in the first place and not yelled at you when you asked me about Dillon, none of this would have happened.''

Anthony tried to raise an eyebrow at her but flinched, and there was a delay of rubbing and sympathetic noises before he groused. ''No, none of this would have happened if Layne was anywhere to be found. Where was she?''

''Way ahead of you and Jim. After Charles said the rock thing, she made more phone calls and borrowed Geoff's laptop to check Dillon's credentials again. If you weren't quite so smart, she would have been back to raise the roof in time to stop you. Only missed her by a minute or two.''

''Well, you know me. Gotta fix the problem.''

Emma sighed. There was so much she wanted to talk about and none of this was on the list. ''Please stop. God only knows what might have happened if you hadn't gotten there when you did. If he'd started that fire it would have gone up like a bomb, and there are apartment buildings behind it.''

''Sounds like you wouldn't have cared much if it weren't for those apartments,'' Anthony said, picking up a curl that had long since sprung free of her top knot.

One smoky brown eye stared at her until she had to drop her eyes. And then he asked, ''Do you remember what you said to Dop?''

"Not really. Nothing too hideous, I hope."

"Quite hideous. You said I wouldn't want you if you didn't have the store. I hope you don't believe that, Emma."

"No, I'm sure I've given you sufficient reason not to want me. I am so sorry, Anthony. If I'd—"

"Your turn to stop," he told her, leaning forward to touch her mouth with his. A touch was all they could manage with a very sore, very fat lip in the way.

Emma sniffed out a laugh, even though she knew what was coming. Hoping he still might change his mind, she said, "I love you."

"I know you do," he said. "But I'm not going back on anything I said. Nothing that happened tonight changes anything."

"Yes, it does. It changes everything."

"For tonight, maybe. The way you feel right now won't be how you'll feel tomorrow or the next day. And forgive me for saying this, but I know you better than to believe you'll change overnight."

"What happened to the old adage that you shouldn't expect someone to change for you?"

Anthony shook his head. "See? Here it comes already."

"But Dillon was—"

"No. Forget it, Emma. You can't use Dillon as an excuse. Yes, you need to rethink the things he told you, but the problems in your life were there long before he entered the picture. And if you believe I'm asking you to change for *me,* you haven't really heard a word I've said."

"I did. Honestly. And I know you're right. But I can't imagine walking out of here and being on my own again."

"Then that's what you need to do," he said. "You're a smart girl. You'll figure it out. But until then, I can't hear from you because even though I know better, I'll... You own me. You're the one who has to do the fixing now."

Tilting her head, trying to make eye contact, Emma understood him. Understood that it was killing him to admit what he'd just admitted. The proudest, most arrogant man she'd ever met was saying that she had all the power in this equation, and she'd better not abuse it.

"I'll miss you," she said.

"Good."

Emma raised her eyebrows and told him, "That isn't very nice. I've listened to you and I've heard what you've said, but what about you?"

"What about me?"

"I don't think you've changed as much as you want me to believe," she said, keeping the tone gentle but meaning every word. "You still think the only way to get what you want is to bulldoze me into giving it. And then you act insulted when *I* bulldoze you. The general manager issue, for example."

"I wasn't insulted. If things were different, I'd have accepted your offer in a heartbeat. You'd understand that if you ever bothered to listen."

"I always listen to you," Emma said. "I don't always like what I hear, but I listen. You're not so hot at that yourself, you know. And if there's only one thing I can ever make you hear, I want it to be this."

"What?"

Emma threaded their fingers together and said, "I know your father hurt you, and you don't trust him. Can't say as I blame you, but if you're going to preach to me about what's important, you'd better look in the mirror, Anthony. Okay, maybe not at the moment, but soon. You're the one who doesn't speak to Maxim when you should be thanking God your father's still alive to drive you nuts."

It was the best and worst timing for the nurse to arrive, telling her in no uncertain terms to get out.

Not so much as a goodbye and Emma was out the door, feeling almost as scared as she had earlier at the store. She didn't know how she'd get though this, or even what to do.

But she'd have to deal with it—on her own. Not as though she had a choice. Anthony wouldn't listen to her.

No, he'd just make his accusations and leave her alone with the consequences when she needed him most.

If he loved her, he wouldn't do that. But everyone else left. So why not.

Too tired to scare up much anger, she cried all the way home under the nervous eye of a cabdriver.

By the time she got to the store, she was beyond tired. And Jim, who had to be fit to drop himself, proved to be the white knight in disguise. Deserting a horde of evidence people hard at work in the vault and workroom, he walked her to the apartment and even helped pack a few things.

"How's Anthony doin'?" Jim asked, the Southern accent putting in an appearance. She'd noticed it cropped up when he was tired so the quicker she let him finish his work, the better.

"Rotten."

"You two get things worked out?"

"Yes and no," Emma said. "But it'll be okay. Eventually."

Jim grunted a laugh. "Got everything you need?"

Emma stared at Jim. Anthony might be leaving, but something told her Jim had been instructed to deal with some consequences, and as the conversation unfolded, the proof piled up.

"Yeah," she said.

"Where do you want to stay? I'll take you."

Emma decided on a hotel across the river in Minneapolis. On the way, Jim explained that they'd called Peter Carlson and he'd be coming in soon to assess the damage, so there was no need for her to go back to the store if she wasn't up to it.

Once he'd helped her check in and carried her bag upstairs, Jim stopped at the hotel room door and said, "You'll have to meet with the prosecutors this week. And later a grand jury and trial."

Emma nodded. "As long as Dillon ends up behind bars, I don't care."

"Yeah, well, y'all are gonna care when the media gets ahold of this. They'll be going nuts in a few hours. You think you can handle that without..."

He let the question dangle, finishing it with a hand wave.

"Without screaming at anybody?"

"Yeah."

She managed a ghost of a smile and said, "I don't think I'll have it in me to scream for a while."

"Emma," Jim said. "Are you sure you're all right? What did Anthony say to you?"

"Nothing that didn't need to be said. Don't worry. I'm not contemplating harming him or anything."

Jim laughed. "Go to bed. Call me when you regain consciousness."

By Tuesday afternoon, the media had worn themselves out, and Anthony was feeling almost human. Well, a human train wreck, but he'd lived through it once and he'd do it again.

He was in Jim's office, waiting for Emma.

It would be the first time he'd seen her since the hospital and to hear Jim tell it, she'd seen precious few people since then. She'd visited Brady every day and she'd met with the prosecutors, but hadn't left the hotel otherwise. Hadn't even been back to the store, unbelievable as that seemed.

Charles had seen her and said she looked all right on the outside. How she felt on the inside was anyone's guess.

And here he sat, so nervous about seeing her that his knee was bobbing. He knew he'd been taking a risk, sending her away, but he'd promised himself he wouldn't care. He'd done what he needed to do.

The door finally opened and Jim said, "There you are."

"Sorry I'm late," Emma said quietly.

Anthony managed to look at her and she surprised him by leaning down to kiss his cheek. "Hey. How are you feeling? Your eye looks better."

He raised his brows in reply.

"Yeah, I know," she said. "Considering what it looked like last time I saw it. So, what's the news?"

Jim leaned back in his chair, the way he always did, and said, "Just some things I'd thought you'd like to know. Like how he fooled us with his credentials."

Emma's face soured, and Anthony watched her while Jim explained that Dillon's real name was Paul Ketter, near as they could determine. He'd accomplished the university degrees, practice history and just about everything else he'd done, by hacking into computers all over the place.

The FBI might have caught on sooner if they hadn't checked Dillon's so-called references before Melinda pointed out Dop was using an electronic device to alter this voice. The references Jim had called were both male. And both *Ketter,* through the high-tech magic of his device, and the low-tech magic of call forwarding.

Anthony tuned Jim out. None of this seemed important anymore. And Emma looked tired. The sundress she wore was light blue. Even with the tan, that telltale exhaustion showed through.

Jim said, "Melinda confirmed through his computers that he'd been in Emma's e-mail accounts a couple of times. Deleted messages on at least one occasion. He's admitted he intercepted the real e-mail you got from the referral site and deleted it, so that site can't be faulted. But believe me, as we speak, there are universities and psychiatric associations beefing up their computer security like nobody's business."

Emma made no comment, and Anthony didn't bother looking away when she glanced over and caught him staring.

Jim kept talking while they read each other. Neither one of them was happy apart. He knew she was mad at him for leaving but he had to stand his ground.

"Hello," Jim broke in. "Are you two even listening to me? I'm trying to tell you this guy has a ten-mile-long rap sheet with Interpol for jewel theft. And the military's got warrants out for rape and assault with a deadly weapon."

Emma looked away to ask, "Is that a surprise?"

"Yeah, it's a surprise," Jim said. "This guy brags about everything like we should praise him for what he'd done. But all he's said about the military was that he oozed past the filters with a fake ID. Which is very bad news because he's got identities that'll take us years to sort out."

"How does that affect the court case?" Anthony asked.

"I don't know. All I know is we might have trouble getting him past a competency hearing. If what we're finding is correct, I couldn't even count the conditions our initial evaluation is hinting toward."

"So what does that mean?"

"It means what we've got is a whole lot of evidence but no real culprit to blame it on. He knows right from wrong but his mental condition screws up the part where he's supposed to care. Either way, we can get him off the streets. It's just gonna take some time and a whole lotta headache for the prosecutors."

Emma asked, "Will my stones be in evidence long?"

"I don't know," Jim said. "They're not really something we need to have sitting around, so I'll see what can be done."

"Thank you."

"Least I can do," Jim said.

His phone rang then and he was gone a moment later, leaving Anthony unprepared and alone with Emma. If he didn't know better, he'd swear Jim did it on purpose.

"Don't get nervous," Emma said. "I only asked about the stones because Charles is going crazy." She paused. "I'm not going into business with Neville."

"Then what are you doing?"

"I don't know," she answered, then smiled vaguely, her eyes on her feet. "We have repairs to do, I suppose, and in the meantime I'll have to figure out the rest."

"You're staying shut down the entire time?"

"I don't know," she shrugged.

What did she mean she didn't know? What the heck was going on over there?

Whoa. Okay, time out, Anthony thought. None of your business. Keep your nose out of it.

She asked, "Are you going up to the lake?"

He hadn't planned on it but after that little control spasm, maybe he'd better. "Yes. And staying up there unless Jim calls me down for something."

Her eyes cast down again, she nodded. "You'll keep in touch with Charles, I hope. He misses you."

Oh. God. Anthony rubbed the part of his forehead that wasn't sore, fighting the urge to fix it. He couldn't stand this. She looked so alone and scared, it was like watching her die right in front of him.

"I'll call him," he said.

"Thank you."

Emma got up and left before he could even say goodbye.

He closed his eyes, warring against the million and one ideas flooding his mind. Don't go after her. Going after her was the wrong thing to do.

Definitely against the rules, he reminded himself. The woman rule was long dead, may it rest in peace. He'd given up taking himself seriously. He was so weak where she was concerned it was almost funny.

But keeping life simple was what it was all about. If he ran after her right now, he'd spend the rest of his life running after her. So, as much as he'd like to make everything okay again, he wouldn't.

He'd just rearrange his plans a bit. Con Maxim into coming up to the lake. No way was he getting off that hook.

If Emma was biting the bullet, so would he.

Chapter 15

A faint *eau de gasoline* still hung in the air as Emma stood at the base of the oak staircase, feeling like an outsider there for the very first time.

The store was deserted. Silent.

Looking around, she saw memories everywhere. The dent in the bottom step from her tricycle. And the book counter where she'd taken her first steps under the astonished eyes of her mother, Brady and Brady's dad.

Eyes astonished like Anthony's had been when she said she didn't know what they'd do with the store. She honestly hadn't a clue. It was up to Charles now. She'd handed it over to him yesterday and told him to do whatever he thought best.

Back in Jim's office, she'd almost asked Anthony if he'd help Charles. Anthony probably knew fifty times more than they did about contracting, and she didn't feel right about leaving Charles with all that work.

She'd stopped herself, though. Anthony had made it very clear that she was the one who needed to do the fixing now.

No. He hadn't been talking about the store. She needed to get her priorities straight and find out how to be a whole person on her own, without the store, the label or Anthony. How that was possible, she couldn't fathom. Not without Anthony's help.

Standing there, she understood for the very first time why her father had just...given up. When her mother died, they might as well have buried Dad, too.

The person you love most in the world leaves, and you have to go on somehow. Dad tried. But his version of trying had been to find a replacement. He'd failed three times—a mistake Emma hadn't made the last time Anthony left because she'd seen firsthand that it was pointless.

She'd made a different one, trying to fill the dead hours with empty successes because without Anthony, that's all the hours were. Dead. Lifeless.

Unlike her parents, she and Anthony had been granted a second chance. Even though she'd wanted to maim him when he showed up again, he breathed true passion back into her life. And the passion she'd felt for that Neville deal was an insult in comparison.

She got it now. Everything Brady had been trying to tell her and what Anthony had meant about choices and decisions. There wasn't room in her life anymore for passions that didn't matter. The only passion that mattered came from Anthony. From *them.* Together. Not just in bed. In everything.

Anthony understood that. And he'd left because she hadn't been ready to understand.

Well, she was ready now. Ready to get her head on straight. And in order to do that, she had to take the first step. Even if that step was to hand the store over to Charles.

Smiling a bit, she shook her head. How could she go wrong with Charles? He'd brought Anthony back. Charles had some decidedly meddleish tendencies himself and it neither surprised nor upset her that he'd confessed to expecting that phone call from Anthony long before it happened.

She snorted a laugh and trudged up the stairs. There was so much to do. Help Wanted ads to place and bags to pack and a plane to catch.

It still felt wrong, leaving Charles alone to deal with everything, but he'd insisted he'd be fine. The department heads were on board with her taking a vacation, even if several of them looked like they might faint when they heard she was leaving.

Emma passed the workroom door and the silence was deafening.

So many things had come to an end. Dillon. Brady's constant presence, reassuring in its own way. But other things were about to begin.

She made her phone calls, placed her ads and packed her bags. It was time to run away from home.

Ten days. Ten days and the new scar was itching like mad.

Anthony pressed his shoulder into the deck chair, half-asleep in the heat of a late July sun.

A loon shrieked on the other side of the lake and drowned out the gentle sound of waves hitting the beach.

When he'd first found this place he thought he'd never get tired of that sound. Well, he was now. The same old thing over and over and over again. He couldn't wait until winter when the lake would freeze and the silence would be deafening.

Something blocked his sun. "Jeez, Brac. You look like crap."

Anthony cracked an eyelid. "You're early."

"Like that would make a difference."

"Nice to see you, too, Jim."

"Lighten up. Passed your dad on the way in. He going back to the Cities, or just out to buy you a razor?"

"Would you stop already?"

"Only if you get your butt off that chair and take me fishing," Jim said. "Time's a-wastin'."

"Do you have to be so cheerful? It's annoying," Anthony muttered.

The two of them grabbed their gear and set out, opting for the bay after finding the sandbar packed with boats.

They had their lines out before Jim asked again about Maxim.

"He's headed back to St. Paul," Anthony replied. "We've had enough of each other for a while. How's Melinda?"

Jim didn't answer right away, saying finally, "Well, she's pretty ticked off at me for leaving her with a deskful of work, but she'll get over it."

"Is it just the deskful she's mad about or something else?"

"Brac, how many times do I have to tell you? There's nothing going on between us. You ask me about it again and I'll bring up you-know-who."

"How is she?"

Jim gave him a cautious look. This was the first time he'd asked, and Anthony didn't know why he was bothering now.

Jim said, "No idea. She's not back yet. She sent me a postcard from that island place. But no word on what's going on downtown."

The words *None of your business* echoed in Anthony's head. Over and over again, like the waves that drove him nuts.

Out came the question, anyway. "What about Neville?"

"Still nothing. I think she meant it, Brac."

Anthony nodded and changed the subject, asking about Jim's cases. That kept Emma out of the conversation until dinner.

"What do you think they've got planned for the store?" Jim asked.

"How should I know?"

"Don't you and Charles talk about it?"

"No. I haven't talked to him since Emma left," Anthony said.

"Why not?"

Anthony laughed. "You can't help yourself, can you? It's none of my business what's going on down there. None of yours, either."

"I'm just curious. And Layne asks me about Emma all the time. Wonders how she's doing. I mean, we did spend four days there and it bugs us that you don't care what's happening."

"What makes you think I don't care?"

"Hey," Jim said. "The coast is clear, you know. She's on vacation, the store's closed. Might be time for a visit."

"You're hopeless," Anthony told him. "If you need to know what's going on, you visit. I'm almost over the withdrawals and you're not helping."

Jim drained the rest of his beer and set it down, giving him the "you idiot" look.

"What?" Anthony prompted.

"No way. You said the next time I feel the need to advise you about women, I should take a deep breath and fight it. So I did. Can't have it both ways."

Rolling his eyes, Anthony said, "Just say it."

"This whole thing is stupid. Emma loves you. You love Emma. Stop being such a hard-ass and go after her."

"Don't do this to me."

"Fine. Subject closed."

Sure. Now that the damage was done.

By two o'clock that morning, Anthony was wishing Jim hadn't come up. If he hadn't, Anthony wouldn't be tossing and turning, thinking about Emma.

Having Maxim around had gotten him through this far, and trying to silence those particular demons hadn't left much time for brooding.

However, Maxim hadn't found the lake very exciting and Anthony suspected there was another reason Maxim had gone home. A woman kept calling the cabin. Celia, who'd dumped him a few weeks before the attack. She sounded like she'd just turned eighteen but that was none of his business, either.

So he'd finally made peace with his father, but what if he was making a huge mistake with Emma?

There wasn't a second of these last two weeks he hadn't asked himself that question. As always, the argument stood up to be counted—the arguments for giving in. They were letting Dop win. Maybe they could have worked it out if he'd stayed. That this time he was invisible because he'd *made* himself invisible.

But he'd put the ball in her court. If he took it back she wouldn't thank him for it.

Now, somehow, he'd have to get her out of his head again.

He managed to sleep and got up late, catching his reflection in the mirror. He did look like crap. He needed a shave, a haircut and sleep.

And Emma.

He was halfway to the phone before he realized what he was doing. Absolutely forbidden. She wasn't back yet, anyway.

Okay. Get a grip, he told himself. You need to think before you do something that could backfire.

Jim's news was bothering him, though. Especially that part about Emma sending Melinda a postcard. Did he get one? No.

Anthony tapped the razor on the edge of the sink with a little more force than necessary. What if he was screwing up again? What if this was all a mistake and the doubts were getting to Emma?

They were sure as hell getting to him. What if she was down there right now with some guy from wherever, having the time of her life?

Nice one, Brac. It'd be his own fault, if she was. He'd sent her away and if she found someone who'd treat her well, he'd have to be happy for her.

He flinched as the razor nicked his chin. New rule. Never

shave while thinking about someone else touching Emma. He'd lost enough blood this year.

And he'd stewed long enough. He missed her so badly he couldn't breathe. The logical thing to do was wait until she got back and call her. Ask her is she was all right. Tell Emma he loved her and whatever happened from there, happened.

Anthony looked at himself in the mirror and made the fatal admission. Maybe Emma had been right. Maybe he wasn't so hot at listening. Because had he bothered to listen in Jim's office, he might have understood what happened there. In hindsight, it looked to him like someone had just gone cold turkey from the store.

She was trying, and Jim was right, too, damn him. This whole thing was stupid. They loved each other. And they'd both be better off with someone to help them keep it between the lines.

He and Jim were at breakfast when a phone call cut Jim's stay short. Ten minutes later he was gone and Anthony had already started packing when Charles called.

He said he only had a minute, and sounded like he was being run ragged. "Would it be too much to ask that you check your e-mail once in a while?"

"Oh, yeah," Anthony said. "Let me race to the in box after the whole Dop situation."

Charles sighed impatiently. "Go check it. Quickly. As in *right now.* I must go. Someone is swinging a very large hammer alarmingly close to a display case."

Didn't have to tell him twice.

He hadn't checked his e-mail since he got to the lake. If Emma had sent him something he hadn't replied to, he'd hop the next plane to wherever she was.

But there was nothing in there from her, only a message from Charles. Blowing out a breath, he opened it.

Anthony—

I heard from Emma early this morning. I know you

were hoping there would be some miraculous cure-all for her heart where you are concerned, but I am afraid there are some things no one can fix because they need no fixing.

On the other hand, there is the store. And I am afraid there are some things no one can fix because none of us have any idea what we are doing.

All of this has happened for a reason, and I have never believed that more than this morning when Emma refused to come home despite my complaints. And she forbade me to call you for help, but she said nothing of e-mail and I am desperate.

So it is time for you to come home. Our girl needs your help and so do I. Call her if you like but I think a surprise wouldn't be amiss for a change.

I will assume we understand each other and you will call me as soon as you get this message.

At the very bottom of the e-mail was a link to a Web site Charles thought might interest him. Anthony clicked on it, and as a newspaper classified section filled his screen, he started laughing. Charles was a very, very smart man.

Chapter 16

"What?" Emma cried. "Please tell me you're joking. Two hundred?"

Just arrived from the airport, Emma stood in the rubble of what used to be her jewelry department. There was a gaping hole in the wall between the buildings but she couldn't care less about the heaps of brick and concrete at the moment.

Charles was holding a mother lode of résumés in his hand. She hadn't expected this kind of response to their ad and was so exhausted from traveling she couldn't imagine weeding through them all, let alone trying to choose the right general manager.

"Do not worry, Emma. We put the more interesting ones on top and the hopeless cases on the bottom. Tomorrow is the cutoff date so that should give you plenty of time to read them over and get some rest first."

"Oh, man," she sighed.

"You will be fine, my dear. Now, tell me about your trip."

''It was great,'' Emma smiled. ''Kind of weird being all by myself for once, but I got a lot of designing done.''

''Emma,'' Charles scolded. ''That was not allowed, remember?''

''Oh, come on, I had to have something to do. Blue water, blue sky, sandy beaches, no one for miles. Gets boring after a while, you know.''

''You were only gone two weeks.''

''Stop scolding me. I had a good time doing absolutely nothing stressful. So what's with the hole in the wall?''

''A slight concession,'' Charles told her. ''For Beautiful Things. Everyone seemed to concur it was too crowded up here, and the label deserves its own space. And come here a moment. I want to show you something.''

She followed Charles through the hole, checking with a slightly anal but relieved eye that the floors were exactly level between the two buildings.

He stopped at a mountain of something covered by a tarp. When she saw what was hidden beneath it, her mouth dropped open. There was enough oak paneling under there to cover every inch of the place.

''Charles! Where did you find it?''

''I didn't find it. Someone else did.''

''This is amazing. It's exactly the same as the old stuff! I don't believe it.''

''You will believe it when you get the bill. Trust me.''

Emma laughed. ''Home sweet home. Speaking of home, please go. You look tired. I'll see you tomorrow.''

He disappeared into the workroom and Emma carried the résumés up to her office. Unbelievable. Two hundred?

Yet after two weeks of doing nothing but designing and resting she was highly motivated to find the perfect general manager. It was the right thing to do, although it would take a while before she'd feel comfortable with all this freedom. Even on pristine beaches, every now and then Emma had that sensation of slipping on ice, catching herself at the last second as she realized the store was just fine without its owner.

Sinking into her office chair, Emma let her mind wander, not horribly surprised when it settled on Anthony. He'd be the perfect general manager. He had the know-how, the interest and the love of this place that it would take to keep it running. But she couldn't ask him to do it. He had to be here because he wanted to be here, and it looked like the jury was still out.

She knew she shouldn't be thinking about him, and she tried to stop herself.

She failed. Miserably. The vacation had helped somewhat and for the first time ever, she didn't feel as though the store and label were her entire, pathetic life. It was amazing what letting go of all the stress could do. She felt like a different person.

Except for one thing. If she didn't see Anthony soon, she'd fall apart. There was so much she wanted to tell him. But she'd promised herself she'd give him the space he needed. Dop had done a number on him, too, and she had to be patient even if it killed her.

After a while Emma dragged her mind, kicking and screaming, off Anthony. Before her on the desk was a stack of messenger envelopes, one of them neon purple and marked urgent.

Curious, Emma opened it, disappointed to find another résumé. And not even a good one. If the applicant couldn't be bothered to put their name and phone number on the cover letter, she couldn't be bothered to read it.

Emma dropped it over the side of her desk into the trash but as it fell, the pages came apart and Emma caught a few words. Diving after them, she gathered all the pages and landed with a thump in her chair.

Jerk. Meddle. Those were the words she'd seen.

Reading the cover letter this time, Emma raised a shaky hand to her mouth and felt tears prick her eyelids like cinders.

"I believe this job was offered to me some time ago and I mistakenly turned it down on a technicality. Enclosed, please find my résumé..."

Emma breathed out a watery laugh, reading a section titled "problem areas." He'd listed "Not a talker, major meddler, arrogant, something of a jerk."

Next came a list of "special skills" that made her blush.

Charles had told her about Anthony's rules the day before she left and Emma found them listed on the last page. "One: Keep life simple. Two: Never take yourself too seriously. Three: Only sleep with the boss if she asks nicely."

Three was a bit skewed, but she loved him so much for those rules that she'd forgive him the liberty. Especially that kind.

The last thing she read before tears won out was the salary requirement: "Marriage. I believe the preliminary answer was 'maybe' We may need to negotiate a more suitable final answer."

If she only knew where he was, she'd give him a final answer he'd never forget.

Emma spent a few minutes pulling herself together, too happy and nervous to know what to do. She reached for the phone but hesitated. Patience. When he's ready he'll...

Her eyes went to the ceiling as footsteps passed toward the staircase.

"Jerk." She smiled, seeing untied high-tops coming down the steps. She might have known he'd already be here. And it would appear he'd been here for some time, smashing holes in her walls.

"I heard that, witch," Anthony said, and stopped to lean against the stair rail.

He looked incredible, even though he was filthy. His jeans were covered with concrete dust, and a T-shirt that might have been white once upon a time had a hole in one sleeve. The black hair was also liberally dusted, yet just as wiry and shiny as she remembered.

But all Emma wanted to see were the smoky brown eyes.

Goose bumps were already in the works and a swarm of butterflies were fighting for wing space in her stomach.

At a loss, she asked, ''Why can't you ever tie your shoes?''

''They're only untied when you're around. I like to be reminded,'' he said, still staring.

Emma bit her cheek, trying not to start crying again. But there was something that needed to be said. ''We have a problem.''

Anthony raised his eyebrows and crossed to take the chair across from her desk, waiting expectantly.

She took a deep breath and said, ''Before we begin our negotiations I want to make sure there's no technicality this time. Given the choice between a husband and a general manager, husband wins. Always. If there's any doubt in your mind, I'm fully prepared to spend the rest of my life proving it.''

There it was. The look that kept her awake at night. She didn't know how he did it, putting his whole heart in his eyes. But she figured she'd learn in time.

He sat back in his chair and said, ''Can we stop with the résumé thing? I love you, Emma. I want this for us and it'll work if we help each other keep things in perspective.''

Nodding, she said, ''Right. The store is great. It's security, it's challenging, it's home. For both of us, because you love it as much as I do. At least I hope so, because it's half yours now.''

''Half mine?'' he repeated, brows up.

''Yes, half. Well, unless you think I should keep fifty-one percent. That way, if the store ever became more important to you than I am, I could sell it. And you'd be stuck at home with me and your daughters for the rest of your life.''

Emma's heart turned over as Anthony's eyes fell, but not before she'd seen a suspicious shine.

Yet another Anthony moment committed to memory.

When he looked up again, he said, ''I love it when you're

subtle. But you're right. So, in the interest of beginning as we mean to go on, I have one demand and it may cause our first fight."

"What is it?"

"We are *not* living upstairs. Either we live in the Ashland house or buy a different one."

"Done. The Ashland house it is."

He grinned. "Well, then. That was easy."

"Anything else, or would you like to see your office?"

She got up and went to the door separating their offices as Anthony warned, "Emma, don't you think there are more important things to discuss right now?"

Emma turned, raised an eyebrow, and Anthony's mouth snapped shut, the charcoal glinting in his eyes as he came after her.

He caught her while she was still fumbling for the light switch. Slowing things down a bit just to be sure she'd said it, Emma cupped his face and told him, "I love you. When can we get married?"

"Patient as ever," he said, then lowered his head.

By the time he raised it again she'd almost forgotten what they were talking about, too busy showing him how much he'd been missed to remember for a moment.

Anthony reminded her with, "I suppose I should ask you properly this time. But I'm having trouble with the ring issue."

"I'll take care of it."

"But I have to get you something."

Donning a haughty face, Emma told him, "I already saw the paneling and I'm assuming you're responsible. I'm also assuming I'd drop dead if I saw the bill that came with it."

"Then I guess I won't be showing it to you, will I?"

"Anthony—"

He cut her off with his mouth, backing Emma up to the desk and pushing the blotter onto the floor.

"I can't believe we won't even make it past dinner,"

Anthony complained. "Now I'll never be able to concentrate in here."

"That was the general idea," she told him, nipping his neck.

"Shameless."

Emma stood at the window, staring over a snow-covered lake, talking to Jim on the phone. "And for the icing on the cake, they found out yesterday that she's pregnant. Maxim's elated, but Anthony's scandalized, becoming a big brother at age thirty-one."

Jim laughed and asked, "What time does the wedding start?"

"Soon. I'm supposed to be getting dressed, but I wanted to check in. Try not to work so hard."

Emma said goodbye and hung up, smiling as she went to the closet. The dress hung on a satin-covered hanger. Rather racy for Emma's taste, but it wasn't her wedding. She supposed she'd get used to being part of a family and doing things she'd rather, not because that's what families did.

Halfway to the bed, Emma yelped. Spider. Big spider.

She loved the lake house but did not love the wildlife that came with it.

The spider crept in her direction and Emma grabbed for a shoe, then stopped herself, to scramble on the bed instead.

"Anthony!" she shrieked at the top of her lungs. Anything to get his mind off this wedding.

Footfalls rocketed up the steps and the door flew open. "What's wrong?" her husband demanded, his tie flipped over his shoulder.

She pointed at the spider, chirping, "Get it!"

"Oh, please," he grumbled, snatching a handful of tissues and scooping up the offending creature. Anthony went into the bathroom for a second, the toilet flushed and he came out wearing a tolerant look. "Nice try, honey. I probably couldn't count the spiders you've stomped on since we got here."

"Yes, but those were small. This one was huge."

"Is there a particular reason we're stroking my ego today or were you just showcasing the lingerie?"

Emma made a face and then hopped off the bed to straighten Anthony's tie. "I thought you needed a little cheering up."

"Keep hopping around in that strapless thing and I'll be very cheerful. But aren't you supposed to be dressed?"

"I have zipper issues."

Anthony helped her into an emerald green sheath, kissing her neck as he zipped. "I hope he doesn't screw it up."

"It'll be all right. She loves him and he loves her."

"Not as much as I love you."

"Anthony," she scolded.

"Stop. I do remember today which one of us is the parent. I hope he does, too. If he screws up my baby brother or sister I'll pound him." He shook his head. "And while we're on the subject, when are we getting pregnant?"

Emma turned and put her arms around his neck. "We've only been married a month, for God's sake. Patience, anyone?"

He laughed. "Okay, okay. Changing the subject. Hurry up or we'll get started late, and the weather doesn't look good."

Twenty minutes later they were staring at each other across the living room. He stood beside his father and Emma was lined up with Celia, her twenty-four-year-old future mother-in-law.

Everything was going to be fine between Maxim and his new bride, she knew. The age difference wouldn't matter because Celia didn't take any of the Bracco crap, either. And Maxim looked positively moony.

Smiling at Anthony first, Emma looked over at Sophia and Geoff. Only Sophia would cry at her ex-husband's wedding. Emma winked at Geoff and turned back to Anthony, who was rolling his eyes at his mother.

Afterward, Sophia brought Celia's parents to see Emma's

ring, a simple diamond solitaire surrounded by tiny daisies. Emma had designed Celia's, too—an iris in white diamonds.

Lunch was a rushed affair, by male insistence. Everyone needed to get on the road or they'd be stranded.

When everyone was gone, Emma and Anthony stood in the doorway together, watching Maxim and Celia pull out of the drive.

"Stop brooding," Emma said. "She can handle him. Besides, we need to finish cleaning up."

Anthony leaned against the doorjamb, lifting her chin with a gentle hand. "I love you."

"I love you, too," she whispered, and practiced putting her heart in her eyes.

"Ah, Emma. Don't do that. Not until after we're done cleaning."

She laughed as he showed her again how it was done. "Totally unfair. Do you have any idea what that does to me?"

"Why do you think I do it all the time?"

He kissed her, raising goose bumps.

"Mmm. Think anyone would notice if we didn't show up for work on Monday?" she asked.

"Funny you should ask that. I might have warned some people we wouldn't be back until Thursday."

"Meddling. Always meddling."

"Hey," he said, pointing. "What was that vow? I choose you every day over—"

Emma finished for him, "Over shiny things and worries. I won't forget."

"No, you won't. And no chance I'll let you."

"Right. And yours is I choose you over..."

Anthony repeated, "I choose you over numbers and 'that guy thing where I have to fix the problem.'"

Laughing, she said, "That's not quite it, but close enough. Let's go clean up. I'd liked to be curled up in front of the fire by the time we get snowbound."

"Fire?" he asked dubiously.

Emma pushed onto her tiptoes so she could whisper in his ear.

Anthony's eyes widened, his mouth dropping open. ''Can we skip the cleaning and do that part first?''

''Nope. Absolutely not.''

''Witch,'' he laughed, scooping her up and carrying her to the kitchen.

* * * * *